NUNS
with
GUNS

SETH KAUFMAN

Sukuma
Books

This is for Theo and for Hilary.

Chapter 1

"*Nuns and Guns?*" I sputter into the phone.

"That's exactly what I said, Rick. It seems absurd. But he's offering me two million dollars."

"Two million? Are you kidding me? Did he give you any details about the show?"

"No, not really. He just said he represented a very motivated, passionate group and that they thought I was the perfect person for the series they're developing."

"Sister Rosemarie, I gotta tell you, that's a nice piece of change. Nobody's offering me a friggin' nickel these days."

"But you just had the number one show!"

"Well, I'm a marked man at the moment. The networks are all wondering what's going to happen with the lawsuit. Not only do I have a reputation as a creative jerk, now I'm a *litigious* creative jerk."

"I'm sorry to hear that, Rick. Really. You certainly did wonders for the Mission."

That was collateral success, of course. Totally unintentional. My last show, *The King of Pain,* was not conceived to help Sister Rosemarie Aria's magnificent Mission of Mercy School, Shelter, Bakery and Community Center. But she became a fan favorite. And when viewers opened up their wallets for her embattled mission at the end of the season, it was a feel-good story on my feel-bad reality show which featured contestants getting tortured.

"I'm glad we could help," I say, because I really am glad. "How did you leave things with Mr. Nuns and Guns?"

"I thanked him for his offer and said I would have to think about it."

"You're damn right you have to think about it. You need details. What is the show about? What's expected of you, who are the other nuns?"

"He said we would explore the wide world of firearms. The fascinating history, the exciting power. Those were his words. Not mine."

"Amazing."

"So you think I should consider it?"

"You want my honest opinion?"

"Yes, please."

"The title is pretty genius. Really. I mean, I don't know what they plan on having you do, but it sounds like the most intriguing thing this side of *The King of Pain*, to be frank. Whoever thought of it is one cynical bastard. I would watch in a heartbeat and so would half of America, just to see what it is."

"Oh my," said Sister Rosemarie.

"That said, I would tell this guy that you don't think the project is right for you. I mean, you are a very hot property, Sister Rosemarie. You could probably get a million bucks for doing *Nuns Weaving Baskets and Saying the Catechism*. Think about it: You got over a million in donations from viewers who were tuning in to watch people get tortured. You have star power. You're like a Kardashian for good or something. You need an agent to help you figure out what to do."

"Who do you recommend?"

"You remember Jay, my lawyer? I'll email both of you, and he'll get you a list of agents and managers. Top guys. But you can always run them by me."

"Thank you so much, Rick. I tell everyone that you really are a very sweet man. How are you feeling by the way?"

"Marta is my greatest influence. I exercise, I eat well, and I only drink at dinner and parties."

"That sounds great."

"Oh it's great. I almost feel like my old self."

"That's so wonderful to hear. Give Marta my love. And thanks for the advice."

I hang up the phone and have Jasmine, my new assistant/slush-pile reader/office eye-candy, bring me a cup of chamomile tea. The thought of Sister Rosemarie getting this offer really burns me up, and I need to calm down. I found Sister Rosemarie. I made her a household name. And I *still* can't get any respect around town. Plus, if anyone should do a show with her, it should be me.

I'm sipping my tea when Little Ricky, my associate producer, sticks his head in the door. "Got a minute?"

"Come on in."

"On the way in today I had an idea for a show. Are you ready? It's a one-word pitch."

"Is it better than *Nuns and Guns*?"

The excited smile falls off Little Ricky's face for a moment and then returns. "Are you kidding? *Nuns and Guns*? Oh man! That is loud."

This kind of reaction is why I love Little Ricky. It's

as if God created him in my own image, except I'm taller, smarter, richer, older and I curse a lot more.

"I know," I say. "Sister Rosemarie called. She got a mysterious offer. I'm betting the NRA is behind it."

"That is one hell of a title."

"That's what I told her. Sells itself. Although, personally I think *Nuns with Guns* might be better."

"Either way. Kinda takes the wind out of my pitch a little."

"Sorry. How about you go out and come back in again?"

"Once I tell you this idea, Rick, you must swear to never, ever give me credit for it."

"Whatever you say. Remember, it's just a pitch. At this point, you can only be accused of a thought crime. Not actual perpetration."

Little Ricky looks at me. He's clearly nervous. He takes a deep breath as if to brace himself. Then he says it:

"*Catfight.*"

Some pitches need a sentence. Most need a paragraph. In Hollywood, when studios assign a reader to "cover" a book or a screenplay, the reader delivers a log line, like, "*Sesame Street* meets *Rambo.*" Then there's a one-sentence summary, like, "Vietnamese TV puppet show is infiltrated by a renegade CIA agent who mutates puppets into murderous live furry beings that go on a rampage looking for MIA vets." And if that's not enough, there's also a short paragraph summary, a one-page summary and a full, multi-page, blow-by-blow, detailed plot summary, followed by comments and analysis by the reader. Today, however, I have just heard two pitches that really require almost nothing beyond the imagination of the listener—because the titles themselves are so good.

"Little Ricky," I say, "Before I tell you what I think, I have three questions for you. Number one: Has there ever been a movie or TV show with that title?"

"I couldn't find any."

"Incredible. Number two: how would you pitch it in a sentence?"

"Springer on Steroids."

"Nice. I'm not sure everyone in Hollywood remembers Springer. He's sort of faded, hasn't he?"

"He still brings the chaos. What's the third question?

"Is this show worth destroying your relationship with Amanda?"

"Yeah, well, that's a problem."

Amanda is Little Ricky's fiancée, the VP of Development here at Salter Entertainment, and my sometimes-unwanted moral barometer, which is to say that she frequently disagrees with my more inflammatory projects.

"That's a pretty enormous problem, don't you think?"

"I know. That's why I came to you, Rick. You like it, right? If it became your idea, if you adopted it, it could be your brainchild and our little secret. I could just advise you."

I'm a little touched. In our 18 months together, Little Ricky has become my pal and protégé and now, it seems he's asking for both guidance and help. Or maybe he really wants to dump a money-making idea in my lap. Either way, it's touching.

"I'm not getting a lot of network interest at the moment," I say. "But tell me what you're thinking."

"Each show opens with a mini-doc about two women that sets up their problems with each other. Then the women come out and have a verbal exchange. Maybe they comment on the mini-doc. Then the audience members vote on who has the better grievance, and the woman who wins gets to choose the kind of catfight."

"What do you mean?"

"I'm thinking we offer different combat options: ultimate fighting cage, standard boxing ring, or a special ring where you fight, but there's also ropes and levers so a contestant could pull a rope and dump mud or freezing water on their rival."

"That's pretty good. I like that—the special ring. The Cat Cage. No, the Cat Box!"

"And maybe the audience votes on the winner. Or there's a panel of judges. I'm not sure."

"Nice."

"You like it?"

"It's catchy."

"Thanks."

"And very offensive."

"Yeah, well, that's part of the marketing charm."

"I'm sure someone will buy it and we could make it a real spectacle. But I'm not sure I want any part of this. We took a lot of heat with the last show. This would be worse. It's pretty blatant."

Little Ricky nods.

"Let me think about it."

"Thanks, Rick." He cracks the door to my office open, sticks his head out looking for any possible witnesses to his thought crime, and scoots away like a mouse trying to make it back to his hole.

• • •

I frequently come home for lunch these days. I go for a swim and then eat with Marta. Usually our conversations touch on the following subjects:

1. Her morning, my morning
2. Our impending wedding
3. Her grandkids
4. Our honeymoon trip around the world, which I apparently promised her after she saved my life, and which leads us back to #3 and #2
5. Me, my shows, the lawsuit, Hollywood gossip, anything she heard on the news

I have explained to Marta that this will be my fourth wedding and that, frankly, whatever she wants to do will be fine with me. If she wants the Imam of Mecca and Dalai Lama flown in, fine. I don't fucking care, as long as we do it soon, so she's not deported. And if she wants to spend a million bucks, that's fine, too. Here's the thing about Marta and me: She's been my housekeeper for 21 years. She pretty much raised my son Jared. And a few months ago, after my "Accident"—when my humongous home entertainment system collapsed on me and I spent an entire weekend pinned under it, hoping to be rescued—Marta was the one who saved my life. So when she told me the immigration police had been to visit her apartment and that she needed me to marry her, I immediately agreed. It didn't hurt that I have had the hots for her during most of those 21 years and that, as I have discovered in recent months, the feelings were mutual.

"You crazy, papi," she laughs whenever I tell her I don't care about the wedding ceremony and that she can spend a million bucks. "I would never waste money like that. And

Hector and Mikey, they won't charge so much."

Hector and Mikey are Marta's two sons. They own a taco joint and they are Marta's caterers of choice.

"I just want you to have the wedding you want, Marta, that's all. And the sooner the better, so we can get you citizenship."

So I drive home and on the way I realize I have not talked to my lawyer Jay today. Every phone call to Jay costs a fortune, but it's worth it, considering I have a one billion dollar lawsuit heading into court about my old TV show. That's right: One fucking billion dollars. An absurd amount of money. That's what the head of The Network, Walter Fields, told a *Wall Street Journal* reporter *The King of Pain* was worth. And since I created the show, and The Network fired me and shut it down, well, you do the math.

"Any news?" I ask when Jay picks up.

"A little bird told me The Network is planning on filing a countersuit. If that's true, then that's going to mean delays, Rick. We'll file a motion to dismiss, just like they did. And the judge will probably order a hearing to examine the merits of each suit."

"What can we do to bring them to the table?"

"We can take your story public. 'Heartless network actions put producer in hospital.'"

Me going to the hospital—what I refer to among a very small circle of friends as "the Accident"—is a highly embarrassing subject.

"Not an option. I don't want this to be about me. I want it to be about them."

"I got it," says Jay. "We leak your email to Fields. The one where you say you'd rather just cancel the show and pay off the finalists. That's part of our case. If you were incompetent, how come they stole your idea for ending the show? Plus, we submitted the email as part of our discovery package. That means it could have come from them, as well as us."

"I dunno. You still like our chances if we go to trial?"

"Rick, it's a no-brainer. They kicked you off the number one show, which you created. They tarnished your reputation, devalued your creation and impinged on your character."

"Thanks," I say. "If you think the leak will work, do it."

• • •

When I pull up to my house, I sit in the car for a few moments. For someone actively trying to avoid crazy, I seem to be living it today. *Nuns and Guns* and *Catfight*. They are both good. And by good, I mean they are loud, loud, loud, which is the reality TV industry's chosen word for sensational, controversial and probably very entertaining. Very loud shows generate lots of viewers and dollars, which is something I'm interested in, normally. But my crazy-warning defense system seems to be working. Part of me feels wary; I'm not leaping in. And anyway, I want to make a movie. Something for the big screen. Something like *The Gizless Days of Thomas Binder*, which is what I've sent Amanda to New York to option.

I'm all about titles. A lot of research goes into naming things in this brand-obsessed world, but I'm sorry to say that it's an art, not a science, as much as branding pseudo-scientists want to bullshit about it. If it were science, then products wouldn't tank, movies wouldn't bomb, bands wouldn't crash and burn, books wouldn't die, and every new cell phone or car or pair of pants would sell out. So if choosing a name is not a science, what is it? Inspiration, smarts, quality and luck. A good title can get you two-thirds of the way there. Today's pitches were clear and magnetic; they were inspired and clever. Luck? They'll still need it.

I get out of the car and notice a MINI Cooper parked by the kitchen door. Rental plates. I try to remember if we are expecting anyone, but I come up empty.

As soon as I walk in the front door Marta calls out: "Rick! I have a surprise for you!"

I head toward her voice. She's in the kitchen.

"Hi, Dad."

My son Jared is sitting at the table, a plate of fried plantains and a glass of milk in front of him—his favorite Marta-made snack since he was about three.

"Hey, Jared! Come on and stand up! Let's see you."

He stands, towering over me, and this makes me laugh. I throw my arms around him and pull him in for a hug. It's been at least 18 months since he's been in L.A. His mother is on a soap opera in New York, so he stays with her on most holidays.

Jared pulls away and says, "Forget about me, let's see you. You don't look half bad for a cripple."

"Oh my God," says Marta. "You should have seen him when he was stuck in the Accident. He looked like death and he smelled worse than that!"

"You do 48 hours pancaked by a thousand pounds of shelving and hardware, and we'll see how you look, honey."

"Did you take any pictures, Marta?" asks Jared.

"Oh, no! It was serious, Jared. Your papi almost died."

"I think Marta has video of me using a walker when I came out of surgery."

"He was cursing so loud. At the physical therapist.

Poor guy."

"Don't believe a word. I was a complete gentleman. I wish I'd known you were coming, Jared. What is the occasion?"

"Marta knew. She's been after me to come, ever since the Accident, which I'm still not too clear about. How did it happen?"

"Bad construction, a freak thing," I say, waving my hand, as if I can push the subject away. "How's school? And what about the band you were working with? You never sent me a tape."

He swings his long straight black hair off his face, my tall and handsome son. I see he has inherited his mother's strong jaw line, dark eyes and swarthy skin, all of which is a good thing in my book. It's not like he needed my craggy schnozzle.

"Dad, I'm kinda maxed out on school. I need to take a break. I've been pretty down."

Let's get one thing out in the open. I have not been a model parent. I never, ever, will be. So when I hear the words "Kinda maxed out on school," a trio of reactions—all probably wrong—zip through my head:

1. Are you fucking kidding me?
2. But you only have a year left!
3. A break from what? Bong hits?

But before I utter any of these warm and fuzzy thoughts I look over to Marta, who has a concerned, empathetic look on her face, her full lips pursed, her eyes narrowing on Jared, her head slightly tilted. So I catch myself.

"Oh, really?"

"Yeah, Dad. I want to finish. Don't worry about that. I

love school, in theory. It's just that—"

"How about we stay with reality?"

"I just don't know what I'm doing. Everything is screwing up. That band I was working with? The singer went into rehab and they broke up. And Lizzie dumped me after two years."

"*She* dumped *you*?"

"Yeah."

"I'm…I'm sorry." Actually I'm not, because Jared could do *a lot* better than Lizzie, who smelled like a patchouli patch, was a marketing major, and was the kind of pretty, zaftig girl who is tragically doomed to fight a losing battle with easily gained weight. I know that's incredibly shallow of me. But it's the truth. They were doomed as a couple. "Jared, I know that must hurt now, but I'm going to tell you two things: One is that time heals all wounds, unless you're a crazy bastard like your old man. And two is that you are a helluva good-looking kid. There are going to be other women in your life."

"Thanks, Dad."

I look at Marta. Her two sons are a little older than Jared. They own a Mexican restaurant. They have kids. They may even be married—I have to ask Marta about that. Neither spent a day in college. But Marta is all love and sympathy.

"Rick, Jared is depressed. That is like a disease, you know?"

"I know, Marta. I warned you: It runs in the family."

"That's okay. I tole you I'm not having no kids with you, papi!"

"How much pot are you smoking, Jared?"

"Not that much. No more waking and baking."

I just nod. Because that seems like the safest thing I can

do. Anything else is liable to sound pissed off, judgmental, non-supportive and, basically, mean.

"Your room is just like you left it, Jared."

"Don't depress him more, Marta."

"Hey, I love my room!" says Jared.

"Good. Great. Does your mom know about all this? You quitting—I mean, withdrawing—from school? And that you're here?"

"No. I wanted to talk to you first."

I wonder if that's because he thinks I'm softer than his mom. Or because I'm the guy who pays his tuition. "So how much longer do you have to finish?"

"A year and a half. I basically fucked up the spring semester this year."

"So if you're here, what do you want to do?"

"I'm thinking that working for *L.A. Hunt* would be cool."

"*L.A. Hunt?* The gossip site?"

"Yeah. They know everything. Everybody reads it. They even have a TV show."

"That's what they read in college? *L.A.* fucking *Hunt?*"

"You check it out when you have a spare moment."

"So do you have any connections there?"

"Yeah, my friend Sara from high school, she's been promoted from the phones to a researcher. She thinks she can get me her old job."

I'm trying to hold it together. To be a nicer person. I'm always trying to be a nicer person. Every goddamn day. Nicer, nicer, nicer. It's my annual New Year's resolution. But this is painful. *L.A. Hunt?* Jesus Christ. At least Jared doesn't want to be a real estate agent. Or branding expert.

"Great," I say. "Hey, is that lunch I smell, Marta?"

"Oh, sorry, Rick. *Sí,* it's ready. Jared, you want more?"

"No thanks, I'm going to go for a swim. There's snow on the ground in upstate New York."

"I love the snow," says Marta, "I just saw it for the first time at Christmas with Rick."

"It gets old after a while, Marta," says Jared. "I love L.A."

• • •

I take a siesta after lunch. When I wake up, I check my phone. Lewis, my other lawyer on retainer, has called. He's my immigration lawyer, or rather, Marta's immigration lawyer. But somehow, Marta's legal standing has become my responsibility. That's okay. She's taken care of me plenty.

"You are *still not married?"* he says, when I call him back. "What is it with you two? Aren't you a producer? Don't you make big things happen?"

"Whoa! I do make things happen. But the secret to that is money and the quest for more money. Big things happen because movie and TV executives think they are going to make more money. Marta is not after money."

"Did you explain the risks to her?"

"Of course. She knows. She doesn't say no, but every time I bring it up, she says she wants a proper wedding with her mother there. Sometimes she starts crying."

"We need an intervention."

"Do you do those, too?"

"We do whatever needs to be done. As long as it's legal, of course."

"Really? Do you have some man of the cloth show up and do the ceremony? Is it like Dial-a-Rabbi or Minister Home Delivery?"

Lewis laughs. "That's a good idea, actually." Then he tells me what's going to happen.

That night we take Jared to Hector and Mikey's restaurant.

"I'm a little worried," Marta tells us on the drive. "Hector tole me that men are coming to the restaurant and demanding protection money."

"Wow, that sucks," says Jared. "But I guess it means business must be booming."

"Guaco-Taco is getting them famous. They sell *cerveza* now. Five dollars for one beer!"

I admit it. It was hard for me to imagine mullet-coiffed Hector and his brother Mikey becoming major restaurateurs, but they have their mother's recipes, which are delicious, and her genes, which are encoded for hard work.

"How much are they asking? The goons?" I say.

"A thousand a week."

"Jesus."

"I know, right?"

"Are they *cholos*?"

"Nah. White guys."

• • •

It's impossible to miss, the enormous sign proclaiming GUACO-TACO - HOME OF L.A.'S BEST MEXICAN FOOD!!! Inside, it is pretty bare bones. Formica tables and matching chairs that Hector got dirt cheap at a foreclosure auction. The walls are lined with posters of matadors and *narcocorrido* stars. Marta has told me about narcorridos: it's basically Mexican gangster music, played by Mexican guys in cowboy hats and super flashy embroidered suits. I'm not sure why guys dressed like gay, spangled cowboys playing accordion polka music is considered really badass in Mexico, but it is. There are lots of plastic flowers everywhere. I mean, tons of plastic flowers. It is not in any way ironic, because Hector and Mikey, who are 27 and 26 and still wear mullets, do not do irony.

"Who designed this place?" Jared asks. "It's awesome."

"Hector's wife, Miriam, did all the flowers," says Marta. "You like it?"

He nods and admires a sign behind the counter:

Taco y Burrito Heat Index
Gringo: Totally mild
Chica Mestiza: Nice 'n' sweet
Santana: A good burn
Cholo: Killer hot (Order two drinks)

Guaco-Taco is crowded. It's a self-service, cafeteria-style joint, and there's a line that is pretty backed up. Of course Hector spots us, and leads us to a table near the front that has a "reserved" sign on it. He kisses his mom, bumps fists with me and squints at Jared.

"You remember my son, Jared, right?" I say.

"*Hermano pequeño?*" he says.

"*Sí, gran hermano!*" laughs Jared.

I have no idea what they are talking about, but they are both laughing now and they share a soul handshake that turns into a bro hug.

"*Hermanos!*" cheers Marta.

"*Cuatro cervezas!*" Hector calls out.

Mikey comes out. The bro-hugs multiply. I even get one.

After we finally sit down I am reminded that this trio of boys would frequently play together and Jared would insist on being called little *chico* or *pequeño hermano*. I nod. I feel bad. I think I knew this. Maybe. "My memory is a little hazy," I say.

"Yes, you gotta remember!" says Marta. "You used to throw them in the pool. All the boys. They loved you. I got pictures. Your memory...it's just too much working and drinking."

Her words make me feel slightly better. Now I understand some of the affection her sons seem to have toward me. But it's pathetic that the memory of tossing my kid and his friends in the pool has vanished.

The grandkids—Hector and Miriam's duo, Zorro and Zoraida, and Mikey and Yolanda's younger boys Victor and Thomas—join the table, and then some staff come from behind the counter to heap tacos on the table. It's really a nice celebration except for the fact that we've come to discuss this protection-money issue.

As always happens, the conversations shift into Spanish. So I take the moment to ask Jared how his day was. I'm scared to ask because I don't want to go apeshit on him. Really, I've been thinking about how to sway him. I'm sure he doesn't want to work for me. So I've been thinking about other contacts. But my world has sort of shrunk, especially with the lawsuit being unresolved. All my connections are either super big shots, solitary screenwriters, or have gone into churning out porn films, which is not that far a cry from *L.A. Hunt* in my book.

"It was awesome," he says. "Totally awesome."

"What did you do?"

"I stopped by *L.A. Hunt* and helped my friend all afternoon. Answered the phones. Read the trade mags."

"What? Like *Variety?*"

"No, Dad. *The Enquirer, People, Us.* The gossip trades."

"Right. Of course."

"I got to meet people, too. Norman Gorelick, who founded it and is the star there. And that foxy Josie Malone."

"I'm not familiar with their work."

"Really? Well, she asked if I was related to you."

Jesus Christ. I take a sip of beer. "You don't say?"

"I told her we were distantly related. And she said there was something very mysterious about you."

"She said that?"

"Yup."

"Listen, Jared, I hope—"

"Don't worry, Dad. I'm not going to trade on my family. Give me some credit."

"Thank you, Jared. I'm very proud of you. But you have to understand I don't share your enthusiasm for the dirt-digging part of the media. They have not treated me very well. They do fucked-up things."

"Yeah, well, sleazy guys like Mel Gibson and Donald Sterling, those guys are worth taking down."

"It's hard to argue there. But you know what? Right now, there are people, like Network head Walter Fields, say, who think I'm worth taking down. And I can tell you firsthand, power and pressure and alcohol can make anyone into a monster. But listen, if you are really serious about this, Oswald MacEntire at *Star News* owes me a favor or two. So when you finish school, we can get you off the phones and into reporting."

Then I notice a shift in the level of chatter at the table. I look up. Hector is at the restaurant entrance having a conversation with a musclebound gentleman in a tracksuit, which is the internationally recognized uniform of goons. I look over to Marta, but she's not in her seat. She's marching toward Hector.

"Hector, ¿Es este el hombre?"

"Mamá, siéntate!"

"Yo mister, you want money?" Marta says. "Why you don't go work for it?"

"Get the fuck out of my face, lady."

I'm up out of my chair. Jared grabs my arm and Yolanda says, "No, Mr. Rick, wait." And as I pull away, my tiny Marta reaches up and slaps the behemoth across the face.

"What the fuck?"

But Hector steps in between the two of them, saying something to his mom in Spanish on one side of his mouth, while ushering the big guy away.

"You fucking psycho!" the thug spits at Marta.

"You a crook! Go get a job, *gilipollas!*" Marta says.

"Come on, man, let's go outside," Hector says.

"You gonna pay! The price is going up, bitch."

I finally make it to Marta. "Honey!"

"Mierda! You hear how he disrespected me?"

"I know, honey, but we've got to let the cops handle this. We're trying to get you legal, remember? Getting arrested for assault is not going to help anything."

"The cops? They ain't gonna do nothing."

"Come back to the table. Zorro and the kids shouldn't see this stuff."

"Ay, you are right, Rick."

I give her a kiss. "Damn right I'm right."

But I'm wrong. When we get to the table, the whole family and everyone in the restaurant erupts. Zorro and the other little ones shower her with kisses and hugs. Marta is beaming and laughing and chattering in Spanish.

• • •

Later, when business has slowed down, Marta goes with the grandkids and their mothers to the apartment above the restaurant. Everything has gotten wiped down and the staff is putting up chairs so they can mop the floor. Hector empties the register, stuffs the wads of cash in a rubber pouch and then stuffs the pouch into a pocket on the inside of his jacket. Then he joins Mikey, Jared and me.

"What can I do, guys?" I ask. "You wanna hire guards? 24-hour security? I can bankroll the whole thing. On me."

"We got to pay, Rick. And now we got to pay more."

"How much?"

"It was a thousand. Now it's 1,500."

"A month?"

"Every two weeks."

"And if not, what happens?"

"No garbage collection, and then…bad things."

Jared pipes up: "Hector, I got some of that on my camera. You could bring it to the cops. They could ID that guy."

"Yeah, but he says the cops get paid off, too."

"Well, my offer still stands," I say.

Hector and Mikey speak Spanish. Mikey is shaking his head.

"You filmed it?" I ask Jared. "With what?"

"My phone, Dad. I'm training for *L.A. Hunt.*"

I shake my head.

"I'm not gonna post about anything to do with you or the family, Dad. Don't worry. Never."

"Good. Remember that next time I piss you off," I say. Then I turn to Hector and Mikey. "What are you guys going to do?"

"We starting to make good money, man! We should just

pay," Mikey says.

"What if they keep asking for more? What if they ask for a piece of the business?"

Marta returns bestowing hugs and kisses. "You don' pay that man. He is no good. And the money, it just go up."

• • •

That night at home Marta weeps for her boys. I bring her some mint tea and try to console her, but I'm not particularly good at it. "Hector and Mikey are smart, Marta. Good businessmen. They will figure it out. And if they can't, we'll get them help."

"You gotta call the mayor, Rick," Marta says.

"Sure," I say. Even though I don't know the mayor.

"Thank you," she sniffs.

"I am so proud of you, Marta. You were a dynamo! But I have to say, you scared the hell out of me."

"I scared the hell out of me! That was crazy, Rick."

I move closer. My right arm is around her shoulders. My left hand is on her thigh.

"See? I'm rubbing off on you. Crazy is contagious."

"Maybe, papi."

"Well, I am definitely rubbing *against* you."

Marta looks up at me. She's not smiling. She moves my hand off her thigh.

She gets up and heads to the bathroom. "You need—how they say it?—rewrite, papi. Big time." And before she closes the door, she shuts off the bedroom light, leaving me in the dark, wondering what the hell is going to happen tomorrow.

Chapter 2

I come home for lunch. Marta is babysitting all four grandkids: Zorro, Zoraida, Victor and Thomas, who are ages 6, 4, 3 and 2. Plus her friend Inés has come for a visit.

"Marta," I say, walking into the kitchen, "Lewis is sending an assistant out in about half an hour to talk to us, a Ms. Jackie Oberwand."

"Okay, but Inés is here." Like Marta, Inés is an illegal alien. She used to work around the corner, many years ago. Now she works in Silver Lake, so Marta doesn't get to see her that often.

"Hi, Inés! Great to see you. You're looking well."

Inés lights up. "Oh, thank you, Rick. I joined Weight Watchers."

"Whatever you are doing, it's working. Listen, this lady is coming to talk to me and Marta, so when that happens—"

Marta interrupts me with a barrage of Spanish directed at Inés.

"I'll take the kids out to the pool," says Inés to both of us. "Don't worry, I love that pool."

"Thanks," I say to Inés. To Marta, I say: "Lewis says this is very important."

"Okay."

A giant limo pulls up. A redhead gets out. She's tall and beautiful with a big-hair coif out of a shampoo commercial. We go to meet her at the door.

"I'm Jackie Oberwand," she says, in her one-hundred-percent Southern-as-sunshine-accent. "From Lewis' office. Can we talk?"

Marta gives me a look.

"Sure," I say, shaking her thin, soft hand. "Rick Salter. And this is—"

"And you must be Marta," Jackie says, her green eyes transmitting warmth and concern at my fiancée.

Marta forces a smile and nods. But once we walk to the kitchen, she attacks the refrigerator, pulling out food as if to start cooking.

"Oh, no," says Jackie. "I'm not here to eat. We need to sit down and talk. Please. Rick, did you tell Marta why I'm here?"

"I was going to last night, but we had kind of a crisis."

Marta sits down. I sit down.

"Well, there's never a good time to tell someone something they don't want to hear," Jackie says. "Isn't that true, Marta?"

Marta shrugs. "I guess. Some times must be worse than others."

"Well, you have a point, but, Marta, Rick has something to say to you, don't you, Rick?"

I open my mouth, thinking fast, but not fast enough.

Marta waves her hand at me, scornfully. "You want me to sign a pre-nup, right? But you don' have the *cojones* to tell me? You think I don' know about all the other divorces…

Your wifes tole me how much they got! But I tole you I'm don't care about the money. You are such a dummy, sometimes!"

"Pre-nup?" I say, trying not to smile. "No. No. No! I don't give a shit about a pre-nup. I never had one before. No. Lewis and Jackie aren't *marriage* lawyers, remember? They specialize in immigration! That's why Lewis is always talking about the marriage."

Marta looks at Jackie, "Oh, I thought he did, like, both."

Jackie gives her a serious nod of affirmation. "Rick, do you want to try again, please?" she says.

"Marta, honey. I don't care about a pre-nup. We have to get married. Like now. Like today. Lewis says they are cracking down on illegal aliens in a bad way, and that me being famous and all, they would love to arrest and deport you. It would make headlines."

"*Today*?!" Marta explodes. "You couldn't tell me before? Damn, man! You couldn't tell me so I could get a dress and tell some friends?"

"I've tried to tell you!" I say, which is sort of true. "I tell you what Lewis says. Every week I come home and say, 'Lewis says we need to do a civil ceremony as soon as possible.' And right away you start talking about having your mother here. Well, by the time your mom makes it here, you'll be fucking deported."

"You still could have told me!"

"I'm sorry, Marta. I apologize. I'm bad at this. I see you planning and dreaming. I want you to have the wedding you want. And then last night, after all the shit down at Guaco Taco…"

"We are worried about you, Marta," Jackie says. "We are hearing about more and more people getting picked up every day. The administration is trying to look tough…"

"Marta, this is perfect. We've got Inés and the grandkids and a limo. And I called Hector and Mikey and Jared, so they will be there, too."

"Where?"

"Downtown. Courthouse." I get down on my knees and grab her hand. "Marta, will you marry me today? And then marry me again when your mother is here?"

She is shaking her head. She reaches down and holds my face between her two hands and says: "I should *keel* you, not marry you. I must be crazy."

"That makes two of us."

"Inés!" Marta yells. "Everybody outta da pool!"

• • •

We all pack into the limo—Jackie Oberwand sits up front with the driver—and the conversation starts in English for my benefit, but it takes about a minute for Spanish to start ricocheting around the limo between Marta, who is studying herself in a mirror and applying make-up, and Inés. This is fine by me. There's a TV screen in the back and the kids are watching the greatest formula this side of Pythagoras' theorem. I'm talking about *Scooby-Doo*, which employs the same plot over and over and over again, and yet the kids watch it like it is the most engrossing thing ever made.

We park and Lewis meets us in the lobby of the Los Angeles Superior Court. Marta gives him a kiss.

"This is great!" Lewis says. "I'm so thrilled for you guys."

"Are they really arresting everybody?" Marta says.

"Yes. Yes they are. So this is a big relief for me. Plus, tomorrow is the last day to file for a green card lottery drawing. That would be the biggest win, but with you guys married, you will be a citizen no matter what. Eventually."

Marta's hand presses against her lips. "Dios mio."

"You can still get married in another ceremony, which I know you're planning, Marta. But we need to do this. Rick tells me he's working on new shows and will be back in the news again. We don't want to gift wrap you to the NIS."

The three *hermanos*—Hector, Mikey and Jared—show up with Yolanda and Miriam. And at the sight of them, Marta starts crying.

I step closer and grab her hand, the one with the big diamond ring that I gave her after making one of my first post-Accident solo excursions. I won't describe it because, number one: It's a ring. Number two: I have no idea what makes a ring special because, three: I'm the kind of man who doesn't give a shit about rings. But I kiss her hand. "Come on, Marta. Let's get married. Who else do we need? You want me to call the paparazzi?"

"No." She laughs a little through the tears. "But even if I had one day, I would have got a new dress."

"You look gorgeous. Look at me. This jacket—I can't even remember when I bought it."

"I know," she moans.

"Come on, let's do this. Everyone is terrified of you getting picked up. Especially me."

And it's true. I'm crazy about Marta and my domestic life right now. I like the fact that my house, which sometimes felt like a mausoleum with a pool, especially when Jared went to college, feels like a 24-hour party, with swimming, music and cooking and kids and even fucking *Scooby-Doo en Español*. I suppose the grandkids need to go to school one day. And that homework and age will rein everyone in. But for now the chaos is fun.

We get the license and Marta's mood has lightened. "It's no use being upset," she says, and forces a smile on her teary face.

"Hey," I say. "There are songs about what we're doing," and I start singing the chorus of "The Chapel of Love."

"Ow, papi, don't. It's embarrassing."

The justice of the peace or city clerk or whoever does the job asks if I'm the guy who made "that show." And of course I say, "No" because for all I know this clerk will be on the phone to *L.A. Hunt* in a second and the paparazzi will show up. But that doesn't actually happen. The wedding is a perfect civil ceremony of flawless "I do's," and me fishing two rings out of my pocket. I kiss the bride hard and she kisses me back. Everyone cheers. And I feel fucking great.

• • •

We head straight to Guaco-Taco. But we only stay a few hours. Then Marta and I drive up to Pasadena to the biggest suite the Ritz-Carlton has to offer. Marta loves hotels. I discovered this when we went skiing, or rather, when we went up the mountains to watch other people ski, because, let's face facts, most Jews my age don't ski. We just look at all the snow, try to stay warm, and wonder if this is what our ancestors fled the desert for. It was Marta's first hotel and she marveled at everything. The TV in the bathroom, the room service, the paintings on the wall. The Gideon Bible in the night table drawer.

"Why is this here?" she'd asked.

"Bibles are always in hotel rooms. They just are. In practically every hotel in the U.S., as far as I know."

"This room is not made for praying," she said then,

kicking off her shoes and flopping on the bed.

Now at the Ritz-Carlton she is oohing and ahhing at the living room, the leather couch, the chandelier, the TV with the video game console. She grabs the phone and says, "Room Service, please," and flashes me a gigantic smile. "Yes, this is Mrs. Rick Salter. An' I need a bottle of champagne and some grapes, please…I don't know. A good one. Thank you!"

She hangs up and pats the place on the couch next to her, motioning for me to sit down. "You know what this is, papi? This wedding today?"

"Marriage?"

"Practice. Now come here."

• • •

We spend the weekend in Pasadena. Marta has never spent any time here, so we go to the Huntington Library and walk in the gardens and look at famous books we can't actually read or touch. "Ooh, more bibles," says Marta. "Maybe you should convert. It's a sign."

I give Marta a look.

"I'm kidding, papi. I like making potato pancakes and matzo balls, even though the crumbs get everywhere. Damn."

"But you still hate gefilte fish, right?"

"That's gross! How could God choose the Jews, and then you make that stinky fish to eat?"

We drive into the hills to the Mt. Wilson Observatory, we eat room service, we enjoy the piano bar. Then Sunday evening we go home. Married.

Chapter 3

There are few better ways to start the day than waking up to find a well-planted story in *Daily Variety* at the breakfast table.

EMAIL BOLSTERS KING OF PAIN CASE vs NETWORK

A viciously worded email obtained by *Variety* suggests that *The King of Pain* producer Rick Salter provided The Network with the plan it used to shut down the controversial #1-rated show. It then fired Salter before putting his plan into action.

Just days before his dismissal, Salter wrote Network honcho Walter Fields that he would rather "pay off the finalists and end the show than see you milk it and ruin it."

The email was sent Friday, April 20. Two days later, The Network canceled the show and announced that the remaining four contestants would share the allotted prize money.

The dismissive missive – in which Salter calls

Fields a "eunuch" – seems to bolster Salter's billion-dollar wrongful termination suit, according to NBC legal analyst Colby Colon.

"It seems pretty damning," Colon said. "How can they paint Salter as irrational if they used the exact same strategy he proposed? Unless The Network has some shocking memos or video tape of Salter endangering someone, they are in a tough spot."

Both Salter's lawyer, Sanjay Thanda, and Network spokeswoman Marcy Mitchell refused to comment on the ongoing case.

I go for a swim, then put my ear against the door of Jared's bedroom and listen to the sound of him snoring. I'm glad he is here, *L.A. Hunt* be damned. I was such a fuck-up as a father, I should be honored he even sets foot in my house.

• • •

I arrive at the office at about 10:30. Jasmine, who is wearing a low-cut top that is hard not to notice even if you are a 61-year-old newlywed guy who would really, on some small level, rather not notice, hands me a stack of while-you-were-out messages.

"The phone has not stopped ringing, Rick. What did you do?"

"Story in *Variety* this morning. Let me go through these and start calling people back. Thanks."

"Oh, Boss," she says, springing up as if she's just remembered something.

"What is it?"

"Congratulations!"

She gives me a hug. The old me would have been thrilled by a hug from Jasmine, who has better curves than a circle. I would have silently focused on the sensation of her breasts pressing against my chest, marveling at their magnificent, calibrated-by-God density, wondering about their details. Are her nipples large and pointed? Are her aureolas wide and stretched or small and taut? So much to think about with breasts. Are they as tan as the rest of her, or paler, which of course would only serve to make the nipples look darker and more striking?

I still think about this stuff, but not with as much focus and ardor as I used to. I swear. I'm married.

"Who told you?" I ask.

"I never reveal my sources."

"I already know. Marta called, I bet. She wants to know if I'm wearing my wedding band, right?"

"No comment."

"Listen, she checked my hands to make sure I was wearing it before I left the house this morning."

"It's none of my business, Boss."

"I told her, men of my generation, we don't wear jewelry. I never even wore a peace sign when I was dealing drugs in the '60s and '70s. And look at me now: no watch, no gold chain, no chai. Nothing."

"Too much information, Rick!"

"Okay, Jasmine the Spy, I'm done. The ring is still on, but not for long."

I give her a wink, and she smiles, a little flushed. I strut to my office. I may be married, but flirting dies hard, even if the whole thing is ridiculous; I'm old enough to be Jasmine's grandfather. I've got a slight post-Accident limp. I'm about as dangerous as an unconsumed Viagra pill. And still, I flirt.

In my office, I sort the messages into order of importance.

> Jay
> Lance Cruz, CBS
> Torrance Long, NBC
> Ned Davis, ABC
> Oliver Dose, Fox
> Amanda
> Little Ricky
> 25 media reporters

About two months ago, when I felt ready to start working again, I rang up a handful of network execs, but they never returned my calls. So the deluge of big names is a little surprising. But then again, not *that* surprising, given this is the entertainment industry, which is driven by such easily quantifiable and meritocratic metrics as status, envy, connections, greed, heat, who your agent or manager is and who is on their client list, who you are sleeping with and who you slept with (yet another variant of connections). Oh, and box office and critical reputation can help, too.

I make my first call.

"You a happy man?"

"Jay, that was perfect."

"I hope so. You sure you didn't try and sleep with Sister Rosemarie or anything like that?"

I have wracked my brain on this matter. Not about actually trying to sleep with Sister Rosemarie—that's ridiculous. But I can't recall doing anything that shows me as an irrational nut job. Nothing, at least, that I can remember.

"No. I think I was a model citizen. For me."

"Well, I'm guessing they are reviewing their options at The Network. I can't imagine Fields will keep pushing to fight us. The sooner he can make this go away, the better."

"I dunno, Jay. I imagine he's pissed off."

"Yeah, but his counsel doesn't want to lose. They will settle."

"Okay. Keep me posted. And good work."

I study the list of phone messages. I figure I'll start at the top and so I have Jasmine call Lance Cruz's office.

"Rick!" he explodes when we get connected. "You almost killed me this morning with that 'eunuch' line. I was choking on my brioche! It made my day."

"Glad to brighten your mood, Lance."

"Listen, so it sounds like this *King of Pain* thing may be winding down. We should get something on the calendar. Seems to me you're gonna come out of this looking good."

"I can't look any worse, Lance. They took away the number one show in the country and canceled it."

"I know, I know. Insane. Listen, have your assistant connect with my assistant, and let's grab an hour soon. You have something for me?"

"I have a ton."

"Good. Looking forward to it."

This conversation basically repeated itself all morning. There's nothing a network head likes more than seeing a rival stabbed in the back, especially when someone else is doing the stabbing.

I send Jasmine to get me a coffee and Little Ricky slinks into my office again. "Did you think about *Catfight?*" he wants to know.

"Not really. I'm busy being hailed as a hero for calling

a man a eunuch while I was in a drunken rage. But it turns out we might be able to pitch the show. So I need you to write it up."

"Okay. Amanda is flying back soon. We need to keep it on the down low."

"Little Ricky, you've got to step up here. If I order you to do *Catfight,* what can Amanda say? She is 99 percent of the way to a green light for her movie. As far as she's concerned, a project like *Catfight* will just ensure her movie gets funding."

"I'm not so sure about that."

"Let's cross that bridge when it yells at us."

"Okay. But let's try and keep it on the QT."

"I really think honesty is the way to go here."

'No question. But there's a time and a place for honesty and this is not it."

"Are you quoting me to me?"

"Of course."

. . .

That afternoon Jay calls with the big news. They want to settle.

"They are offering $15 million. You get the show back but they get a piece of future earnings."

Fucking lowball offer if I ever heard one.

"Rick?"

"I'm here. I'm just stunned."

"I told them the numbers have to grow."

"You're fucking right they have to grow. They better order some steroids."

"You okay with them retaining a piece?"

"Sure. That's fair. They grew it. They invested in it. Plus, then the other networks won't be scared of working with me. And I'm not even sure I want to keep the show going."

"It's a billion-dollar baby, Rick."

"That show almost killed me. And people think of me as a torturer. Me!"

"I hear you. So what's a good number? 25 million?"

"Are you kidding? My bonus payout was 12 million. Get me 50 up front and they can have 30 percent of the show. You can give 'em 50 percent if you need to."

"Great. I think we can close this soon."

"Did Sister Rosemarie call you?"

"Yeah, I owe her a call."

"Don't make her wait. She is the real deal. Utterly without guile."

"I know."

"So she needs a great agent, not some make-a-fast-buck, morally bankrupt scumbag."

As soon as the words "morally bankrupt" are out of my mouth, I get an idea.

"Jay, can you trademark something for me?"

"We have someone who handles that stuff."

"Please get me the trademark for *Nuns and Guns* and *Nuns with Guns.*"

He laughs. "What is that?"

"A potential TV show and maybe a book. And put a rush on it. Like for yesterday."

I hang up and dance out of my office, feeling like the evil genius I am.

• • •

When I arrive home after work, there are two more cars in the driveway, Hector and Mikey's white and black Broncos. I open the door and Zorro is standing on the couch blasting a toy ray gun with sound effects at his sister and cousins. They are all in bathing suits. I notice there are suitcases and plastic garbage bags in the foyer. It's very disorganized, which is not Marta's style at all.

Zorro looks at me and I put my hands up. "Don't shoot me!" I plead. "I have four grandchildren to buy presents for and take to the circus."

"No!" yells Zoraida, and she runs over to shield me. Her smaller cousins, who were rolling on the floor while Zorro was blasting away, have come to join her.

"What are you smurfs doing here?" I say, bending down on one knee so I'm at their level.

"We are going to stay here with you and Abuela Marta," Zorro says.

"Oh, right!" I say, even though I have no idea what he is talking about. "But if you kids are going to stay here, I need to make sure you guys are in tip-top shape. And that means it's time for a….tickle test!"

And with that declaration, I reach out and tickle each one in the crook of the neck, repeating "Tickle test, tickle test!"

I leave them squealing with laughter and rolling on the floor, and head to the kitchen, where Marta and her daughters-in-law, Miriam and Yolanda, are sitting. I lean down to give Marta a kiss, which does nothing to stem the tide of *español rapido*. I go get a glass of water and think about the unopened Rosetta Stone Spanish language CDs I keep in the glove compartment of my car.

I sit down at the table and smile at my new

stepdaughters-in-law, but they are nodding intently at Marta's lengthy monologue.

After about a minute I say, "Hey, I—"

"*Momento, papi.*"

I listen in. Words I know, like *policía, restaurant, evidencia, casa, Hector y Mikey*, and *aquí* zip by among words I don't: *bala, gilapollas, ventana*. But eventually, Marta's monologue ends and she turns to me.

"Last night they shot out the window of Guaco-Taco."

"Are you kidding? Is everyone okay?"

"Ya, but I tole Miriam and Yolanda they have to stay here. They can't live upstairs from that."

"Of course!" I turn to our guests. *"Mi casa es su casa.* Is that right?"

"*Bueno*," says Miriam.

"Too bad the guest house isn't ready." I say.

"The architect, he gonna have the plans tomorrow. But for now, I move in with you." She means into my bedroom. We've had separate rooms as we've eased into our relationship. "I hope you don't drive me crazy with the snoring, papi."

"Me, too."

"Hector and Miriam can have my room and Mikey and Yolanda get the guest room."

"What about all the kids?"

"They'll sleep with us, " smiles Yolanda. "They come into bed anyway."

"How are Hector and Mikey?"

"They're okay. They have insurance. But they are worried about what happens next."

"They could have a fire or a bomb," says Marta solemnly.

"If you owned it, Rick, what would you do?"

asks Yolanda.

"I'd stop paying and I'd hire a boatload of security guards or bouncers."

"They are doing that."

"Then I'd start thinking about other locations, other neighborhoods," I say, "I love Guaco-Taco, but let's be serious. It's not worth dying for."

• • •

The next morning Amanda walks into my office wearing a light blue sundress and semi-high-heeled Greek style lace up sandals. I'm sure they have a name, but I as I've told each of my ex-wives, I don't speak fluent shoe. Whatever Amanda's bondage boots are called—Spartacus Lifts? Aphrodite Flops? Grecian Sex Sandals? Roman Porno Pumps?—they work.

"How was New York?" I ask. "We have *Gizless* all sealed up? How was the nutjob?"

"He reminded me of you."

"What? Me? Him? I would never pass up a free trip to meet a rainmaker. And I could never think up that crazy shit." You have to understand, this book we are trying to acquire the rights to is written by this wacko from New York. We offered to fly him out first class for an all-expenses paid, Chateau Marmont extravaganza on my dime. And he turned it down! Now I loved, loved, loved this guy's work. His story, *The Gizless Days of Thomas Binder*, which is about a world where everyone is obsessed with their phones and there are no physical books, is going to be a goldmine. But refusing a free trip to L.A.? That's crazy, right? I don't deal with crazy that well. So I sent Amanda, who found the book in the first place.

"I can't believe Kaufman reminded you of me," I say.

"He's very…authentic."

"Come on, Amanda, what the hell does that mean? Everyone is authentic."

"I mean, Rick, that he seems to say what he thinks. There are not a lot of checks and balances going on. And he has a potty mouth."

"My spiritual brother."

"He's more neurotic than you, though. He said the reason he didn't want to come to L.A. is that he's afraid he'll like it too much."

"Gee, that makes a lot of sense. Did he explain that one?"

"It means he thinks the weather is unbeatable, and the beaches are beautiful, but he loves mass transit, hates driving and believes people should live in apartment buildings, because that's better for the planet."

I'm horrified. I love driving. "He said all that?"

"Sort of. I'm summarizing."

Fucking writers.

"So what happened? Did you get the deal?"

"We agreed in principle. I've asked Jay to draft one up. $100,000 with another $200K bump when it goes into production and then the standard percentage."

"Fan-fucking-tastic! Lets get busy casting *Gizless Days*. It's a teen movie. See if the Disney Channel or Nickelodeon has some kids for us. Let's get some names attached and slice this pie."

"Slice this pie?"

"Get some partners. Some funding to limit our exposure."

"I'm on it."

I watch her rise, turn and walk out, calves curved and elongated, hips swaying inside the dress. Each step a reminder that God is great.

• • •

That afternoon Marta calls, sobbing. Someone has been shot. At Guaco-Taco. She's on her way there in a cab.

"Hector or Mikey?"

"No, no, no! Omar!" she wails and hangs up.

I have no idea who Omar is, but I get in the car and drive to meet her.

Yellow police tape is already strung up around the restaurant. An ambulance is parked outside, lights silently whirling. The medics just seem to be hanging out, which I take to be a bad sign. I see two investigators in poorly fitting sports jackets duck under the tape, which I approach. There's a cop patrolling the perimeter.

"Excuse me, officer," I say. "My sons-in-law own this restaurant. Can I see them?"

"I'm sorry sir. This is a crime scene. Until the detectives tell me different, no unauthorized personnel are allowed behind police lines."

I think about mouthing off, but the cop is just following procedure. The old me would have dropped my credentials and tried to get in. The improved me—who remembers my mantra to be a nicer person—nods and goes to sit in my car.

Eventually, Marta, who has somehow gotten through the yellow tape, calls and summons me to go around the block and enter the back of the restaurant. Mikey is lugging suitcases downstairs under the eye of his mother.

"They are getting everything out of this place, Rick," Marta explains. "Everything. They shoot out the windows, then they kill Omar. Next, they burn it down. Everybody stay with us, Rick."

"Of course," I say. "What happened? Who was Omar?"

"He worked behind the counter. With a pony-tail."

"That skinny kid? He was so young," I say.

"Only 20 years old. An' he has a son!"

"Jesus. That's awful. Where were the security guys?"

"Inside, by the doors," says Mikey. "What could they do? The car pulls up, a kid gets out, pulls a 9mm, shoots out the window and fires into the restaurant."

"It doesn't matter now, but maybe they should have been *outside* of the restaurant. You know, like bouncers or guards."

"They were. They just came in for a break."

· · ·

As you can imagine, it is a very long, grim evening as we migrate from Guaco-Taco land to my house and get everyone settled. I sleep in the next morning and when I finally get up, I walk out to the deck and see Jared is swimming laps, snaking his way between his step-nieces and -nephews who, outfitted with flotation devices, are splashing around the shallow end of the pool.

He is in remarkable shape for a Salter, but that's because he's a Van Peters on his mom's side. And being a Van Peters means you have 400 years of gorgeous, DAR/Mayflower, hard-working, land-grabbing, prep-school educated, Ivy League fornicating, stock-tipping, club-swilling, square-jawed, long-legged, Protestant DNA coursing through your cells. And that code is so powerful, not even the crappy *shtetl*-honed Salter chromosomes can louse it up. I remember thinking that when Jared was born, a grievous error had been committed: He was a boy. His mother and his aunts and his grandmother were so damn beautiful, it seemed a waste of genetic gold to have a boy, as if somehow we had deprived a new generation of perfect, flawless feminine beauty. But I see in Jared, in his long lines and defined muscles, that the male specimen of the Van Peters is no slouch either. And watching him swim, I can't help thinking that the awful, zaftig Lizzie who broke up with him was probably issuing a preemptive strike for self-preservation, because her genetic makeup and her looks were no match for his. All Jared needs is the confidence to match his looks, and everyone will want him. Hell, look at me. I was once a hot ticket. Me! A 5'10", slightly bowlegged Jew with overly generous schnozzle. Yeah, I was funny. And successful and I could focus, focus, focus during foreplay's foreplay, conversation. But looks? Let's just say that I looked okay in the reflective glow of my Oscar.

When he's done with his laps, Jared tosses the kids around. There are screams of delight, the joy of being safely terrified as a friendly giant picks you up and hurls your 40-pound body through space. And suddenly I do remember throwing Jared, Hector and Mikey, just as they said I had. Just like what I'm watching.

After Jared finishes using the kids as barbells, doing curls with them and then finally lifting them over his head and dropping them into the water, one by one, he comes over and sits with me, big smile on his face.

"These kids are laughter machines," he says.

"I really enjoyed watching that. You were all having so

much fun." I have a stupid fatherly grin on my face, the doting enchanted smile of a parent amazed at the marvel he has set in motion. "It was the best part of my week, hands down. Especially after what just happened with your *hermanos*."

"Yeah, that was insane. Listen, Dad, I was going to tell you last night... I got this call at work. About you. I'm not sure I played it right."

"What call? From who?"

"Some high school girl in the valley. She says she taped you insulting fat people at her school. It was during *The King of Pain*, she says."

It takes me a second to place this. "Oh, that? I was with Amanda. They booed her off the stage, so I went up to defend her and they booed me, too. So I let them have it."

"She says you come off like a total jerk and that it is news because she heard you were in a trial. I told her *L.A. Hunt* wouldn't be interested in it—that you're not a celebrity."

"Good thinking."

"But then I was worried she might take it to another show like *E! News* and that this might hurt your case with The Network, so I told her I might know someone else who would buy it."

"Double-good thinking. I don't think there's anything damning about my performance. But I wasn't a choirboy either. And if Amanda isn't on the tape, then I probably do sound like a nut."

"I have her number."

"Great. Tell her you want to buy all rights to the tape. I'll give her five thou, eight maximum. Whatever it takes."

"I'll see what I can do. First I need to see the tape, right?"

"Right. Jesus, Jared, you might have just totally saved my ass. This tape gets out and The Network might think they have a case—which they don't. But still."

"I guess I was in the right place at the right time."

"I'd say so. Yeah. I might have to change my tune about your job. But don't count on it."

I walk into the cold air of the living room. I have to work to get the smile off my face. Hector is sitting like a zombie on the couch.

"You okay?" I ask.

It's a stupid question. But he has the good grace just to shake his head.

Chapter 4

The idea comes to me at the funeral of Omar Naxos.

It's up there with the worst funerals in the whole history of shitty funerals, which, now that I think about it, is pretty much every funeral. Nobody ever says, "I just came from a kick-ass funeral. You really should have been there." Memorial services, that's different. Great stories get told. Life is celebrated. But funerals are not about remembering. Funerals are about saying goodbye. This funeral is made worse by a shit storm of rain and wind. Very, very un-L.A. Plus, it's a stupid funeral. Twenty-year-old guys making $10 an hour scooping rice and mashing avocado aren't supposed to get shot. It's not like they are running cocaine rings or knocking over banks.

Hector and Mikey look like crap.

Marta is crying a river and her makeup is double smeared by the tears and the rain that is blowing in under her hat. Omar's young son—I'm talking 2 years old—is howling and breaking everyone's heart.

My umbrella is stripped and shredded, black fabric

flapping against the silver metallic skeleton of the ultimate planned-obsolescence device. We can fly to the moon, but we can't make an umbrella that survives a 15-mile-an-hour gust? Are you fucking kidding me? And you can't just toss a busted umbrella in a graveyard because, guess what? *There are no trash cans in cemeteries.* Never, never, never. And this is a fucking outrage, really, because people constantly come to cemeteries to clean their loved ones' and ancestors' gravesites and tombs. But cemeteries want families to pay them astronomical fees for plot care. Fuckers.

The priest is murmuring in Latin.

I start to wonder, what did we do wrong here? Were Hector and Mikey wrong to stand up to extortion? Should I have told Marta and her kids that sometimes you just have to play ball and settle? We always play ball making movies: greasing palms for locations, getting union guys to do a little extra here and there for a handful of C-notes, because who wants to wait three hours for an extra gaffer to drive across L.A. to plug an extension cord into a socket for scale pay, right? But I didn't know the rules of the game in the shakedown business. I didn't think anybody would actually rent a 16-year-old—under 17, you don't get tried as an adult, is what a detective tells us—to be a drive-by douchebag. Or rather, I guess I knew you could, theoretically. I had heard about things like that. But that only happened somewhere else. To other people. In other neighborhoods. Fucking gangs. Fucking guns.

And then, in an instant, I know what to do.

Revenge.

And a goldmine.

• • •

I run it by Jay first, who says it's crazy and loud and genius. That's the vote of confidence I was hoping for. I decide to make the big phone call.

"Sister Rosemarie, it's me, Rick Salter."

"Oh, Rick! How is everything? I have you on my to-call list."

"Good and bad, Sister Rosemarie. I went to a funeral today for a young man who worked for my stepsons."

"My goodness! I'm so sorry."

"Abso-fu—" I catch myself. "Absolutely. It was senseless. And I started thinking about guns. Remember that show you got pitched? *Nuns and Guns*?"

"Yes."

"I want to do a show called *Nuns with Guns*. It's the opposite of what they pitched you."

"I'm not sure I understand."

I stand up at my desk. I'm amped. I'm going to pitch like the all-star I am.

"I'm thinking of doing a show starring you. *Nuns with Guns*. Four nuns tour the country to see who can collect the most guns."

Silence.

Silence, of course, is a great negotiating technique. But not when it is used against me. I start to wonder if I've said something wrong.

"Sister Rosemarie?"

"Yes."

"What do you think?"

"Rick Salter! You make me think a million things at once. Isn't that stealing?"

"They haven't announced a show that I can find. And even if they did, you can't copyright a title, and I know they didn't trademark it, because I did. We could write a book and call it *The New Testament* or *Jaws* or *Cat in the Hat* and nobody could stop us, if those books aren't trademarked. But this is a different title anyway. And a completely different show."

"How in the world are we going to convince people to give up their guns?"

"Sister Rosemarie, you got stone-broke viewers to donate to your mission. You raised, like, a million bucks in a week. They'll give up guns for you. Anyway that's the competition: Marketing, figuring out where to go, what cities, what to offer."

"Gee, Rick. I don't know."

"Winner gets $2 million."

Silence.

"And thousands of guns off the street. Tens of thousands."

Silence.

"That's a huge thing, Sister Rosemarie. Really. You can't put a price on that. Guns don't beget liberty or safety in this country so much as they beget fear, violence, crime, loss of property and loss of life. Thousands of senseless, accidental, heartbreaking deaths. Tens of thousands of suicides and crippling injuries."

"I know. It just seems so serious. *The King of Pain* was a lot of fun."

Fun. She said fun. *The King of Pain was a lot of fun.* I'm stunned. I wish I had a recording of that. No one will ever believe me. That show subjected contestants to torture, starvation, sleep deprivation, branding of human flesh. But Sister Rosemarie called it fun. And she's right; it was exciting.

"Yes!" I say, doing my best to cheerlead. "This show will be even more fun. It will be a competition, just like *The*

King of Pain, except that we will be improving America."

"I need to think about it."

"Sister Rosemarie," I say, careful to vanquish any possible hint of joy or bullshit from my voice. "I really do hope you'll consider it. I think this is going to be the most important show in the history of TV. After the senseless funeral I went to today for a hardworking, 20-year-old young man with a young son, well, I want every damn gun in this country melted down and used to build schools and housing and factories. I *need* to do this."

Silence.

"Me, too, Rick."

I've got her.

• • •

I head home for lunch and tell Marta, who still dressed in black to mourn Omar. She's going to wear black all week. She even has an all-black bikini.

"That's a good idea, Rick." She beams at me. I love that she still beams at me. How long can it last? "You always have good ideas and do good things."

"That's debatable, hon, but thanks. I didn't exactly solve Hector and Mikey's problem."

"That's not your fault, papi. That's too many guns and not enough jobs."

She's at the kitchen counter chopping tomatoes, my sexy, un-college-educated, illegal-aliened wife, distilling the issue down for me, and arriving not far from where I stand. "That's why your show is so good. The idea is good. Stop the guns, get more safer, start the jobs. Go do it, papi," she says, turning around, kissing me and sending me on my way.

During the drive to the office Jared calls from his desk at *L.A. Hunt.*

"The girl with the video called. We agreed to meet at the mall."

"The mall?"

"Brea Mall. She's a kid. A senior in high school. She doesn't know L.A."

"Did you discuss money?"

"I said I could only discuss money once I saw the tape. I also told her she'd have to sign that this was the only copy and that our company would own the exclusive rights if we bought it."

"Our company?"

"Yeah, some bogus company that you own. You can fix it, right? I'll just tell her it's a company related to *L.A. Hunt.*"

The kid is a natural born fixer. I tell him that.

"A fixer?"

"Yeah. You know what another name for that is?" I say.

"What?"

"A producer."

"Really?"

"Sort of. Yeah."

• • •

Amanda and Little Ricky don't quite share my enthusiasm for *Nuns with Guns.*

"Half the country has guns, Rick," says Amanda.

"Actually, I think something like half the country has *two* guns," clarifies Little Ricky.

"So?" I say.

"So you can forget about those people watching."

"You think the people that watch *Biggest Loser* are all fat? You think kosher Jews don't watch cooking shows? That married couples don't watch *The Bachelor*? Anyway, we are going to make them watch. This isn't some Jerry Lewis telethon. This is drama. This is a competition, a war, a crusade, a fight, a national dialogue played out on prime time. There are going be counter-protests. These NRA scumbags are going to buy ads and programming against us. Great! Let 'em. That's more PR for us, and we are going to take guns off the street. This is life-saving TV."

"That's a pretty good tag line, actually," says Amanda.

"Damn right. This is Sister Rosemarie!"

"Rick," says Little Ricky. "What is the show about? What is the meat of the show? You know, what happens?"

"Solicitation, education, stunts and stats."

"Explain, please."

"Each nun has a team that helps her each week in a different location. They have to do things that will get attention. Visit murder scenes, rent billboards, lead marches, give speeches. Whatever. So each week, it's about their effectiveness as a team, reaching people and getting those fucking guns."

"I don't get it," says Amanda.

"What don't you get?" I say. Amanda usually gets everything, plus, she's a liberal.

"Why you are so excited by this? You have so much going on now. The *Giz* movie, and Marta, and Jared. Aren't you supposed to have an official wedding and tour the world?"

"The wedding thing is happening. But the Guaco-Taco crisis got in the way. And we can't travel until Marta becomes a citizen or gets a green card, which is going to take months.

And meanwhile, Amanda, every second that ticks away without background checks on firearm purchases, without tougher laws, without bans on semi-automatic weapons, and with stupid open carry laws, and idiotic stand-your-ground laws that make killing okay—is a second wasted."

Amanda is smiling and shaking her head. She's looking down at the table.

"You are the god of spin. The master of dressing exploitation up as a cause."

I can't believe she's saying this shit. "That's an insult, Amanda. My sons-in-law are getting shot at. This is personal. And for your information, that is the nature of causes. If you don't use them, or in your word, 'exploit' them, is it a cause? Or is it just a thought? Having a cause is the activation of an idea. So if you think that this is me just being cynical, driven by making a buck, you are wrong. Very fucking wrong."

"Interesting," says Amanda.

"And who am I exploiting, anyway? Sister Rosemarie? She *wants* to do it. The people who bought guns but now have legitimate doubts about them? Listen, Amanda, if you don't like this, or don't want to be here, fine. Just take *The Gizless Days of Thomas Bender* script. Go, run it. You are not going to be involved with this show."

"Really?"

"Really. Ricky and I will do this. Right?"

Little Ricky looks a little dazed. I'm pretty sure it's because I just called him Ricky, without sticking a "little" in front of it.

"Sure," he says, weighing his options, which, frankly, stink. "I think this is a fascinating idea. Risky and possibly dangerous, but fascinating."

"How can it be risky? We've got Sister Rosemarie on our side, for Christ sake."

"There's this little fact that guns are involved, Rick. That seems a little fraught. To me anyway."

"Touché," Amanda says.

"That? Guns? Ricky, we'll go to Brooks Brothers and get you a tailor-made Kevlar suit, okay? And you can stay inside the remote truck, too."

"Rick, it's just a fact, is all."

"And that's why it will be a hit show. The danger element! But that's only one reason why people will watch it. There are plenty of others. Sister Rosemarie and three other amazing nuns! To see who comes out—the gangbangers, the rednecks, the nervous dads, the pistol packin' mamas. Gun fans will watch it too, to see what kind of guns we get. It'll be like *Antiques Roadshow* to them! Then there will be the testimonials, the stories of the mothers and fathers who lost their children through stupid fucking accidents, and the brothers and uncles who were just cleaning their guns when they went off. You know what? We are going to preach! The message will be impossible to miss. Guns are bad. Too many guns kill too many people. The less guns the better."

"Lines like that haven't exactly sent the NRA running for cover. It makes them see blood."

"I guess we'll see about that. This is a no-brainer."

• • •

But it's not a no-brainer to sell the thing. Most of the big-name flacks completely freak out when we ask if they want to be "mentors" for the contestants. Just like Little Ricky, they are uncomfortable dealing with guns. "Listen," I tell

Julie Marks, "You can stay in L.A. the entire time. We can film you giving advice in phone conferences."

"Guns make me nervous, Rick. I'm sorry."

As for the major networks, four of the big five have instant cold feet.

"Too politically charged," says Lance Cruz.

"Why don't you throw in an abortion angle while you're at it?" says Torrance Long.

"Love it, but we are booked solid right now," says Jarvis Daniels, who might actually be telling the truth since his network is crushing everyone.

I don't even bother with cable. I want ratings. I want viewers. Say what you want about network TV, but nobody can compete with amassing eyeballs the way they can. They understand marketing. They understand spending power.

And that leaves me with only one more place to turn.

Walter Fields and The Network.

The thing is, I think I actually might have a tiny, minuscule iota of a chance with Walter Fields because the man has been taking a beating over The Network's massive ratings decline. There are rumors in the press that his head is heading to the chopping block.

I call Jay to discuss the situation.

"Word I'm hearing is he will finish out the season. He even has his team working on the fall lineup. But I can't believe he'll be around. He canceled the number one fucking show, without developing a strong franchise replacement. That's an unforgivable sin," Jay says.

"But he led them through some very good years."

"What town do you think you're living in?"

"See if you can arrange a meeting," I say. "I think this is one of those marriages of convenience."

"A shotgun marriage of convenience."

"Not bad, Jay."

"Thanks!"

"For a lawyer."

• • •

Walter Fields insists on neutral territory and total secrecy. So we rent a conference room in the most un-Hollywood place we can think of, a Best Western on Valencia. There are sanctioned hip hotels in Hollywood, and this isn't one of them. Jay and I get there early. There's full spread of coffee, tea, mountains of fruit, bagels and huevos rancheros that I paid Hector and Mikey to provide. None of us are going to eat a morsel, but it's the thought that counts.

"You think he knows the other guys have passed on the show?" I ask Jay.

"I honestly don't think so. He doesn't have many connections at the other networks. And a bunch of his development team have jumped ship and gone over to the web."

"True."

"Also, the world is interested in green lights, not red ones. If *Variety* covered passes and rejections, it'd publish a hundred pages every day."

Actually that's not totally true. Many Hollywood development people never actually say the word "pass," if they can help it. They simply stall and don't respond to queries, that way they can't be accused of turning down a project that later becomes a big hit in someone else's hands. But Jay is right, at least when big names and major talent is involved. Then you can't stall or you'll piss off the wrong people.

When Walter Fields enters with his layer, Gene Mossbach, he says not a word. Instead he walks around the room, looks at the floors, the ceilings, under the tables, and the food spread.

"No hidden cameras? No secret recording?" says Mossbach.

"I gave you my word," says Jay. "We have our cell phones and nothing else besides $200 of smoked salmon over there."

"What about the help?"

"They don't even speak English."

"Here," I say, pulling out my cell. "I'm turning my phone off."

Fields sits down. We all do. He looks at me.

"You are the last person I ever expected to hear from," he says.

I smile, nodding in agreement. I'm a little embarrassed, which is rare for me.

"And you are the last person in the world I want to see, too," he adds.

"I'm glad you came, Walter. I know it must be difficult."

"My staff has a lot of respect for Jay."

"Oh, absolutely."

"So why am I here?"

"Because I'm not entirely happy with the way things turned out. You green lighted the greatest show in history. Nobody seems to remember that. The way I see it, we had a major hit, then it got crazy and mistakes were made. But at the end of the day, we took a highly original and daring show and turned it into a worldwide phenomenon. And yet, you're getting pounded in the press and in the ratings. I thought maybe we should explore a new project and see if we can restore some good karma after our battles."

Walter Fields doesn't look at me while I'm talking. And when I'm done, he looks from Gene Mossbach to Jay and says: "Can you believe this?"

But he doesn't go anywhere. He doesn't tell me to go fuck myself. So I just go for it. I pitch *Nuns with Guns*, spinning it as the logical step from *The King of Pain*. "Except this isn't about creating pain," I say. "It's about stopping it. You know the perfect tag line for this? Life-Saving TV."

I explain the vision: a competition between four nuns to see who can collect the most guns nationwide. Instead of having auditions in city after city, like, say, *American Idol*, we'll go from city to city collecting guns.

"How will you collect guns? Won't cops just arrest everyone standing on line with their weapons?"

"Great question!" Always tell the decision maker they've asked a great question. "Jay's been researching it."

"It looks like we can partner with most police departments and D.A.'s offices for a gun amnesty day or week," Jay says. "Law enforcement agencies generally love gun amnesties. They call them gun exchanges and they usually give money in return for the guns."

"Obviously, we won't pay for guns," I say. "But we'll give them a photo with their nun that they can retrieve online. And the nuns will be working to track down freebie giveaways—T-shirts, hats, that kind of thing."

"Get me a proposal," Walter Fields says to Jay. "I need it by Monday: Budget, time-line, rollout. I still have one spot in February that might be open. And you—" he turns to me. "Fuck you, Rick. Not for the lawsuit, but for leaking the email."

I could say many things in response. I could say the

email was part of the court record and could have come from anywhere. I could say firing me for defending my own show was dirty pool. Or I could say I gave him the show on a silver platter and earned The Network its greatest year ever and got burned for my efforts.

But I don't.

"I didn't do that, Walter," I say, which is technically true, because Jay did it, not me. "But even if I did, we both have legitimate grievances. Both of us. Let's the two of us look forward, not backward. I want to do this show. It's important the same way *King of Pain* was. More important, actually. And if we pull this off, we'll become legends in this town. Legends all over the world. Not just me, but you and me. Legends."

"We'll get back to you."

"We'll send the proposal and give you three days. Then I have to take the show elsewhere. You understand?"

Walter Fields nods.

• • •

Back at the office, Little Ricky summons me to our conference room.

"I thought we should talk to some gun exchange experts. Tabitha Shaw and David Ryan, please meet the deservedly infamous Rick Salter."

We exchange hellos.

"Rick, Tabitha and David work for the Gun Control Alliance."

They are kids. And when I say kids, I mean they look like Little Ricky's younger cousins, and he's all of 26.

"Great to meet you. Did Little—did Ricky tell you

about the show?"

"Love it," says Tabitha.

"Ditto. This is the kind of national conversation-starter we need," says David.

"What the country needs!" says Tabitha.

"Great. I'm thrilled to have you guys here. We need people who know the landscape and the issues. Experts who can provide us with talking points and facts. But I need to talk to Ricky in private, so if you'll excuse us for one second…"

We step outside. "What are you doing?" I say in an urgent stage whisper. "Are you stocking the show now? We don't have a green light!"

"No, Rick. I'm just doing background."

"Yes, but don't you think we should have the nuns—which we don't have yet—getting the lowdown with, you know, *cameras rolling*?"

"Actually, no. I don't."

"Why not?" I say, ending my whisper.

"Because this is background research, Rick. Because this is *a super volatile issue*. And I'm not going to bring the cameras in until we know what the show is, who the stars are, where we'll be going, and what the gun laws are in each place we shoot. And if we have those answers, then maybe you'll be able to get underwriters to insure us. And then, at that point, we'll be ready for cameras."

I catch Jasmine looking at us and then looking away. I take a deep breath. "Good points," I say. "You are right."

"I know."

"How very gracious. When you beat your boss in an argument and he concedes, you say, 'Thanks, boss.'"

"Thanks, boss."

"What's the matter with you?"

"This show has me…scared, is all."

"Really? You think viewers are going to hate on nuns? Who hates nuns besides their students and Islamic extremists?"

"We are stepping into the middle of a shit storm. We are going to need *heavy* security. Remember those women who shouted Amanda down after the hunger episodes on *The King of Pain?*"

"Of course. Jared and I were just discussing that."

"Those women were saints compared to what we are going to run into. Here, come listen to these kids."

Back in the conference room Little Ricky says, "Tabitha, David, can you tell Rick the kinds of harassment you guys face?"

"The prank phone calls?" says Tabitha. "The giant food deliveries we never ordered? The anonymous phone calls and death threats that forced me to unlist my number, and forced my mom to as well?"

"Yeah, we've had our web mail hacked, and bomb threats."

"Bomb threats!" I say. "What do you do then?"

"We call the L.A.P.D.," says David. "And they tell us to leave the building and notify neighbors, which of course makes us really popular with the neighbors. They complain to the landlord, and he threatens to evict us."

"Jesus," I say.

"Plus, I get messages and calls always advising me to arm myself, because they are coming for me," says David.

"Yeah. Me, too. That's pretty normal," says Tabitha.

"You guys are heroes," I say. "We need you to help us prepare our show and help us select the places we should hold events. I assume Ricky told you what we are doing."

"Yes. The basics," says David.

"What do you think?"

"I think…well, you don't want to know what I think," says Tabitha.

"Of course we want to know. That's what we're going to pay you for—for telling us exactly what you think."

"What about the advertisers?"

"You mean you think they will pull their ads?"

"I think there will be huge pressure, a huge negative campaign against the show. The talk radio jerks will be out there rallying the troops. The conservative bloggers and talking heads will rattle off talking points and accuse you guys of being anti-American conspirators. Fox News will air any and every negative slant they can, 24/7. It will be like *The King of Pain* outcry to the tenth power."

I'm smiling. I even laugh.

Little Ricky interprets for them. "Mr. Salter, I'm afraid, does not see any of that as a negative."

"Damn right," I say. "If we get that kind of response and coverage, the ratings will spike so high it will damage the ozone. Advertisers will do anything to get at those concentrated eyeballs. Anything!"

"Mr. Salter, nobody wants you to make this show more than we do, whether we are involved or not," says David. "But don't underestimate the volatility of this issue. It is even more of a hot-button issue than abortion rights. You know why? Because nobody 'loves' abortions, but people love their guns. Nobody collects and fetishizes abortions— well, some of the deranged right-to-lifers do, I suppose. Gun owners spend $7 billion on weapons and ammo each year. They give guns as gifts to loved ones. They cherish them. They scrimp and save for them. They buy accessories for their guns the way people pamper their pets. Seriously! Holsters, sights, silencers. They spend a fortune at gun ranges. Americans love their guns and despise anything perceived to be an attack on their right to own guns."

"But this is a *voluntary* gun collection program."

"It doesn't matter. As Tabitha said, the NRA and other groups will react with venom."

"Ricky," I say, "let's schedule a debate. Sister Rosemarie vs. Charlton Heston. The Nun vs. Moses!"

"Heston is dead, Rick."

"Mr. Salter, you can joke all you want," says Tabitha. "Sometimes we laugh at the situation, too. Look, a 2-year-old boy shoots his mother to death in Walmart, and yes, that is a horrible tragedy. But it's laughable that no politician stands up and says the obvious: that this was 100 percent avoidable. In a case like that, no gun equals no death. But those would be words of war to the NRA."

"What Tabitha is saying, Mr. Salter," adds David, "is this is dead serious."

· · ·

Marta wants me to meet her later at Guaco-Taco, and when I get there I see the front window covered by an enormous poster of Omar Naxos, emblazoned with "Never Forget."

Inside, there is a party going on. Spanish rap—which Jared later informs me is called reggaeton—is thumping, the grandkids are running around like maniacs, and Yolanda and Miriam are dancing with a group of friends, Hector and Mikey are behind the counter, handing out food and drinks. Nobody is manning the cash register.

Marta comes up and kisses me hard. She is smiling

again, finally. "They caught the shooter, Rick. At a traffic stop. He still had the gun, stupid *pendejo*."

"That's terrific."

"And he named the guy who hired him. The detectives are very happy. Come dance, papi."

When a 61-year-old gringo hits the dance floor the hoots and hollers start. But the teasing doesn't go on for long because I can hold my own. I'm not great, but I'm not an arrhythmic train-wreck, either, especially when half the songs are bouncy Mexican polkas.

Jared is on the dance floor with a dark-eyed stunner whose tanned skin and exotic, slightly Semitic nose could make her Italian, Greek, Turk, Arab or Hispanic.

Her name, when Jared introduces us, is Nadia, which gets me nothing in terms of her background—Russian, Slavic, French, I got no idea. But I do learn that she is from the land of fantastic smiles. Really, when she greets me, she lights up like a centerfold for the American Association for Collagen Studies and the American Dental Association. It's a thing to behold: Glistening, shining, symmetrically aligned teeth encased by full, blossoming red lips that let a fraction of pink gums into the scene. This glorious smile almost outshines her eyes, which are both black and not black at the same time. And by that I mean black absorbs light, but Nadia's eyes, in full smiling glow, seem to emit rays of their own.

I shake myself out of this smitten spell and look proudly at Jared. On a purely aesthetic level, this young woman has a lot more charm than that dumpy and dumping Lizzie back at college. A thousand million times more.

When Nadia excuses herself to make a call, I turn to my son and state the obvious. "That is a very attractive young woman, Jared. I hope you know that."

"Yes, Dad. I have 20-20 vision."

"Did you meet her here?"

"I invited her here. I know her from work."

"Great. Great. She's lovely. What a great day! Omar gets some justice, you get a girl, and I might sell a show."

"Thanks, Dad. Not to ruin your streak, but the girl with the video called. She's pissed."

"Why?"

"She says she knows who I am. She says she traced my license plate when I met her at the mall."

"How'd she do that?"

"I guess either she or a friend followed me to the parking lot and she got my plates traced. You can pay for all that stuff on the Internet."

"Little sneak."

"She said she's not going to release the video. But she might tell reporters about the video and the deal."

"Hmm."

"Which might put me in a bad position."

"And me, Jared. I just met Walter Fields this morning. We have a deal on the table. Fuck."

"*Dad…*"

"I know, I know. Forget about me. What do you want to do for you? You have totally delivered. I'll do whatever you want."

"I'm going to talk to her and explain that she got a great deal. It's not like you are Brad Pitt or a household name or were filmed having sex, so it wasn't worth that much in the first place to a news organization. We actually gave her more than it was worth."

"That's a great point. Slightly insulting to me, but great."

"And I'll offer her some more money."

"If she wants a few more shekels, fine. Offer three grand, settle for five, and we're done. But whatever you want. I know you like your job."

"I met Nadia there."

"What does she do there besides break hearts?"

"You can ask her. Here she comes."

Nadia is in ad sales. I am thrilled to hear this because it means that Nadia is not a reporter or on-air personality for the show. And I have this idea that ad sales people often move from gig to gig. So maybe she'll leave *L.A. Hunt* and Jared will get the idea there are other places to go. The fact is I'm not sure how this is going to work when my show gets hopping and he's still working there. He'll know everything about us.

Marta joins us and coos over Nadia. "Ooh, you are so pretty. You look like Cleopatra."

"Thank you," Nadia blushes slightly.

"Are you from L.A.?"

"Yes, but my family is from Iran."

"I don't think I ever met someone from there."

"There's a big community of Persian Jews in L.A."

"Really?" Marta looks at me. "He's Jewish, too, but he likes Christmas, right, papi?"

"Sure, sure. It's un-American to not like Christmas."

"I love Christmas!" Marta chimes.

"Listen, honey, I need to be at work early to work on a deal. Are you staying?"

"Sí." She stands on her toes and gives me a quick kiss. Then she grabs Nadia's hand and leads her to join the dancers.

Chapter 5

The discussion with Tabitha and David and Little Ricky stays with me, and the next day, while I'm waiting for Walter Fields to make up his mind, I call Little Ricky in.

"Yes, boss?"

"I wanted to thank you. For bringing in Tabitha and David."

"No problem. Having any second thoughts?"

"Only one."

"Just one?"

"Yeah, about *Catfight*. Their remark about joking all you want. That really hit home."

Little Ricky nods, but I can see he has no clue what I'm talking about.

"I started thinking about everything. What have we got at Salter Entertainment? I don't want to do *The King of Pain* anymore. The Network can sell that on Japanese and Italian TV, but I'm not going to be involved. I'm really jazzed about *The Gizless Days of Thomas Binder*, but that is going to take a while. And then there's *Catfight*, which, to you and me is sort of a cynical joke, right? Titillating theater that we could justify to ourselves by talking about empowerment and conflict resolution and providing a sense of closure. And do I really want to do that?"

"That's a great question, Rick."

"And the answer is no. I don't. Fuck it."

"That's great, Rick."

"So I'm passing on your idea—and it was a good idea if you want to make another loud, cynical, exploitative reality TV show. Or is that redundant?"

"You nailed me, Rick. I was just trying to come up with an outrageous title and premise. Totally cynical."

"Yeah. What I'm saying is we need to focus on *Nuns with Guns*. There isn't another show I want to do. Are you with me?"

Little Ricky takes a deep breath.

"The way I see it," I say. "It's our patriotic duty to make *Nuns with Guns*. Don't laugh! I fucking mean it. It's the most important show since..." I'm searching, I'm thinking the Watergate hearings, or *Roots*, or—

"*The King of Pain*," says Little Ricky. "I'm in."

Who am I to argue? "Great! And I guess this means you don't have to hide *Catfight* from Amanda."

"I already told her about it."

"*You told her?* And you're still alive. Congratulations."

"After she calmed down, it went really well."

"How's that?"

"She realized that I have what it takes. What you have: vision and moxie."

"She said that? About me?"

"Both of us."

"Wow."

"You're telling me. I was sweating bullets. But she says she likes that I'm being creative and aware and proactive and honest. She says that's just what she expects out of her partner, even if she might disagree with some of it. It went really well."

Little Ricky gives me a huge smile. I nod wisely, like I understand what he's saying. I think he might be telling me they had sex. But I'm not sure.

This of course reminds me of Marta, who was a tigress last night when she finally got home. You have to remember that our romance has progressed slowly. About 21 years, actually, if you go back to her coming to take care of Jared. But the actual heat started, of course, after the Accident. At first we spent endless days in the hospital together, her urging me on, bringing me food, scratching my back. When I came home with my fucking walker and painkillers I was hardly a Lothario. But slowly we've evolved from shy, awkward, do-it-in-the-dark dalliances to unabashed action. And last night things were off the charts. It was the kind of sex that, afterwards, when I'm sweating and panting and close to passing out, makes me wonder if I'm at the age when I should be worrying about heart attacks.

Chapter 6

Two days later Walter Fields calls. The show is on.

Walter isn't very interested in the details at first. He wants to talk about announcing the show in a way that controls the story and makes him look like a man with vision. His lack of announcements and new shows for this fall has been—and this is his spin—"due to legal issues that held up what we thought could be our biggest show. Issues like gun safety, indemnification, things like that. The controversial nature of the show required secrecy while The Network conducted our due diligence."

"Walter," I say, showing up at his office with Jay. "The alibi is good to have. I like it because it makes the show seem calculated and that you and I have been collaborating instead of being at war. But let's focus on the show, the show, the show and the show. That is what we have to sell the world. We don't want to overshadow it. You know industry rags are going to say we are the strangest couple since Michael Jackson married Lisa Marie Presley. But everything needs to come back to the show, the show, the show."

"Absolutely."

"How Sister Rosemarie is a new kind of icon, the selfless celebrity."

"I like that!"

"How this is a show about saving lives."

"That seems a bit of a stretch. No offense."

"None taken. I'm riffing. But we need to create competition, drama, uncertainty and even danger."

"I'm concerned about the level of tension here," says Walter. "I love the show, but are the nuns cutthroat enough to compete? Aren't they all, you know, sisters?"

"The tension? The tension?" I say, searching for the perfect answer. Usually two or three contestants hate each other on every reality show, but how likely are we to get major personality clashes with four nuns? "The tension is everywhere. The sisters are competing, of course. But there's the statistics of gun deaths, the NRA, the conflicted gun owners, the victims of gun violence talking to the camera, our visits to the sites of gun massacres."

"What? Don't tell me you're going to Columbine?"

"We're considering it. This is a national march. A big fucking televised march to stop the madness, to confront a national crisis."

"Wow," says Jay. "Crazy."

"Explosive," I correct him.

"Sounds a little dangerous," says Walter.

"Walter," I say. "Did I give you a show America had to watch? I did. This is the same thing, only better. Clearer. There was a lot going on in *The King of Pain* that viewers didn't get. This is much more black and white. And we are going to have a terrific cast. We found a nun who runs marathons for God. She's like Sister Rosemarie 2.0."

"Is she on the show?"

"We're finalizing things." Which is true, since I made this woman up on the spot.

"Okay," says Walter Fields, "I think this is going to be a go. There's one final clause."

"What?" asks Jay.

"No interviews. We can't have another CNN meltdown due to your unchecked mouth, Rick. Sorry."

"Are you kidding?" I say.

"You can talk to the press as long as one of our PR team is with you."

"I need a minder? *A babysitter?* I'm 61 years old."

Jay stands up. "Come on, Rick, let's go."

"Give me a minute, Jay. Walter, can we talk privately for a second?"

Walter Fields nods.

When the room is clear I say, "Walter, what did you think would happen when you raised this issue?"

"I thought you'd have a shit fit."

"Has that happened?"

"Amazingly, no."

"The thing you are nervous about? I get it. But that's the thing that gives us heft. Drama. Buzz. This winter you will be the biggest story of the press tour in Pasadena. You saw it happen last time. You were there. *The King of Pain* was the biggest story going."

"Yeah. I had a front row seat, but I took a lot of heat from my bosses. A lot of calls from the board members."

"I know you did, and I appreciate it."

"And when we announce this, they are going to call again and I have to tell them something."

I'm thinking about walking out. But I'm also thinking

that this is my only hope. I don't want to do *Nuns with Guns* on cable. I want America to see this.

"Okay," I say. "How about I leave all the announcements and interviews to you and the PR team. I want to meet with them. I have ideas and talking points. But I won't open my trap unless I have a network flack at my side, as fucking humiliating as that is."

"You totally surprise me."

"People change, Walter."

"Really?" He offers me a handshake.

"A little. Sometimes." We shake.

"Have Jay call legal."

Chapter 7

"St. James here."

"Sarge, it's me, Rick Salter. Where are you?"

"Vegas. With Mike Tyson."

"Doesn't he need security to keep him away from himself?"

"The same could be said about you, Rick. How's that home entertainment system doing?"

"Thanks to Marta, the home entertainment system and I have both recovered. I'm no longer a danger to myself, thank you very much. But my threat level is probably going to go up."

I explain the new show.

"I'm not big enough, Rick. Call Boyle."

"The stalker expert with the stupid name?"

"He's the man."

"But he's one guy. I need coverage at the office, of the nuns, and at my home—I've got a fucking refugee camp over there with Marta's family. Plus, we'll need a ton of security at the actual shows."

"He's got a team. He's the face, but the dude has an army of ex-Special Forces and Secret Service agents. He is the guy you need. Sounds like you are going to be pushing buttons faster than a psycho playing *Call of Duty*. Call him. Now. I'm texting you his number."

The tone in Sgt. St. James' voice leaves me a little scared. Not for me. I've had a good run. I'm 61. I'm having fun. I love life. I want to make movies, do interesting things, and enjoy my time. But I'm really concerned about Marta and Jared and everyone who is jammed into the house. And my staff—Amanda, Little Ricky, Jasmine and Sister Rosemarie, of course.

Sgt. St. James is right. Little Ricky is right. *Nuns with Guns* is going to be a crazy show. Half of America is going to hate us. Or hate what we stand for. And that half is the fucking half that loves guns and has guns. Millions and millions of guns. And now what do I want? Protection. Protection from guns. And, if I'm honest, I'm happy to be protected from guns by people who have guns. How fucking insane is that?

True to his word, Sgt. St. James texts me Boyle's number. Here's what I know about Lance Boyle: He's a former Navy Seal who got a degree in criminal psychology, worked on a number of high-profile stalker cases and parlayed that into gigs as an international security consult. Also, he has an unfortunate name that is a sentence, and that, in hindsight, is the perfect name for a guy who gets rid of any pains in the ass you might have.

When I get through to the man, he has a deep, slightly gruff, all business, confidence-inspiring voice, like I imagine General Patton to have had. After establishing that we are familiar with each other's work, I take him through the broad strokes of the show.

"This is a very complex situation," he says. "Knowing what I know about gun rights activists, I would say you are presenting a perfect target for an extremely motivated and easily agitated opposition."

"Fanatical," I say. "A classroom of little kids gets shot up, and all they care about is their right to have the same gun the killer used. I guess you could call that extremely motivated. In my book, I call that fucking nuts."

"My initial understanding is that we have, potentially, a very high threat level. It could be a perfect storm. A movement led by multiple high-value targets on a national stage versus well-funded opposition groups with a 24/7 noise machine for propaganda, and an unknown army of faithful ready to lend materiel support to anyone who wants to be a provocateur."

I'm sifting through Boyle's terror-speak, wishing I had my Tom Clancy jargon thesaurus handy. "Listen, Lance. What do you mean? Who are the high-value targets?"

"The nuns, the hosts, you, your family, anyone on your staff. I guess it could even extend to The Network."

"My *family*?"

"It would be very rare for someone to attack your family. But not out of the realm of possibility. I would compare this to the threats abortion doctors have faced with extremist right-to-lifers. The extremists harassed clinics and clinic workers, but they only murdered the actual doctors."

"In this analogy, I'm the doctor, right?"

"You and the nuns, and maybe the hosts."

"Jesus."

"It's unfortunate. I love guns, but as a law and order man, I appreciate what it sounds like your show wants to do."

"Thanks. What would you do to prevent these current high-value targets from becoming former high-value targets?"

"You are going to need bodyguards. I would move the nuns to new secret locations every week, blanket your office with security checkpoints and keep it under 24-hour surveillance."

"Can you come to my office? I need to hire you."

We agree to meet at Salter Productions at "1500 hours," per Boyle. And I immediately call my long-time director, Rittenhouse, and tell him two things.

1. Watch your ass.
2. Get a film crew to the office asap. We have a new story line.

• • •

When Lance Boyle, whose can-do efficiency and confidence drains any comedy out of his name, is done explaining his vision of security detail for the show, I'm in awe. This guy is a major producer. By tomorrow there will be security guards outside the office. There will be Kevlar body armor for all employees of Salter Productions. An advance team of security analysts will go scout our locations and facilities. There will be two coordinators, ensuring everyone is outfitted with the correct security passes, and there will be a man named Sampson Smith sharing Little Ricky's office.

"Sampson Smith is an ex-marine who went back to Annapolis for a masters in covert warfare and surveillance," says Boyle. "He's the best we have."

"I didn't know those were fields of study," I say.

"They are."

"If you and"—he turns to Little Ricky. "Is your name really Little Ricky?"

"It's Ricky," I answer. "Sometimes I slip up."

"Sampson is going to need to know every single detail. If you organize a photo shoot, a dinner out, a catered affair in, Sampson needs to know. And he needs to know a week before it happens, so he can strategize and work out logistics. Do you both understand?"

"Yes," says Little Ricky. He looks grim.

"I tend to run things spontaneously, Lance," I say. "Reality TV can throw you curveballs."

"Mr. Salter," says Lance Boyle, "I realize you are running a potentially very successful TV show. We will be running an equally successful security operation. To do that, nobody can cross a street without us knowing about it. The nuns don't go to Mass and you don't get a cup of coffee without Sampson Smith or someone on his team knowing about it."

"Ok, I get it. Let's start tomorrow. We'll need to introduce Sampson to everyone. Also, are you and your men okay with being on camera? I didn't even ask before. We'd love to put this in the show. It's part of the whole dynamic."

"I like guns, Mr. Salter."

"Yeah, but you like law and order, too. And you can call me Rick."

"Most of my men love guns, too, Rick."

"We aren't trying to stop you from owning guns, Lance. That is *not* what the show is about. It's about making the world safer by having fewer guns out there. Eliminating senseless deaths and mass murders."

"Let me think about it."

Chapter 8

The first *Nuns with Guns* casting meeting happens a week later in our office. It's a family affair: Little Ricky, my director pal Rittenhouse, Sister Rosemarie, Jasmine and Sampson Smith.

Little Ricky and Jasmine have assembled a stack of headshots, although most of the pictures barely qualify as headshots, because, obviously, your average self-respecting nun doesn't do headshots, right? So most of what we look at are photocopies from church newsletters and bulletins with mini bios glued to the back of each one.

Little Ricky has also assembled the first draft of a show bible, which is nothing more than a binder with loose ideas for the show. Eventually, it will grow into something more formal, a rulebook for the series, and a massive project management document.

Sister Rosemarie is fascinated. "Is this how most shows start?"

"No," says Rittenhouse.

"Launching a TV show is always chaos with me," I say.

"In a movie you have a pretty tight script that you have to follow. It dictates locations, crew requirements and so on. There's a lot more discipline in the movies. A show like this is…"

"Completely the opposite," finishes Rittenhouse. "This is what we call unscripted entertainment in TV land. It's formulaic, but unpredictable. It's reactive. You react to us. We react to your reactions and adjust the show."

"We need to address the hosts and judges for the show, too," says Little Ricky

"We need judges?" asks Jasmine.

Sister Rosemarie nods. "Why would we need them if the show is just about collecting guns? The biggest collection wins, right?"

"Backup," says Little Ricky. "Narrative flow. There are potentially complicated issues here. We could face obstructions from protestors that influence the outcome. Also, there are going to be huge crowds. So having a host or judges to interact with them could be helpful. I don't think this is something that we want to leave to an anonymous voice-over explaining things. It needs a face. Or two."

"Agreed," I say.

"And I wanted to kick around the idea of the hosts being the judges."

Gotta love Little Ricky. He's not saying it, but I'm sure he's thinking about the bottom line. If a host is a judge, then that's one less mouth to feed.

"Bingo," I say. "The host is all-powerful. He's the judge, jury and MC."

"*He?*" It's Jasmine.

"Correction: co-hosts, one man, one woman. We need more than one anyway, as we'll be shooting in different locations."

"Are just four contestants going to be enough?" asks Sister Rosemarie. "It was so exciting having people get voted off. I mean, the competition factor created tension."

She has a good point. But this is a very different show than *The King of Pain*. "Sister Rosemarie is right. We need to have some kind of voting or rule or change. Something to winnow down the field. But, Sister, it's not like we can send 10 nuns off on an Easter egg gun hunt and the one with the biggest basket of guns wins. With security concerns and all, we need to keep the number of contestants small."

"That sounds good to me," says Sampson.

"Nuns," I say, reaching for the stack of photos. "Let's find our nuns."

• • •

It takes three weeks to map out and staff the show. We need local segment producers all over the country and a supervising producer who reports to Ricky to oversee them. We need legal on the ground for each location. And ironclad N.D.A.s—Non-Disclosure Agreements—with everyone we talk to. Hell, I want N.D.A.s with the people working hotel reservation desks. We need two camera crews and a sound guy for each location and an assistant director to work with Rittenhouse.

The co-hosts? We sign up Maggie Driscoll, a CNN reporter with a warm smile and a slight Southern accent. She's a dirty blonde that gun totin' bubbas might relate to. I really want to bring back one of reality TV's greatest stars, the elegantly opinionated Dr. James Burns, who brought gravitas and charm to *The King of Pain*. But he is hiking through Lhasa or something, according to his agent, and is unreachable. ("Listen," I tell the agent, "He's your client, but I really think you are going to want the commission on what I'm prepared to pay. So my advice to you is FUCKING FIND HIM!") We audition about 10 newsmen and actors, none of whom wow Little Ricky or me. A lot of them had too many skeletons in the closet: NRA memberships or political affiliations. And none of them had that sense of unflappable authority, dramatic timing and humor that the best reality TV judges have.

And then we got a call from G-Mac Treadman's agent. Would we consider him?

"*The* G-Mac?" I ask.

"I hope so," says Jasmine.

G-Mac Treadman, of course, is the incredibly telegenic retired basketball star who, as a rookie, was suspended from the league for "insubordination," which was a nice way of saying he once held his team's general manager hostage, upset that, after scoring 60 points in three consecutive games, he could not renegotiate his league minimum salary for another 10 months.

"I don't want to kill nobody," G-Mac famously told reporters after he ended his self-described "prolonged and very private contractual negotiation" while on his way to questioning by police. "I just want fair market value. My knee could pop any time. I could die in a plane crash. And who's gonna take care of my mama then?"

The charges against him were dropped, but G-Mac was suspended for the rest of the season, and rumors circulated that the irate hoopster had a knife with him when he was arrested. With his enforced sabbatical, G-Mac turned into a beloved breed of sports jester. Not a clown, but a commentator and faux-historian, a sideline kibitzer evoking

Joe Louis, Jackie Robinson, Muhammad Ali, Curt Flood and the too-loud ultra fan who inevitably sits in the next row at whatever game I'm at. "I ain't no way in their league, y'all," went the standard G-Mac line. "I'm just standing on the shoulders of giants, praying not to fall off as I tell the truth."

That was seven years and two major knee surgeries ago.

"Jasmine, how many Twitter followers does G-Mac have?"

"Gimme a sec."

"I bet he has a lot," says Little Ricky. "He might be perfect."

"Two million," says Jasmine

"Let's bring him in," I say.

• • •

In the end, the show has four nuns. The plan is that midway through the season, the two nuns with the lowest scores will help the two leaders, which we think might change the whole interpersonal dynamic of the show. There are two hosts/judges who will have the power to award and deduct points at the end of each event, but the number of guns and gun accessories, like suppressors, holsters and ammunition, are the way contestants will earn points.

Me being a Jew and all, my sum total experience with nuns is as follows:

1. Maria in *The Sound of Music*
2. Sally Field in *The Flying Nun*
3. Mother Teresa in a zillion news articles after she won the Nobel Peace Prize
4. Sister Rosemarie Aria in *The King of Pain*

Put those nuns on a show and I think they'd get along pretty well, except for Mother Teresa, who I imagine was something of a hard ass. I don't mean any disrespect, but you have to be tough to get so much accomplished in the world. Like me. Not that I'm a nun or even a particularly good person, but you have to have drive and a touch of ruthlessness to see things through. I'm sure it's the same, even with Jesus on your side. But I could be wrong about all this. Sister Rosemarie is so nice that she got along with everyone on *The King of Pain,* including me.

"You didn't go to Catholic School, Rick," says Little Ricky. "There's an entire spectrum of nuns. Believe me. Liberal nuns, funny nuns, fascist nuns. Hetero nuns, homo nuns."

"Hetero nuns! Jesus Christ, what are you talking about?"

"I'm just saying. They weren't sexual, really, or anything. But you could tell. Some sisters were more admiring of men than others. And some sisters and some priests have been known to break their vows and get married. All I'm saying is they are not all going to be Sister Rosemarie clones."

He was right. It didn't take long for us to make our choices—mousy nuns got the hook. So did ones with heavy accents—a lot of nuns come from overseas these days, apparently—or who had become too administrative and didn't deal with the great unwashed. You already know Sister Rosemarie, but here are the other three:

Teresita Maria Alves-Rodriguez was the first nun to blow us away. Sister Teri went into the family business, you could say. Her uncle was a liberation theologian who was murdered in Nicaragua when Teri was six years old. Her family moved to Miami and tiny Teri, a popular, fiery teen, got the Holy Spirit after receiving a vision of her uncle during a school trip to the Everglades. On her way to a campsite toilet, Teri tripped on a mangrove root. In the years that followed, she tried to recall if she had banged her head, as if that might explain the vision, or if she had been dehydrated, but her memory of the event remained constant: she tripped, landing on her hands and knees, looked up and there was her uncle, a fuzzy, rippling image telling her to "bring Christ to the world and strive for justice for the poor." She didn't tell anyone about the vision initially. But she knew what she saw and decided that she would follow the words of her martyred uncle.

Sister Teri was a spitfire. Maybe 5 feet tall, she had dark eyes that I knew would stare into the hearts of our viewers. She also had led marches, badgered Miami rich to donate money and time to the city they partied in, even visiting Star Island millionaires to hit them up in person. She was fearless. Asked why she wanted to appear on *Nuns with Guns*, she said: "The prevalence of guns makes us all unsafe. It robs us of our children and loved ones. Guns are the leading cause of violent death in impoverished communities and for battered women. It gives men the power of life and death, but I know only one Being who is worthy of such power."

Sister Constance Grace Onawaru is a first-generation American of Nigerian descent from Cleveland. She has a broad face, and I can't take my eyes off her eyes, which seem especially far apart, and are big and round and expressive. She is an Ursuline nun, which is a mission I had never heard of. In fact, I had never heard of any orders other than the Carmelites and the Dominicans, but what do I know? I liked what I heard about the Ursuline order, even if the name made them sound like a bunch of *Star Trek* fanatics. They are dedicated to social justice. What really gets us about Sister Constance Grace is that she is young and has a law degree. We thought it would be good to have a lawyer on the show and she didn't let us down. "I am a woman of God and a woman of law. What part of the commandment to love thy neighbor has room for semi-automatic weapons or fragmenting bullets? Where is the Second Amendment hidden in 'Thou shalt not kill?' Truly, having guns everywhere in America makes us a nation that does not live under God, but acts beneath Him."

Sister Iris Shaughnessy, the fourth of our nuns, is literally a dream come true for me. I had lied to Walter Fields about a nun who ran marathons for the glory of god. Sister Iris just so happens to turn my imaginative fib into the truth. She is the oldest of our contestants. Mid-50s, thin and feisty, with a short mess of black and gray hair and a warm spirit. In her day, she even finished the Iron Man, hence her nickname, Sister Iron Iris. "Fantastic! Fantastic!" she says when we tell her she's our fourth contestant. "Can you tell me what the name of the show is? You've got to have something better than the Untitled Sister Rosemarie Aria Project."

"*Nuns with Guns.*"

"That," says Sister Iron Iris, after bursting out laughing, "is hilarious. But you know, I'm not a nun."

"What?" says Maggie Driscoll, our host.

"I'm a *sister*, not a nun."

I'm watching in the editing room and I throw Little Ricky a look. "What the fuck is she talking about?"

Little Ricky gives me a blank stare. "I have no clue."

"I'm a sister," repeats Sister Iris. "I think all the women I saw waiting to audition were sisters, too."

"Are you saying there's a difference between a sister and

a nun?" asks G-Mac.

"Hold on," says Maggie, thinking faster than we are. "Let's get Sister Rosemarie in here."

Luckily, Sister Rosemarie's been hanging out in the makeshift studio greenroom, talking to her new colleagues and drinking whatever it is nuns drink to stay so nice. Tea, I think.

"Yes," she says, making her entrance. "Is everything all right?"

I speak into Maggie and G-Mac's earpiece, "I want in. Introduce me as the show's producer."

I stride onto the set while G-Mac introduces me as the man who runs *Nuns with Guns*. "Hi Rick," says Sister Rosemarie, "How can I help?"

"Listen, I've called you a nun before, right? A zillion times, right?"

"Oh, yes. Certainly."

"So, is being a sister the same as being a nun?"

"Well, yes and no."

"Come on, Sister Rosemarie," says Sister Iron Iris. "It's quite clear. Nuns, those solitary women at convents, withdraw for God. We do the opposite. We engage for Him."

"Oh Sister Iris! We both honor the Lord. They have done the work for centuries. We sisters wouldn't be here without them."

"I'm just having a little fun, Sister. You're right, of course."

"Um, I don't understand," I say.

"Technically, nuns are cloistered, while sisters are out in the world, living and working with regular people," says Sister Rosemarie.

"But most people refer to 'sisters' as 'nuns.' And of

course there are many similarities, so it's really okay," says Sister Iris.

"Oh, great! You almost gave us all a heart attack. So Sister Iris, are you really okay with the title?"

"Sure. I guess."

"I think we can say that the greater good of the show is more important than a distinction in terminology," I offer.

"They love terminology in the Church, Mr. Salter. Especially the old guard."

"Whoa!" I say.

"I'm 56, Mr. Salter."

"Call me Rick."

"I'm 56, Rick. I keep waiting for changes. I'm not going to go into details. Just sensible changes that will comfort everyone, include everyone, and make their lives easier."

"The world changes," says Sister Rosemarie quietly.

"Sometimes our world, our bureaucracy seems stagnant."

"Hey, I hear you, Sister Iris," I say, a little concerned that any perceived church- or Pope-bashing is not going to be great for business, no matter how subtle or correct. "But this show is about changing the amount of guns out there on the streets. About collecting guns and protecting lives. So can we stick to that?"

"I love the church. It's okay to have problems with what you love."

I know we are going to edit this into something great, so I just lay it out there. "Listen, Sister Iris, after the show, when you are a rock star, you can kick the Holy See all you want. But for the sake of this show, we need to go easy on religious politics. Are we okay? Can I sleep easy on this?"

"Yes. I'll do my best. Sister Rosemarie, are you a rock star?"

"Maybe in a manner of speaking."

"You bet she is," I say. "If she demanded all green dotted beads on rosaries backstage, nobody would blink an eye. We'd just get them. Right, Ricky?" I say to Little Ricky.

"One hundred percent," he says. "Just say the word."

• • •

The next step is to pair the nuns up with public relations whizzes. We draw them out of a cornette, which is the ornate headgear that nuns wear—you know it; just think of Sally Field on *The Flying Nun*. Apparently, it is not used so much anymore. And some nuns use something called a wimple.

When I first hear these terms, I'm surprised. "A wimple? A cornette? They sound like fucking ice cream cones," I mutter to Little Ricky.

Sister Constance Grace is a little shocked when we present the headgear. "Oh my goodness!" she exclaims. "Are we allowed to do this?"

"I doubt it," says Iron Iris.

"Sorry, ladies," says Little Ricky. "We've got a whole crew ready. Let's just shoot it and we can always re-enact it later if we have to."

I love Little Ricky for this. Keep the trains moving, think on your feet.

The pairings seem—sorry about this—made in heaven. Sister Rosemarie gets paired with the oldest flack of the lot, Wilson Cliff, who was just out of college when he worked for me on *Goldengrove*. I've always felt a little guilty about that. I mean, working PR on one of the biggest film flops in history can leave a nasty scar on your résumé, though not as bad a scar as actually writing, directing and producing one of the biggest flops in history, which was my role on the film. Wilson is an old-school, event-based PR vet. He has stewarded plenty of A-list careers. So I feel pretty good about the pairing. I won't have to worry about Sister Rosemarie doing anything risqué or off-brand.

That isn't exactly the case with Sister Teri's publicity guru, Marnie Blitzer. A former party promoter, Marnie babbles about street teams and Twitter campaigns. She talks about cross-marketing, viral campaigns, brand-alignment and segmented email targeting.

I don't understand half of what she says. And that's also the case with Oona Strike, who speaks a mile a minute about ROIs and GWPs—"instead of 'gift with purchase' we can offer 'gift with pistol' and it will be a great return on investment," she explains to Sister Constance Grace, who nods and seems to understand.

The last public relations "strategist" is Felice Donnati, who did a fantastic job overseeing the release of my smash tween hit, *The Diplo Dynamite Six*. Felice outlined her secret of success for the camera and for Sister Iron Iris Shaughnessy: "Basically, I never take no for an answer. If someone tells me no, I ask what it will take to get them to say yes. I'm pretty accommodating and pretty demanding. It's a great combination."

• • •

With the cast now in place, I get an email from Jared telling me that G-Mac is not, in fact, our ideal host. The list of potential issues:

- Photographed at a Las Vegas shooting range, blasting machine guns at Saddam Hussein and Osama Bin Laden posters.
- Riding in an SUV in which handguns were found. Driver was busted.
- One dismissed DWI case.

This is not good. I'm fucking furious at G-Mac, G-Mac's asshole agent, and, of course, Little Ricky and Jasmine, who are young and supposed to know this stuff. I should be angry with me, but how productive is that?

I start thinking about all our footage with G-Mac, his vetting of the Nuns, his winning on-screen charm. There's only one thing to do.

"Rittenhouse and Little Ricky," I say, "can we get G-Mac in here?"

• • •

"Sit down, G-Mac," I say, 30 minutes later, ushering him into our conference room. It's just me, him, a cameraman and sound guy.

"Sure, Rick. How's it goin'?"

"Not so good, actually. Do you remember when we interviewed you for this job and we asked about your relationship with firearms?"

"Sure. I don't own any guns. Never have."

"Well, what the hell are these pictures supposed to tell me?"

"Oh, shit!" says G-Mac. We add a bleep, later, when we put the footage in our opening episode. "Damn, these are, like, a decade old! Honest. I ain't been to a range in years. That was right after 9/11! My friend's bachelor party in Vegas."

"Really?"

"Swear it, Rick. Swear to my mama and your mama and everybody's mama."

"I think your mama should suffice," I say. I pick up a police report. "What about this ride in 2008, where the cops found guns in the car?"

"What country am I in? Is guilt by association a crime? I got in a friend's car. His driver had a 9mm in a shoulder holster under his chauffeur jacket and another in the glove compartment."

"Okay. Fair enough. So how do you feel about guns, G-Mac? From the heart, please?"

"I guess you could say I like two types of guns, Rick. I like guns in video games, when it's pretend. And I like them when good guys have them and bad guys don't. I don't own any. Never have. Do I have friends with guns? I'm sure I do. But me, I believe the less guns the better. That's why I am thrilled to be on this show. I'm sorry if those photos cause embarrassment and that I forgot to mention them. But they represent a moment in time. Not my true self."

"Thank you, G-Mac. I appreciate your honesty. Are there any other skeletons in the closet we should know about?"

"Nah, man. I'm all about *Nuns with Guns*! I love these ladies. I mean, sisters. They inspire me. I hope they inspire America."

• • •

"Great TV, Rick," says Rittenhouse. "Confronting the host. I don't know that I've ever seen that."

"We had to see him saving himself. And he did it. But it made me realize something."

"What?"

"We need a third judge. Two is stupid. What if they disagree?"

"How about a real activist?" asks Little Ricky.

"How about no."

"Simon Cowell?"

"He's got more irons in the fire than a fucking blacksmith."

"Jason Argyle?"

"From *Cooking with the Stars?*"

"Yeah."

"No."

"Toby Rouse from *Last Chance Romance?*"

"What is Burns up to again?"

"You talked to his agent, Rick. Remember? He's traveling in Asia and he only wants to consider 'meaningful' projects, whatever that means."

"Right. Right. Meaningful! What's more meaningful than *Nuns with Guns?* We've got to find him. This is the last piece of the puzzle."

Little Ricky attaches his cell to his ear and bolts back to his office, leaving me looking at the tentative shooting schedule—California, Texas, New Orleans, Florida, Baltimore, New York—and wondering if I'm insane.

Chapter 9

When I see Jared the next morning, he tells me there's been another call from our teenage witch. "She wants more money."

What does the video matter at this point? I have a signed deal with Walter Fields. I'll have the settlement money soon. It all comes down to Jared.

"You still love the job, Jared?"

"Yeah. It's great. And I met Nadia."

"Did we ever get this enterprising young woman to sign anything with us, like we talked about?"

"Yeah, she signed a one sheet promising not to distribute a copy of the tape. But, as she keeps oh-so innocently pointing out to me on the phone, if a friend 'steals' her copy and decides to sell it, what can she do about it?"

"How about this: Tell her if she wants more, she needs to talk to Jay. No more calls to you. He will give her the money in return for an ironclad agreement that will scare the shit out of her. But that's it. If she wants money, she has to sign. This is the last payday. What do you say? It's your call.

Plus, if you are worried about *L.A. Hunt,* we can probably dig up a scoop for you to get back in their good graces. Like a *Nuns with Guns* exclusive. But honestly, I couldn't care less about this video."

Jared nods, "Okay."

"I'll email it to you. Jay's number."

"I already have it, Dad."

"That's right. I forgot. He's almost family."

• • •

"Burns," I say, driving into work. "I need you."

"That's what Little Ricky said."

"That's what I told him to say."

"But you forgot to tell him how much of me you need."

"I need at least a million dollars of you."

"Really? But your last show was valued at a billion dollars and this one sounds a little dangerous."

"Okay, I need two million of you."

"Two? I'm in Shangri-La right now. Would you leave paradise for $2 million?"

"Three and that's it. That's 400 grand a show. And if you tell anyone, you'll never ever get back to wherever the fuck you are. I swear it. If word gets out you're making more than the nuns, I'll get crucified, and you'll get worse."

Silence.

"Also, you screwing around in Shangri-La means you've missed the start of filming. We're going to have to write you in. You've missed the opening show, essentially."

"I'll do the voice-over for it all."

"We'll see. Rittenhouse is working on all that stuff now."

"Give me a point and a plane ticket, and I will happily

be the foreigner who shows America itself."

I hate giving up points, but he's worth it. "OK, Burns," I say. "You can have one of my points."

"I do believe this might be the role I was born to play."

"Yes. Now come and sign a contract. Where are you, anyway?"

"Little place called Bhutan."

"Well, stop fucking around and get on a plane."

• • •

When everything is ready, Walter Fields and The Network gurus leak the first hint of *Nuns with Guns* to *Variety*. It's an interesting choice. The paper has beaten up on Walter ever since *The King of Pain* debacle—that's why Jay wanted to leak our email story there. He knew they'd love it. My guess is that Walter is trying to kill them with kindness to turn their negative coverage positive.

The next day, The Network publicidettes—that army of attractive young women who tend the celebrity-fueled fires of the entertainment world—shower the media with a general press release about the show, and the entertainment reporters go wild. Jasmine gets 145 media requests and directs every single one to The Network PR department.

The stories that follow are exactly what you'd expect: "TV Odd Couple Reunites, Takes Aim at Guns" is the basic gist of most of the coverage.

A number of reporters call the NRA flack who chooses to "reserve comment until we know more about the show." But leave it to the Catholic Anti-Defamation League to actually beat the NRA out of the box. A reporter calls to tell Little Ricky that Richard D'Angelo-O'Leary, the cranky, rabble-rousing self-appointed defender of the faith who has made himself the media's go-to Catholic layman, has issued a statement condemning the show.

"What did D'Angelo-O'Leary have to say?"

Little Ricky scans a printout. "He says the show 'is abusing a pillar of the Catholic church for both personal and political profit' and that 'a man with the exploitative track record of Rick Salter has no business working with sisters.'"

"Son of a bitch. What does he know about me?"

"He adds that 'the sisters should be very careful about aligning themselves with a politically tainted show that is almost certainly at odds with their nation's constitution.'"

"You got to be kidding me."

"It's here in black and white."

"What did you tell the reporter?"

"That we needed to study the statement and would get back to him."

"Get him on the phone and tell him the American Association of Pediatrics just a released a report that 7,500 kids were admitted to hospitals last year with gunshot wounds and more than 500 of those kids died as a result of those wounds. Our show is committed to getting potentially lethal weapons off the street and out of homes and bringing awareness to the damage and death inflicted by gun ownership. Tell him that these nuns are brave, committed, loving women who will go out in the streets to spread love and save lives. And tell D'Angelo-O'Leary I hope he chokes on a Communion cracker!"

"I'll leave that last part out."

"They should be canonized, not castigated!"

"Of course."

"Maybe we should have a press conference."

"You promised Walter Fields. No press."

That snaps me out of my rage. I look at Little Ricky and offer a grim nod.

"Ricky, I can't talk to the press. Thanks for reminding me. But you can and should."

"I'd rather leave it to The Network flacks. I'm working my ass off as it is."

"Right, right. Shit, if the Catholic Anti-Defamation League puts its statement out, the NRA can't be far behind."

• • •

Two days after the show has been announced, I drive up to the office still feeling great. There are second-day stories everywhere: *Variety, Hollywood Reporter, New York Times, Wall Street Journal.* When I get out of the car, I notice a tall man—white, about 50 years old, wearing army surplus camouflage pants and vest—standing by the road with a sign. "Freedom = Second Amendment," reads one side. "Self-Defense is a Human Right," reads the other.

I walk toward the office and he calls out, "Welcome to a defense-free zone!"

I'm just going to ignore him. Not engaging is the most frustrating thing to a protestor, right?

"Guns don't kill people! People kill people!" he yells.

Of course this line almost stops me. Should I have a conversation with this sad sack about the disingenuousness of this statement? Should I hold a two-minute seminar on the many machines, chemicals and drugs that are strictly monitored because of their potential lethal power? Should I point out that we don't let people walk around with heroin or bombs or cyanide or mercury, or let just anyone pilot helicopters or cruise ships or 18-wheelers? But why bother with this guy? A discussion in causation or semantics isn't going to change his mind.

"Remember, sir!" he calls. "The only thing that stops a bad guy with a gun is a good guy with a gun!"

I make it to the door without telling him to fuck off. I'm so proud of myself.

Entering Salter Productions, I say, "Jasmine, was there a loony gun-nut protester outside when you got here?"

"No, boss."

"Well, he's out there now."

"Just one?"

"Yes. Let's hope it's a passing thing."

"Hope? Let's pray!"

"Loonies don't generally go halfway, do they? Holy rollers roll, protesters picket. It's the nature of true believers. I think this guy might be out there a while."

Unfortunately, I'm right. Mr. Gun Crazy, as we start to call him in the office, is out there every day. On the second morning, he has a friend with him—a short guy with a bowl haircut carrying two signs: "No Guns = No America" and "Gun Ownership Is a Civil Right." On the fourth day, they are joined by an elderly man who walks around with this gem: "Election Reminder: I Vote and I Shoot."

I instruct the office to *never* engage with them, although it's not easy. In the afternoon on the fifth day, with yet more stragglers, they start to sing "We Shall Overcome"—a song that is so loaded with history and struggle and inspiration that I almost go out of my mind. It should fucking be illegal to sing a song like that about gun rights. Mr. Gun Crazy probably thinks he's trying to overcome oppression, even though our show has nothing to do with taking away his guns. Fucking asshole. I am so offended that I go out to my car and pull up to a spot near the Uzi Tabernacle Choir, open my windows and blast Chopin on the car stereo at top volume. It's pretty loud, and I'm probably making myself deaf, but I don't care. I sit there for 10 minutes, looking at these morons, who have stopped singing. Finally, I turn off the engine, get out of the car, spit on the ground, and go back to work.

It takes a whole week for the media to turn the picket men into a story. *Variety* runs an item about Mr. Gun Crazy, whose real name turns out to be William Burr, a tall, unemployed machinist who describes himself as "a gun aficionado, Second Amendment lover and American patriot." Why is Burr standing outside the office building in Burbank? "Because this is where the offices of *Nuns with Guns* are. And I want them to know there are Americans who won't stand for an attack on the right to bear arms."

Variety asks Burr if he is bearing arms while protesting, to which he answers, "No comment."

Later that day, Maureen Moscott, the agent who rented me the office space, calls. "Rick," she says, "We're getting complaints from the other tenants about these guys picketing the building."

"Yeah, Maureen. I'm sorry about that. I thought about calling the cops, but what can we do? This is America."

"Well, I don't know either. The building management company asked me to call you. When your renewal comes up this could be a problem."

"A problem? Listen, does the guy mention any other tenants by name? No. He mentions my show. I think all the other tenants are looking pretty safe from where I sit."

After local TV crew has interviewed gun-crazy Mr.

Burr and his bowl-haircut pal Max Ulrich, Jasmine comes into my office to play the clip for me. "You gotta see this, boss. I think he's threatening you." She puts a laptop on my desk and clicks a video screen.

"Have you met with anyone from the show?" asks an off-camera journalist.

"No. Not yet," says Burr. "No one has approached me from the show that I know of, but I have seen Rick Salter, the show's producer, coming and going, seemingly without a care in the world. Well, he should care. There are a lot of people who hate him."

"See?" says Jasmine.

"Great. Thanks. Jasmine, I want you to know we are gong to be okay. This is just intimidation. It won't work. We have 24/7 security. We're going to get the FBI and ATF involved if we have to. Okay?"

"Okay."

"That guy out there? He's a joke. But we will take him seriously. It's not like he's going to be able to waltz in here and make any trouble. But can you please show this to Sampson Smith? He will follow up with the proper channels."

Chapter 10

The first competition is in our backyard. California. Each team has $4,000 to market itself. We divided the state into four sections: L.A., Orange County, Oakland and the border town of San Ysidro. Then the contestants draw lots.

Sister Maria Alves-Rodrigues gets Los Angeles. Sister Constance Grace gets Oakland. Sister Iron Iris gets San Ysidro and Sister Rosemarie gets Orange County.

I love this draw. Our biggest name goes into the most hostile territory, the youngest and least experienced get the cities, and Iron Iris gets the wild card, which is to say I don't know anything about San Ysidro, except that it is on the way to Tijuana.

Our resident gun-control consultants, Tabitha and David, deliver the raw data on the different areas. "First off, about 22 percent of the state population of California owns a gun of some kind," says Tabitha. "I know that's a frightening percentage. But it's nothing compared to Wyoming, Montana, West Virginia and Mississippi, where over 50 percent of the population owns a gun. Still, because

California has such a huge population, it has the second most guns of any state in the country. In terms of legally registered guns, Orange County is a hotbed of firepower. Exact numbers are hard to find. But given the conservative nature of the county, it is safe to say there is a very high density of armaments here. This is an NRA stronghold, so getting guns donations will be tough."

"Now Oakland and L.A. have much denser populations but not nearly as many registered guns," says David. "To state the obvious, illegal and unregistered guns numbers are hard to come by. Generally speaking, though, there is a high crime-to-illegal gun ratio. So in arrests involving guns, over 50 percent of the guns are unregistered."

"Oh my goodness," says Sister Constance Grace.

"Exactly," says Tabitha. "These communities have a history of gun amnesty programs. So there is a precedent for what you are doing. Also, Oakland has the most violent gun crime of any city in the U.S. at the moment. We are talking about a place that has 11 violent gun episodes a day. So the guns are there for the taking. I would imagine the city will roll out the red carpet for you."

"Wow!" says Sister Teri. "I'm going into the belly of the beast."

"What about San Ysidro?" asks Sister Iron Iris.

"That's the tweener, with not much in the way of solid data," says David. "It's basically a southern part of San Diego, so you can appeal to the whole city. But the proximity to Tijuana—it's the busiest border crossing in the U.S.—makes it a hotbed for gun-running."

"Actually," says Tabitha, "it does have some serious history. In 1984, a man named James Oliver Huberty walked into a McDonald's and gunned down 21 people, and injured dozens more. It remains the biggest massacre in California history."

"I guess we should play that up," says Sister Iris. "I mean, use it to make a point."

"Yes, I'd imagine that that will be something to discuss with your team."

"So it seems you are all evenly matched," adds Dr. Burns. "Sister Rosemarie gets a place with lots of guns but lots of gun lovers. Sister Maria and Sister Constance Grace get cities with unregulated weapons, and Sister Iris gets something, well, a little in between."

"Whoa! Wait," says Wilson Cliff, Sister Rosemarie's flack. "Orange County versus Compton? How is that fair?"

"Sorry, Wilson. The drawings were completely blind. You'll just have to do your best. And with Sister Rosemarie, that should be pretty good."

"It's gonna take a miracle."

"Well, Wilson," smiles G-Mac Treadman, "you are working with the right people."

• • •

It used to be that marketing and public relations were simple. Back when I ran marketing for Visionary Pictures there were a finite number of outlets to promote our movies. Radio, TV, posters, movie trailers and the press, and a lot of it was handled by regional promo men. Sure, we did print campaigns and a rare promotional tour, those meet-and-greets in theater lobbies for fan clubs, church and civic groups, Rotary clubs, or anyone else who'd listen. But that was it. There was no social media, no tweets, Facebook, email, cable channels galore, year-long campaigns, fast-food tie-ins, beer ad tie-ins, book-cover tie-ins. None of that existed. Social media was called word-of-mouth. People talked about what you heard on the radio or late night TV. Movies were still a ritual. And they were fleeting and finite. You either saw it or you didn't, and if you ever wanted to see it, you had to pray it would show up at the drive-in or eventually play on a local channel. There was no "I'll catch it later" attitude, which is what has happened with the on-demand, give-it-to-me-now advent of Netflix and DVR. Real time has been suspended in a way; entertainment now moves at variable speeds for the masses. It's à la carte, instant, rewindable and retrievable. All of which is to say that getting viewer attention and time is harder than ever, and that watching our various PR machines churn for *Nuns with Guns* is kind of fantastic for an "old media" guy like me.

The Network flexes its muscle running a teaser about "the most controversial show of the season. *Nuns with Guns*. From the makers of *The King of Pain*." It's a good spot. But the one that is truly amazing shows a nun, her face obscured by shadows, holding an AK-47, with a voice-over intoning, "Life or death TV." That spot starts just before the Super Bowl. And then on Super Bowl Sunday we fly in Sister Rosemarie to the game and 115 million viewers are told that she is the star of the new show.

The PR for each of the nuns is, frankly, uneven, but when it's good, it's genius. The veterans, Wilson Cliff and Felice Donatti, work the old media channels. But the two younger PR kids, Marnie Blitzer and Oona Strike, are wizards. They get bloggers to blog, tweeters to tweet. They use spam companies that operate outside the U.S., they hire street teams and print up fliers for them to hand out. In Oakland, Oona somehow manages to have a massive graffiti mural pop up overnight of Sister Constance Grace, her smile beaming, her hands pressed together as if in prayer, and big balloon letters saying, GIVE 'EM UP TO NUNS WITH GUNS.

Then they both start using YouTube and Vimeo and other video sites I've never heard of. Sister Teri does a dance video in full habit to a track that Oona gets from her Swedish DJ friends, The House Patrol. Sister Teri struts her stuff, approaching thugs, mobsters, hunters, kids in playgrounds, moms in the hair salons and "warming up the nation for a gun donation" as each person drops a weapon in her big red basket. And together they all sing:

> Turn it in
> Turn it around
> Turn it in
> Turn it around
> Guns turn the world upside down
> So turn it in and
> Turn it around

Sister Constance Grace, not to be outdone, wears a dress made of magnets designed by some fashionista genius at Cal Tech. In her video, Sister Constance Grace walks down the street to a hip-hop beat mashed up with Gregorian chanting while weapons just fly to her, floating out of holsters, gangsta jeans, a granny's purse, zinging through the air and all hitting the dress with a metallic clanging sound.

They call me and ask if I'd be in the video. I agree to take one for the team, if they need me. They come down and have me dress as a priest and make a series of surprised faces: shock, awe, terror, bewilderment, confusion, excitement, elation, all of which they cut into the video. And then they give me one line of dialogue. "She has a certain magnetism," which ends up being sampled and repeated throughout the video.

The videos go viral. Thanks to Oona and Marnie, the maestros of the social media maelstrom, who not only get their other clients to tweet and post about "these amazing videos," but also release talking-head video clips of the smiling Sisters Teri and Constance Grace both discussing how fun it was to make a video about something that is so important. "Not only for me," says Sister Teri, "but for a safer America."

You may have also seen the footage of Oona and Marnie gearing up for future episodes, putting out calls to marketing heads of Fortune 500 companies, fashion houses, record labels and music managers as they looked for giveaways. T-shirts, hats, underwear, anything. "Look, I can't promise you anything. I don't edit the show, but if you can give me three thousand pieces, *maybe* we can work it into the show. We'll give them away to anyone turning in a gun… That's right. Yeah, you can bring them by and maybe we can get Sister Teri to wear one. Cool, right?…Yeah, prime time. But I need to know today."

Watching these two operate and innovate gives me an idea. I go back to the office and get online and register for the NRA, which feels a little scummy to a guy like me, but I have my reasons. The first should be pretty obvious, right? Know thine enemy. By signing up, I get put on their email lists and opt-in to get solicitations from other groups. I instantly become part of a nation within our nation: the most powerful lobby group in the country. Actually, I honestly think they might be the second or third most powerful these days; I'm betting the oil lobby and tech lobbies have more money. But I guess the NRA has the biggest voting bloc.

To be totally honest, if it was just about rifles—I'm thinking about the NRA's name, here: National *Rifle* Association—I'm totally okay with people owning the muskets and blunderbusses our founders used to beat the British. Those were the arms of the day—so no problem. I'm in. You want to hunt? Fine. I'm okay with that. And to be double honest, I loved signing up because I couldn't wait to pronounce myself a member of the NRA, that heinous, bogus American Association of Total Disingenuousness. Yes! When I get accused of being a profiteering, liberal, peacenik Jew who is exploiting everyone—nuns, Catholics, TV viewers, advertisers, the entire free world—I will just pull out my NRA membership card. "I'm one of you," I'll say. "Just like the machine-gun makers and bullet manufacturers are one of you, I'm on the same team."

Oh, I can't wait! Because with less than a month to go before our on-air debut, I love the idea that I may inflict some carnage on these greedy bastards. Little Ricky comes to me with reports, with love letters from police departments, from city halls, from gun control activists. The stars are aligning, as I knew they would, on the most divisive issue this side of abortion. And then the "A" word gets me thinking. I walked down to Little Ricky's office, which he's been sharing with Sampson. His desk is covered with maps, production calendars, Non-Disclosure Agreements and permit applications.

"Little Ricky," I say, ignoring the fact that he is clearly drowning in paperwork, "I have a great idea."

"As opposed to your other merely adequate ideas?"

"Oooh, having a bad hair day, are we?"

"This is the fucking craziest production schedule in history, Rick. Look at this: shooting in four cities for one episode. That's crazy. Four assistant directors, four crews, four sets of reservations, four police departments, four budgets and one me and one Sampson."

"Crazy for you, Sampson?"

"Very, sir. We are here all hours."

"I know. But you are making it happen. You guys are fucking supermen. You should do some press. Get some of the glory."

"How about you just buy me a jacket with a bull's-eye on the back?" says Little Ricky.

"I thought you said we're getting tons of love."

"From the people on our side. It can't last. You know some gun-loving cop is going to rat us out. I can't believe it hasn't happened yet. Once talk radio and the web gets a hold of this…"

"But so far the embargo on our schedule is holding."

"A miracle, Rick."

"This is going to be historic."

"I just want to make it out alive."

"Reservations in bogus names?"

"Check."

"At different locations?"

"Check."

"Transport vetted and booked?"

"Check."

"N.D.A.s signed?

"Of course."

"You and Sampson Smith in lockstep?"

"What do you think?"

"Sarcasm is not needed here. You are about to go down

in history as the second-greatest TV producer of all time."

"I'm just tired."

"How's Amanda?"

"Tired of me being tired."

"So go home. Now."

"Okay, I will. But what was your great idea?"

"The right to life."

"The right to life?"

"Our show is about the right to life, isn't that great?"

Little Ricky sighs. He clearly does not share my enthusiasm. "I think I get what you are driving at," he says. "Many of the anti-choice people, the 'right to lifers,' are going to be pro-gun rights. So aligning our objectives to the right to life will cross them up, too."

"Yeah, I love the idea of stealing their message and twisting it."

"I'm not sure we want to do that."

"We don't have to do it. We can have the nuns do it! It's totally consistent for them. They *are* right-to-lifers."

"True. I just don't think that co-opting a battle call is going to change minds. It's going to be the stories we tell. The facts we share, the images of tragedy and children that we've lost."

Little Ricky has a point. Those were our original ideas for the show. He's gently reanimating them to steer me clear.

"Look, Rick," he continues. "Let's keep that idea in our back pocket. But the original concept still seems very strong to me."

I nod. "Ricky?" I say—it's maybe the third time I've left off the "Little."

"Yeah."

"You are a fucking great sounding board. Don't ever let

me tell you different." I turn to Sampson. "You didn't hear me say that."

"Say what?"

We all share a laugh.

Chapter 11

Reality is a relative term. When push comes to shove, we realize that staging all four events on the same day is totally insane. So we play it safe and stage two events on one day, and two events a day later. That way we can spread our hosts around, and we can edit it to give the appearance of everything happening at the same time. For PR reasons, we decide to do Oakland and L.A. first. Bigger cities, more perceived danger and a bigger bang for our efforts.

Frankly, I'm very nervous about the turnout; other gun buyback programs have paid as much as $250 per weapon. We are offering digital photos of donors posing with a nun, some free goodies and the chance to be on national TV. I never underestimate the power of TV, but if money is tight, I'm not sure I'd give a damn about meeting a nun and *maybe* have a tiny chance of getting on TV for five seconds. But Marnie Blitzer and Oona Strike tell me they are worried about having enough swag to exchange for the guns.

"My street team tells me there are going to be people who show up with multiple guns," says Oona, calling me from Oakland. "They know these donors personally."

"Multiple guns. You think we'll get a lot?"

"Rick, this is *America*. People have *generations* of guns that are just sitting there. Which reminds me, my street team also said that some kids were gonna try and trade in toy guns and pellet guns."

"We know about that. That happens at every buy-back operation. Also, guns that don't work."

"Good. Glad you are on it."

"I think we should take all the guns that come in. It seems to me that a broken gun can be used as a threatening object. The same with a realistic-looking pellet gun. There are too many deaths caused by guns that just look real."

"Okay. It's your show."

• • •

We send out remote trucks with two crews to each site, and Rittenhouse, Ricky and I go to a video production studio on Ventura to pull down six simultaneous feeds. At each site, one crew roams around the crowd, interviewing gun donors waiting in line, talking to bystanders about guns, and what they thought of the series. The other crew films the sisters with two cameras as they interact with the gun donors.

All I can think of is that Oona and Marnie are geniuses. The lines are long and filled with young and old, and men and women.

Each donor gets a few words with the sister and a posed picture. Plus, Sister Teri is sending off gun donors with multicolored Scam Streetwear T-shirts and Sister Constance Grace is handing out Perfect Time watches. The shirts retail for $28.99 and the watches list at $42.99. But as Oona explained to me earlier, "The watches cost about 6 bucks to make, 3 bucks to air freight over for the show. So even if they give away 5,000, that costs them $45,000, which is great publicity and buzz. If they wanted to shoot a commercial and buy ad time, well, that's big money, too. So this does the trick—as long as you don't edit them out, Rick. You get me?"

Rittenhouse is cutting the two segments live. Little Ricky and I are there to help him piece the six different feeds together. But he's a total pro. So I just sit back and enjoy. When a woman with three kids starts tearing up about the people she "personally knew personally" who have died senseless deaths, Rittenhouse just lets her go, careful to work Sister Constance Grace's empathy—her grimacing, her big-eyed concern, her gentle back-patting for this stranger—into the sequence. And in the end, Sister Constance Grace and this woman hold hands, joined by her children, and recite the Lord's Prayer. It is very moving TV. First-class. And as Maggie comments on all this afterward, recounting the emotion and the drama, you can hear the same woman off-screen yelling, "What the fuck you mean you ain't got no purple fucking watch bands? I just saw some out there!"

We'll edit that out later when we do the final cut.

• • •

The next day, Dr. Burns is with Sister Rosemarie in Orange County at Centennial Regional Park in Santa Ana, and he wanders through the crowd. There's a big booth set up in the parking lot with a banner: "Sell Me Your Gun!"

"Hello, sir," says Burns while the camera crew films. "What's all this then?"

"I heard there was a gun amnesty program today. And I thought, if people are going to give their guns away, maybe they'd rather have some money."

"Are you a gun dealer, sir?"

"Yes I am."

"So you are hoping to ride on the coattails of *Nuns with Guns* and actually try to buy guns that people have decided they want to put out of circulation."

"If you say so. I'm just giving the people a choice."

"Indeed, you are. What is your name, sir?"

"Charles Van Slyck. S-l-y-c-k, of Van Slyck Guns & Ammo."

"Have you made any purchases?"

"Not yet. But I'm sure I will. I'll be here offering a lot more value than these nuns are, I'll tell ya that."

Compared to Oakland and L.A., Sister Rosemarie's crowd is whiter, quieter, older and thinner. It is also heavily Catholic and very female. And that's because Sister Rosemarie has fans. "I just came to meet Sister Rosemarie. What an inspiring young woman," one gunless grey-haired granny tells our crew. When she gets to the front of the short line, it's a brief love-in. Sister Rosemarie may be disappointed by the trickle of donors, but she lights up when the woman says: "I didn't bring a gun, but I think you're wonderful."

"Oh, my goodness. Thank you. Can I give you a hug?" Sister Rosemarie asks.

"Of course," says the woman. "I want one of my granddaughters to be like you."

"Only one?" says Sister Rosemarie with a sly smile. "I'm joking, ma'am. You are too kind. It is a blessing to do charitable works, however one chooses to do them."

Dozens more show up, gunless, to pose. And Sister Rosemarie doesn't disappoint.

There are a few "alternative exchanges" lining the street—guys with tables and signs offering "$100-$250 for Your Gun." We film donors deliberating whether to take the money; it's a real struggle for some of them. Of course none of that footage makes it into the show.

• • •

Meanwhile, in San Ysidro, Sister Iron Iris is having a great time. There are more people than at the Orange County exchange, and it's a far more diverse crowd. OC was all white with a few Asian and Hispanic moms. Oakland was largely black. L.A. was more mixed, with Chicanos and Asians joining tons of black donors. But the crowd here is very diverse. It's got everything: old, young, white, black, Chicano, Asian. It has skater boys and surfer dudes, ex-Navy men, young women, moms and old guys like me.

It turns out Sister Iron Iris has a secret weapon: a disarming, unabashed laugh, a laugh with volume and rhythmic delight. When *Saturday Night Live* does a parody, that's the trait they will mock. "That looks like a frightening weapon!" she says, astonished at the AK-47 someone has brought in. "I'm scared to touch it." Then she switches gears: "Look at me! Acting like an old nun!" She throws her head back and laughs. "I'm very proud of you, young man. What's your name?"

"John."

"John what? Not the John the Baptist?" she laughs again.

"No. Rodriguez."

"I was just joking with you. Thank you for bringing this

in. It looks like it can do a lot of damage."

"Yes. In the wrong hands, sure. That's what I'm afraid of. Someone stealing it."

"What did you use it for? Are you a bank robber?" The laugh accompanies the question.

"No. It's fun at the shooting range."

"But you decided to give it up to us. Why?"

"I dunno. I like you sisters. And this gun could really hurt someone. Not just someone… Everyone."

"Well, thank you, John Rodriguez! Would a handsome young man like you pose with me? Yes? Great!"

You can practically hear the laughter in the photo.

• • •

The taping of the first "event" ends. But that's not what airs first. No, the season premiere is our "behind the scenes, making-of-the-show" show. It opens with Maggie Driscoll, G-Mac Treadman and Dr. Burns seated in the studio with our *Nuns with Guns* logo—a nun's habit with a 9mm in a circle with a line through it—in the background.

"Welcome!" says Dr. Burns, "to the premiere of *Nuns with Guns*, America's life-saving TV reality series. My name is Burns, James Burns. Dr. James Burns in fact."

"I'm G-Mac Treadman, America, reporting for duty!"

"And I'm Maggie Driscoll. We are the hosts, judges, and emcees for this series, a show that is about…well. What is it about, James?"

"We asked our contestants. Here…" In rapid fire our four nuns fill the screen, their faces spot lit against a black background.

"Safety."

"Hope."

"Life."

"Love."

"Ending fear."

"Embracing life."

"Reducing accidents."

"Saving lives."

"Getting"

"Guns"

"Out of"

"Homes"

"And there you have it. Those are our nuns, and that is their mission," says Dr. Burns. "To collect as many guns as they can from donors across America."

"But to compete, these women, these sisters, need to connect with America," says Maggie. "They need to reach the citizens of this country and win over the communities we visit. And how will they do that?"

"We'll get to that in a second, but first we'll take you behind the scenes to see our rigorous selection process," says G-Mac.

We roll the clips. A lot of the footage consists of our first meetings with our four stars, but we add a lot of the fun stuff: The hilarious G-Mac asking the nuns where their habits are, and if they can recite the Lord's Prayer backwards.

"I'm just playin' with you!" he booms.

There is a painfully shy sister, who goes mute in front of the camera. "We can't have vows of silence," jokes Maggie Driscoll, prodding the woman. "This is TV!" There is a terrific, spunky Rwandan sister who recounts the gruesome violence she encountered during the civil war there, and then suddenly grows tearful. There is a boisterous former cop who admits she enjoyed target practice but swears she's on board with the show. There's a sister who teaches math. She's older, wide and thick. But she's very passionate about the show. "This is a brilliant, brilliant idea!" she cries when told of the premise. "How noble!"

Spliced between these also-rans are the interviews with our stars. The effervescent Sister Teri, who declares the show "crazy but right," says we have to pick her.

"Why?" asks Treadman.

"Because I need to do it! I *have* to do it."

"That's it? That's all?"

She breaks out with a gospel blast:

Let me shine the light
and make the world a brighter place.
A safer place of love.

Sister Teri's little body has a huge voice, and Treadman rises and gives her a standing ovation.

Maggie Driscoll introduces the next nun, Sister Iron Iris Shaughnessy, with heavy stress on her nickname. "Tell us about your name. What's that about?"

"When I was younger and more foolish, I thought running a triathlon would be fun!" laughs Sister Iris.

"Sister, a rollercoaster is fun," said G-Mac. "Cartoons are fun. Dancing is fun. Playin' ball is fun. A triathlon?"

"Exactly! But I got a nickname out of it. Sister Iron Iris. Don't mess with me. I can do anything."

"Do you think getting people to donate their guns is going to be harder than finishing a triathlon?"

"I won't know until I try. That was the same with triathlons. I didn't know until I started training. But I'm pretty good at getting to the finish line. Whatever it takes."

"Let me ask you something," Maggie says, interviewing Sister Constance Grace. "Have you ever actually seen a gun up close?"

"Of course. Growing up, all my brother's friends had guns. Illegal, unregistered guns. It was frightening. So many guns. Once, we had a plumber come to our house to fix a leaking pipe. My mother was away so he called me in to inspect the work. He had left his 9mm on the sink. I said, 'Excuse, me, I think you forgot something.' He just laughed, tucked the gun in his waistband and told me he lived in a dangerous neighborhood—and he lived four blocks away from me!"

"A gun-toting plumber!" laughed G-Mac. "I guess leaky faucets can be dangerous!"

"As I see it, guns create more leaks than they fix."

"Oh, that's good! Maggie, I think we have a contender."

Sister Rosemarie—"the nun who needs no introduction," per Dr. Burns' voiceover—is smiling and fresh-faced as ever as G-Mac asks for her autograph and Maggie Driscoll asks if she thinks this will be harder than appearing on *The King of Pain*, "where you were starved, kept awake for days on end, and even branded."

My favorite nun hits it out of the park. "Oh, without question, Maggie," she says. "Personal discomfort is nothing for me. But seeing the pain of others is very difficult. And I think we will hear stories of loss and tragedy that will break not just my heart, but all our hearts. So this is going to be hard for all of us. Plus, for all I know, running our own marketing campaigns may be far more difficult than fasting."

We show Burns, Maggie and G-Mac conferring about the applicants. And of course there's some fierce deliberation. Maggie loved the Rwandan sister, but G-Mac liked the former cop and thought she'd add some insight into the show. There's give and take, but the decision was reached by yours truly long before we filmed this segment. Yeah, I know: so much for *reality* TV.

After we bring back the four contestants who are all smiles and kindness, expressing their eagerness to get started, we bring out our public relations experts, and Dr. Burns and Maggie Driscoll explain the premise so viewers will understand the intricacies of the show and that these nuns are vying for attention and guns. In fact, the show is an appeal of sorts, with each nun pitching prospective gun donors: Bring me your weapon.

So how does that do? Amazing: We are the 16th most-watched show of the week. Considering we air at 8 p.m. with no lead-in show running before us, that is huge.

As for our first gun exchanges, the big cities—and the newly media-savvy sisters—carry the day:

Sister Teri: 2,023
Sister Constance Grace: 1,889
Sister Iris: 1,718
Sister Rosemarie: 1,183

Chapter 12

Out of the 20 most populated cities in the United States of America, six are in Texas: Houston, San Antonio, Austin, Dallas, Forth Worth and Waco. It is a beast. That said, shooting four different locales for the first show in California almost killed us. Or at least almost killed Little Ricky and Sampson. So we split it up: Sister Teri and Sister Iris go to Dallas, which, thanks to urban sprawl, brings Ft. Worth into the picture, and Sister Rosemarie and Sister Constance Grace go to Houston.

Sister Teri has a major advantage in Texas. She speaks Spanish. So she takes to the airwaves, blitzing Spanish-language TV and radio shows for the entire week. Her "present" for this week's gun exchange is a goodie bag, as she explains to Maggie Driscoll. "For my gun donors who might be from across the border, a handbook about U. S. Immigration that is written in Spanish, some designer lipstick and hair gel, and two coupons: one for a free coffee at The Donut Hole and $15 off at Sneaker Universe."

"So you have different goodie bags to choose from?"

"Yes. We thought it would be fun to have two choices. The foreign and domestic goodie bags. They are exactly the same, except we have different books. One is an informational pamphlet about how to become a legal alien. And the domestic goodie bag has a little book I put together of my favorite inspirational quotes in English. Look, it even has my picture on it." She holds it up to the camera and laughs: "I'm like a brand!" Teri and Oona are clearly marketing geniuses.

Sister Rosemarie and Wilson Cliff, on the other hand, seem to be flailing. They nail spots on The Network's "A. M. America," but once again they are getting out-maneuvered on the reward part of the exchange. Turn in your gun to them and you will get a crucifix and 2-for-1 meal at Burger World.

"That's a very interesting giveaway," deadpans Dr. Burns.

"Yes, thank you," says Sister Rosemarie, who is so buoyant it's almost heartbreaking. "The crucifix is a true symbol of love and sacrifice and these were made by homeless teens at our mission. The young men and women pounded down aluminum cans, cut and shaped the metal and soldered the pieces together. I'm excited to share their work with the world."

"They are unique," says Dr. Burns. "I'm just a little concerned about donors at the exchange getting swayed by the items offered by your rivals."

"We think it is a compelling spiritual offer," says Wilson Cliff.

The smile falls off Sister Rosemarie's face. "You think it doesn't have the same monetary value compared to other exchange options? Is that what you are saying?" asks Sister Rosemarie.

"I think one of the concerns is that people coming to

the exchange will be donating weapons that are worth some fairly serious money," Burns says. "So some donors—not all—will be interested in getting a certain value in return."

Sister Rosemarie sighs. "Yes, that's a good point, Dr. Burns. We'll definitely think about it. But I hope my message of safety, peace and love will resonate with donors."

Needless to say, Sister Constance Grace and Sister Iron Iris have different icons to offer: trendy $30 earbuds—what a disgusting term; it sounds like something is *growing* in your ear—and red-hot Alamo Slim T-shirts and caps that inexplicably sell for $75.

In the remote truck watching all this, I feel exactly what every viewer will feel as we build toward the actual exchange: Sister Rosemarie is a lamb about to get slaughtered. But nobody feels worse than I do. I'm the one who brought Wilson Cliff to the show and he's dragging my star down. She needs big help in both the social media and swag departments.

• • •

The Texas exchanges go perfectly. As David and Tabitha explain to the nuns in a pre-exchange segment, Texas ranks in the middle of the U.S. death rate from firearms, with 11 deaths per 100,000 residents in 2010.

"Since Texas has about 26 million people, we are looking at about 2,231 'official' gun deaths in Texas annually," explains David. "If you think that's crazy, consider that last year, Texas had the second most gun-related murders—699—in the U.S. Considering that 62 percent of all gun deaths are suicides in this country and that accidental deaths are the third category with over 600 deaths annually, well, that is a lot of tragedy."

"That's outrageous!" says Sister Teri.

"Ridiculous!" says Sister Iron Iris. "We need to put that in the show!"

In the remote truck, Little Ricky says: "We should run the names of all the victims in a crawler at the bottom of the screen."

"Genius," I say.

And we do it. The names of the dead. Is there anything more powerful than a list of the fallen scrolling by to communicate the enormous numbers we are talking about? Well, okay. Yes. There probably is. Still, it's pretty dramatic. Maggie Driscoll opens the show by announcing the scroll. "These are the names of Texans from all walks of life who, in the end, have one thing in common: They died by gunfire. We found 2,231 names. Which means we will run 37 names per minute at the bottom of your screen over the next hour."

The exchange goes very smoothly. And while the scroll serves as a powerful, silent statement on behalf of *Nuns with Guns*, an even more powerful moment happens on the show. We get the first of what becomes a defining feature of *Nuns with Guns*: the testimonial.

Sister Constance Grace is the first of the nuns to witness, or maybe even inspire, this phenomenon. A huge man in a John Deere trucker cap approaches with a 9mm pistol. "Sister Constance Grace," he says, "Is that camera on?"

"Yes, Bradley"—she can see his name tag—"it is."

"Good, because I want to thank you for what your are doing. I didn't know what to with this fu-BEEP-ing gun. This is the weapon that killed my son. My little Darrell. Why? Why did I even have this fu-BEEP-ing thing? Because I thought it was cool? I did. And because I thought it would protect me and my family? It *destroyed* my family. Destroyed it. Killed it. My wife, she has *never* forgiven me. And why should she? This…this death machine stole the thing we loved most. So please"—he's holding the gun out with one hand and wiping tears off his face with the other—"please take it. And take all the other guns you can. And you viewers out there, hear my story. It's real. My pain is real! And pray it doesn't become your own!"

The man's full name is Bradley Boardman, and his story checks out. The poor guy had been cleaning his gun and left it on his workbench to answer the door. A neighbor had come over to drop off a pie. An apple pie! And as Bradley stood there hobnobbing at the front door, his 6-year-old grabbed the gun and shot his little brother.

"God forgives you, Bradley. All will be forgiven and you will see your baby Darrell again," says Sister Constance Grace. "You are a brave man, Bradley, for coming and sharing your tragedy, your heartbreak with us. Please, can I give you a hug?"

The media loves a good breakdown, and so does the public. 15 million people viewed this clip on our website in three days, and Bradley's passion and frankness about his cautionary tragedy made him a natural for morning TV.

The California episode was the 16th highest-rated program of the week. Texas gets us to number two.

As for the competition, Sister Teri cleaned up again. The standings:

> Sister Teri: 5,539
> Sister Constance Grace: 4,238
> Sister Iris: 4,007
> Sister Rosemarie: 3,789

Chapter 13

At the end of the Texas show, G-Mac announces our next episode: "Join us next week when we will roll into the Big Easy, New Orleans, one of the capitals of American gun violence. Every New Year's Eve, locals fire guns in the air, apparently oblivious to the fact that what goes up must come down. The result is that over the years, hundreds of innocent revelers have begun their new year with gun wounds and worse. Are you looking forward to it, Sister Teri?"

"Well, I'm glad it's March, not December 31st," Sister Teri says with a laugh. "But yes. As always, our collection efforts are all about reducing senseless suffering. Because, remember: Even safely stored guns can pose a risk."

This particular quote sends the gun lobby through the roof. They see our #2 rating and they know we are reaching huge numbers. Then they hear this message, delivered by a woman who has given her whole life to serving the poor, the hungry, the downtrodden, a woman who lives to educate, feed and heal the masses. How can they assail her?

The answer, of course, is they can't.

So they attack The Network.
With both barrels blazing.

• • •

Two days later, with Sister Teri trending #1 on Twitter and Google, the gun-loving noise machine is in full swing. Radio hosts have their talking points. The right-wing blogosphere has its collective knickers in a twist, and there are full-page ads in all the major dailies announcing a boycott of The Network and calling for Americans to "Fight left-wing propaganda and force the most irresponsible show in TV history to stick to the facts."

LIE-SAVING TV

Nuns with Guns, *The Network's national attack on the Second Amendment, has been spreading falsehoods and fear across our fair nation. This reality show about four nuns vying to collect the most guns from the public announces tragic gun-related deaths during broadcasts. The show also broadcasts testimonials of the "victims" and waxes fearful about the killing power of the firearms they collect.*

At no point does the show or anyone on it balance their attack. Where are the stories of hunters who feed their families? Of parents and children bonding during annual hunting excursions? Of law enforcement officers who use firearms to save lives? Or the women who have protected themselves from attackers? Or the military who continue to serve our nation?

Last Tuesday the show's popular Sister Teresa Maria Alves-Rodriguez—a.k.a. Sister Teri—stated that even guns safely stored in lockboxes, as our organization recommends, are a potential "risk."

The same can be said about butter knives, hula-hoops and Lego pieces. A locked gun, like a piece of Lego, is an innocent object. But swallow a piece of Lego and it can become lethal. We don't see Nuns with Guns *collecting Legos, do we? That would be absurd. Generally speaking, a locked gun, stored properly, is about as threatening and dangerous as a Lego brick. Actually, it may be safer.*

We believe lies and mistruths about gun safety do not help anyone. They are merely propaganda in a veiled assault on our cherished Second Amendment. And we call on viewers to refrain from watching Nuns with Guns *or any other show on this politicized network until this vicious assault on the right to bear arms is ended.*

That afternoon we have a press conference with all four nuns. Each of them is upset by the full-page ad. But Sister Teri is truly furious.

"I'm a liar? How am I a liar? A gun is a lethal weapon. You lock it up because it is potentially dangerous. But a locked gun can be stolen. A locked gun can be unlocked, too. And when either of those things happens, people, the risk goes up. You understand that, right?"

She's pointing to Julie Russell of Fox News, who does the natural thing and nods. "So did the ad offend you?" Russell follows up, unaware that the combination of the nod and soft-ball question will have her removed as on-air reporter after wingnuts accuse her of being a *Nuns with Guns* "sympathizer."

"Of course! I don't want anyone—my mother or sister or nephews or the viewers sitting at home—to think I'm lying about this issue. It's insulting!"

"Can I add something?" asks Sister Rosemarie, ever the picture of decorum. "All Sister Teri said was guns, no matter how safely they are stored, can still, eventually, pose grave danger."

"And I'm sorry to have to say the obvious," adds Sister Iris, "but the reason we want to collect guns and melt them all down and use the metal to build schools and homes for the poor is because guns are, in fact, more dangerous than Lego."

The room cracks up.

It's a nice moment before the death threats start.

• • •

Jasmine gets the first one:

"Is this the production office for *Nuns with Guns*?"

"Yes, sir. How can I help you?"

"Bang. You're dead."

Click.

Jasmine comes in my office, not wanting to make a big deal of this, but clearly spooked, and recounts the call, first to me, and then to Sampson.

"Let's hope it was just some sad joker," I say.

Fifteen minutes later, she gets another one.

"Same voice?" asks Sampson.

"No. A woman. Can you believe it?"

"Yes. Yes, I can."

Jasmine gets our number changed and unlisted. Then she spends hours sending out an update to all our contacts in the industry, which is a huge headache. But five days later, the phones start ringing again with more death threats— usually right around the time Glenn Beck and Rush

Limbaugh are on the air. Sampson sets up a system that records the phone number and the audio of all calls to our main number, so that we can build a library of the threats.

He advises Jasmine and the rest of the office not to engage any of the callers. "That just encourages them. Better to hang up."

• • •

To my surprise, Marta loves having security guards around the house, which is already bursting with Hector and Mikey's families. Guaco-Taco has stabilized for the time being, but my two son-in-laws spend every day scouting locations and meeting with backers, brokers, realtors and lawyers. They are talking about opening another location, or maybe even franchising. There are now officially 13 of us living here until further notice. So why does Marta like having four permanent guards, plus an electrician installing surveillance cameras outside our property?

"Because look," she says. "Look at Guaco-Taco and what happened. Too many guns, too many poor people, desperate people and stupid people. So these men, they make me feel safe."

"Good," I say. "I want you to feel safe. These guys are the best. And they say that you and the family are low-level targets. And that it's me and the nuns who are the logical targets. But don't worry. If they get me, you and Jared are set for life."

She slaps my arm. "Don't joke. You are doing good. Everyone wants to meet the nuns. They should come for a party."

"If we ever finish planning the post-wedding wedding

of the century, they can come to that."

"My mother is getting her passport. Then we do it."

"When? Where?"

"Couple of months."

"June?"

"Yes."

I remember when Marta's "yesses" sounded more like "d'yes." That was one of the first things I liked about her, beside the obvious fact that she was pretty and took care of my son, and she laughed at my jokes when she understood them, and even, now that I think about it, when she probably didn't.

"What's so funny? Why you smiling?"

"You. Me. This."

"What? That we have security guards?"

"No, I was thinking that to stay with me you must be almost as crazy as I am."

"What, cause I like you? I like that you are a little crazy? Crazy good. You think I'm crazy about this wedding, too. Right?"

"It's just one day, honey. We're already married."

"You make shows every day. A wedding is a personal show. My show. Our show."

"I know."

"Don't escrew it up."

"D'yes," I say. "I won't."

Chapter 14

You may think there is nothing like clicking on a link to a web page and seeing a picture of yourself with a bull's-eye photoshopped onto your chest and a caption reading "Public Enemy #1." But there are similar experiences. Like when the caption is changed on another page to say "Take Him Out," an instruction that could be subject to interpretation, or, say, when the caption is changed to "Kill This Man Now," which leaves very little room for interpretation.

I summon Sampson immediately. He looks at the pictures for about one second and says, "Time to call Washington."

"Who? Who's Washington?"

"The FBI, my friend."

"What about Lance?"

"Lance Boyle will tell you the exact same thing. No question. Here, I'll call him."

"No, no," I say, feeling bad. "I'm just a little freaked out is all. I'm not really used to this kind of thing."

"Lance? It's Sampson. Hold on a sec. Here."

I take Sampson's cell phone and start to explain the situation. And two sentences in, Lance says, "Stop. Didn't Sampson call the FBI?"

"He was going to, but I kind of balked…"

"Rick, this is serious now. The same kind of postings cropped up on Right-to-Life sites targeting doctors who performed abortions. Listen to Sampson and call the FBI right now."

Click.

The FBI agents, Nathaniel Blatt and Nelson Garcia, are nice, although not as well dressed as they are in the movies. They note the web addresses we've found, take the list of phone numbers we've collected from all the threatening calls, interview me, interview Sampson and then speak to us together.

"You realize that it is impossible to assess the actual threat level until we track down whomever posted this and the people who have viewed it," says Blatt. "And that is going to be very difficult, given the likelihood that many fanatics use anonymizers to surf the web and may have posted this stuff by routing it through hijacked computers."

"So what do you do?"

"We start searching," says Garcia. "We'll probably ask for some help from some friends."

"The N.S.A.," translates Sampson.

"Do we publicize this?" I say, and as soon as the words leave my mouth I want them back—a rarity with me. I realize that publicity is my natural response to any issue.

"Mr. Salter, publicity sometimes creates more problems, more work for us. I recommend you tell as few people as possible."

"Agreed," says Sampson.

"We take all this very seriously, Mr. Salter. We'll have a security specialist flying in to evaluate things with you and Mr. Sampson. And have our cybersecurity team dig into this site."

"That's it? Wait! I don't want to sound ungrateful, but is there anything else that you can do for us?"

"Sure. Tell you to keep your whereabouts secret, stay indoors and stay the hell away from windows."

• • •

The Texas episode of *Nuns with Guns* has a 25 share and 14 rating. That means that 25 percent of the audience watching TV during that time slot were watching us. That is friggin' insane. And 14 percent of all the TVs in the U.S. were watching us.

Put another way, the show is a huge fucking hit.

I get Walter Fields on the phone and he immediately starts gushing about the ratings.

"Thanks, Walter," I say. "But I have some serious bad news. We are getting death threats."

"What? Who?"

"Me." I explain the photos and the FBI. "I'm going to need some budgetary relief. Our security costs just got higher."

"Go right ahead. Anything, Rick. Anything."

"Walter, you should have a serious security discussion, too, for The Network. These people are crazy."

"Will do. Thanks."

"And, Walter, do not let this leak. The FBI says broadcasting this will make it worse."

"Got it. Don't fuck around, Rick. Watch your ass."

• • •

Four days later, the *Nuns with Guns* death threats are national news, thanks to an intrepid reporter at the *Washington Post*.

A site called Gunsforall.tv posts an assassin's gallery containing eight photographs with bull's-eyes superimposed on the foreheads of Sister Rosemarie, Sister Teri, Sister Constance Grace, Sister Iris, Dr. James Burns, Maggie Driscoll, G-Mac and yours truly.

According to the *Post*, the URL is registered to a post box in Switzerland and hosted by an Internet service provider in Estonia.

The federal authorities quoted in the article say there is little they can do about it. The *Post* also reports that calls for comment were not returned by The Network. This, of course, sends me through the fucking roof, because maybe—*maybe*—if we had talked to the *Post*, we could have quashed the story, pointing out that the FBI asked us *not to publicize* my earlier bull's-eye photo. I call up Walter Fields to let him know just how much I think they've fucked up.

"I know, I know," he says. "I'm trying to see who fumbled it. All I can say is we are very, very sorry."

"We need to address this, Walter. Now. I need to address this. I need a press conference, a prepared statement, something that attacks this, that demonstrates our commitment to the contestants and staff and to the very idea of the show. This is fucking terrifying. But we have to double down."

"No question. Do what you have to."

"Is my shut-up clause dead?"

"I will email you and Jay right now, lifting your gag order."

At 4 p.m., I'm ready.

"Good afternoon," I tell the reporters and camera crews assembled at The Network's Burbank offices. "Thank you for coming. I am Rick Salter, the creator and producer of *Nuns with Guns*. This morning, the stars of my show awoke to discover that some sick individual or group posted a series of disturbing images on a web site. The images turn photos of the cast of *Nuns with Guns* into assassination targets by superimposing bull's-eyes on the cast members. You've seen the pictures. They are awful. Their message is clear: Each one says, 'Shoot this person.'

"Federal law enforcement agents are trying to trace the ownership of this site and the origins of these photos. My picture was among those on display with a bull's-eye on my forehead. Now, I am an American. I believe in freedom of expression. I do not believe in freedom of intimidation and incitement to murder, however, which is what these photos represent.

"This is the work of someone or some group that has gone completely off the rails. I would like to remind everyone again that despite what you may have heard on talk radio, despite what you may have read on some misinformed comment board or right-wing news site or in statements from gun rights organizations, *Nuns with Guns* is not trying to take away anyone's right to own guns. We are not trying to change legislation or challenge the Second Amendment."

At this point, I think about pulling out my NRA membership card, and showing it off, like I had dreamed about. But I decide not to. I don't want to steal the spotlight or go off the main story.

"We are, however, celebrating the right to *not* own guns. The right to live in a safe world where there are no tragic gun accidents or easy, irreversible suicide attempts. That is the goal of *Nuns with Guns.*

"The four sisters competing on our show are four of the most giving, compassionate, selfless women I have ever had the pleasure of meeting. They inspire millions of Americans every day.

"Do you know how dedicated these women are? We have to hire people to monitor them, to stop them from talking and listening to every gun donor who appears on our show. They want to hug every child that comes to exchanges. These women are trying to make the world safer, to reduce heartbreak and tragedy. They should be celebrated as the heroes they are, not threatened by cowards.

"And so I call on Americans of all stripes—conservatives, liberals, Democrats, Republicans, gun lovers and gun control activists—to speak out against this horrible, intimidating act. To turn this threat of violence into a loud refrain for peace and safety. *Nuns with Guns* is not about challenging the right to bear arms. It is about the right to live more safely. And somehow, the pursuit of safety has resulted in death threats. But this will not stop our show or our mission. We will not be bullied or blackmailed or terrorized. And I call on the law enforcement agencies—many of which have lent their full support to *Nuns with Guns*—to monitor the extremists who are threatened by our work. Thank you, and have a safe day."

I don't take any questions. I bolt with my security team and head home to pack before heading to one of the most deadly cities in America.

Chapter 15

Sister Rosemarie doesn't seem upset about being in last place, but I sure am.

"I guess I'm just not getting my message out," she says.

Always a diplomat.

Of course, this is bullshit. Her flack, the old-school Wilson Cliff, is getting totally played on the social media front, on the marketing tie-in front and every other fucking front there is. "I'm going to help you, Sister Rosemarie. Just give me a day or two to come up with a plan."

I call Little Ricky in for a meeting to do a post-mortem on California and Texas.

"The numbers are horrible for Sister Rosemarie," he says, like this is news.

I just drum my fingers on the table. Waiting.

"But the ratings are great," he adds.

"Nobody's happier about the ratings than I am. But we aren't going to beat *The King of Pain* without Sister Rosemarie fighting to the end."

"Why do you say that?"

"It's obvious. Because she's Sister Rosemarie."

"You've lost me," Little Ricky says.

"Sister Rosemarie is Sister Goldmine. She got us the show. She's poised to become the number one all-time favorite reality show star. She constantly trends on Twitter."

"Actually, Sister Teri has taken over."

"Yeah, Sister Teri is great. But I'm talking about more than the gun numbers."

"So am I."

"Sister Rosemarie got us here. We used her face on every damn spot we could nail. We put her on network news and every talk show. You know this. You arranged it. She's why people watch."

"Well, there's also guns. The controversy. The danger element. People think something is going to go wrong."

"Yeah. That goes without saying. But people love nuns, too."

"True, but they don't just tune in to see Sister Rosemarie anymore. The data shows that viewers like the other nuns, too. Almost as much as Sister Rosemarie."

"What data?"

"The Network's data. There's a new VP of analytics."

"You have the reports? Lemme see."

Little Ricky hands me two folders, each stamped "CONFIDENTIAL" with legal mumbo jumbo announcing that this is the sole property of The Network and that it should not be viewed by anyone outside the company. Inside are reports on viewer surveys and a summary sheet. The viewers have been asked to rate the nuns in terms of "likability." Sister Rosemarie is at the top of the list but just barely. Tiny Sister Teri is just below her. I'm not surprised; she's a spitfire and cute as a button. She dances, listens to hip hop and salsa, loves sports. Then just below her, and also rated highly likable are Iron Iris and Constance Grace.

"What do we do? I can't have Sister Rosemarie get trounced and bounced."

"Wilson Cliff could have a health emergency."

"Ah, I can't do that, either. I've worked with him for years."

"Well then I don't see how she's going to rise above this. All the other sisters are terrific, too. And so are their PR teams."

"It's my fault."

"Rick, it's not your fault. Wilson Cliff is not the first guy to get screwed by social media."

"Thanks for saying that. Even if I pay your salary. Let me talk to Wilson Cliff. I have an idea."

Before I can call Wilson, Jasmine comes into my office and motions toward the window. "Burr is gone. So is Ulrich."

"Burr?"

"Mr. Gun Crazy. He's not here, and neither is Mr. Bowl Cut. The protesters."

"Great!" I say.

"Well, the others are out here. But those guys are gone. They weren't here yesterday, either."

"Okay."

"I thought you should know. I already told Sampson. They creep me out. Guys that play military dress-up like that—the camouflage and the boots—belong somewhere else. Like, far, far away from wherever I am."

• • •

Nuns with Guns features a bunch of strategy meetings. Our hosts Dr. Burns, G-Mac and Maggie visit the sisters to discuss upcoming plans and then periodically check in to see how they are going. Most of the time, these are 100 percent unscripted, unengineered. But before Sister Rosemarie's session gets rolling, I consult off-camera with Wilson Cliff and lay out the situation. Then I make a few phone calls and the turnaround for Sister Rosemarie begins.

The hosts go into a conference room and find only Sister Rosemarie.

"Where's Cliff?" Maggie asks her.

"I don't know."

"Okay," says Dr. Burns, "how are you feeling about the competition?"

"I'm a little disappointed with the number of guns I've collected. But I'm thrilled the others are doing so well."

"Are you surprised?"

"Yes and no. When I saw what the others had done—the marketing ideas, the rap videos, the giveaways with major companies—well, it's no wonder. If you tweet great offers and email millions of people in a specific location, and I don't, well, you are going to do a much better job of getting the message out and getting guns off the street."

"But you have three million Twitter followers, Sister Rosemarie."

"I know, but I just forgot about all that. We both did. We thought doing radio and TV interviews would be enough. I'm new at this social media stuff."

Just then Wilson Cliff bursts in.

"I'm so sorry I'm late. But I have terrific news."

"You're going to donate 10,000 guns to Sister Rosemarie yourself?" asks G-Mac Treadman.

"No. But I have a plan."

"I'm all ears," smiles Sister Rosemarie. "We need to do something."

"Let me ask everyone a question. Before Sister Rosemarie and Mother Teresa, who was America's favorite nun?"

"The tennis player? Andrea Jaeger?" wonders Sister Rosemarie.

"Julie Andrews from *The Sound of Music*," says Burns, who always sounds like he knows everything.

Wilson Cliff shakes his head and smiles. "Close. The Flying Nun!"

"What does that have to do with Sister Rosemarie?"

Wilson Cliff goes to the door and calls out, "Come on in, Andray."

The man who walks in is, by any standard, a truly impressive specimen of humankind. His close-cropped hair frames a perfectly symmetrical face with smooth, dark skin covering his high cheekbones, dark eyes, a perfect nose, medium-lipped mouth and a chin that has been calibrated for squareness. He is wearing a flight suit that shows off wide shoulders and a torso that tapers into dancer's hips. He's about six feet three inches. His name, appropriately, is Andray King, and Wilson Cliff introduces him as Las Vegas' top parachute jumping instructor.

In all the episodes of *King of Pain* and *Nuns with Guns*, Sister Rosemarie had been a sea of tranquility, enthusiasm and positivity. But here, in this moment, something has changed. She shakes hands with Andray, but she seems a bit flustered, confused.

"Wilson, what does Andray have to do with the show?"

"Oh, sorry! The next show is in New Orleans. The show

after that is in Miami, Sister Teri's home turf. So we really need to step up our game stunt-wise and promotionally. So I've done a deal with Made in the Shade to give away 5,000 of these new sunglasses. Check it out."

Wilson Cliff pulls out a pair of aviator sunglasses with metallic lenses. On each lens is a reflective image of an encircled pistol with a line through it. The internationally understood symbol for "No Guns."

"These retail for $69.99. But we can give 'em away for free with any gun trade-ins. It's a lot cooler than T-shirts, don't you think?"

"I guess. But what does Mr. King have to do with this?"

"He's going to teach you to parachute—wearing these shades."

"Me?"

"You! A real flying nun!"

"Does anyone even remember *The Flying Nun*?" asks Dr. Burns.

"Older folks, but it doesn't matter. It's a great name!" answers Wilson Cliff.

"But Wilson, I'm scared of heights. I don't even like flying in planes!"

"Oh my god, Sister Rosemarie. Please tell me you're kidding. Because Made in the Shade are air-freighting 5,000 pairs of these over right now from China."

"Oh, Wilson, you should have asked me. I can't do this. I'm sorry. But I can feel my heart racing just at the thought of this. How could you not discuss it with me?"

I'm in the truck with Rittenhouse, who wears a headset to communicate with Burns. "Burns," he says, "suggest they talk in private."

I understand this direction. It gives us a perfect cut-away to a commercial just at the height of the drama. But before Burns can get there, Andray King says, "Excuse me, Sister Rosemarie."

"Burns!" I yell into the mixing board mic. "Let this guy speak."

"Yes, Mr. King?"

"I'm sorry about this being a surprise. But I just want to say that people pay me a lot of money to help them to skydive. I've never lost a student yet. I've made over 2,500 dives and I have loved every second of them. May I tell you why?"

"Yes, please do."

"Because there's nothing like it. Nothing. The view, the sounds, the freedom, the speed. You are flying, falling, moving faster and faster, heading for a target, feeling the wind, between heaven and earth, defying nature by even being in the sky and yet surrendering to it, propelled by gravity and your own weight."

Sister Rosemarie doesn't look convinced. Andray King continues: "You know that fun you had playing video games on *The King of Pain*?"

"Of course!" Her face lights up at the memory of mastering Roller Coaster Space Race, which contestants had to play while severely sleep-deprived.

"I saw that episode. You looked like you were having the best time of your life. If you skydive with me, it will be a thousand times more fun."

"But I'll be terrified. I'll panic."

"I'll be right there with you. In fact, that first jump I'll be joined at the hip with you. And I'll never pull my cord until I see your chute is open."

"Really? How can you stop panic?"

"Meditation, prayer, focus, and the fact that survival instincts just take over."

"Yes. Prayer and God have helped me do so much. Can I see a video?"

"Sure."

"Are we a go, or what?" asks Wilson Cliff, completely shattering the intimacy of this exchange.

"We are a maybe," says Sister Rosemarie, working her rosary beads and throwing a glare at Wilson that we edit out later. Sister Rosemarie is tremendously competitive, smart and sly. She likes a challenge. And likes fairness. Working with Wilson hasn't been fair.

"But," says Sister Rosemarie. "I'm going to need a lot of help."

"Whatever you need," says Wilson Cliff.

"Not just from you." She smiles. "From on high."

Chapter 16

The New Orleans exchange is going beautifully. Before donors enter Tad Gormley Stadium in City Park, they must register and present the weapon they are donating so we can check that it is not loaded. You'd be surprised how many people have no idea whether the gun they are donating is loaded. And you'd be frightened to know how many are in fact loaded. A lot. There are lines of donors snaking along, guided by the belted crowd-control stanchions you see at airports, taking fans to the nun of his or her choice. When each donor hands the gun to a nun, we snap a photo and ask if they are okay with us posting the picture on our website, which they can download for free in exchange for their email address. This, of course, is part of the "sell" to get the gun donation, but it also means our site gets huge traffic as everyone sends links around pointing to their big moment with a nun, which generates a pretty penny in ad sales. Plus, we can email these fans when the DVD and download of the episode are on sale. But I digress.

Dr. Burns and Maggie Driscoll thread through the

crowd interviewing donors as they wait in line, gathering B-roll for the special looking-back episode and the after-show reunion program and for our syndicated video news clips. We have six crews on hand, one for each nun and two roamers who wander around filming the thousands of fans and donors. It looks like our biggest turnout yet, which is thrilling. I am amazed at the excitement and buzz in the air. There are food trucks. And craft vendors. And there seem to be entire families coming out to make donations and see the sisters. Like it's a state fair or something.

Then the crack of a single gunshot rings out. Two seconds pass and there's another blast, followed by a rat-a-tat-tat. Looking over the footage later, you can see the instant terror; and you can hear the screams, the holy shits, the what-the-fucks, the sweet-Jesuses and the oh-my-gods.

"Holy FUCK!" I yell inside the remote truck. "Rittenhouse, tell your cameramen to scan the crowds 360 so we can see what is going on! Sampson, what is this shit?"

Sampson has got a headset on and is giving orders to his security guards. "Shield the nuns," he intones evenly. "Tell everyone on the lines to remain calm and stay low."

"Down! Everybody get down on the ground!" yell the cops, crouching and prowling, their own guns drawn, searching for the source of the blasts.

I'm scanning the crowd shots. Our crew near the entrance shows people running like mad to their cars. Rittenhouse is aghast. "The cops have to freeze everything, or people are gonna get trampled. Fuck!"

"Jesus! I can't believe the cops are drawing their weapons," says Sampson, pulling his phone to his ear while simultaneously cranking up the police scanner. It is filled with cross-talk babble. But as far as I can tell, nobody is reporting a shooter or a victim.

"Let's pray they don't panic," says Little Ricky. "And that it's just some asshole shooting in the air, New Orleans style."

Rittenhouse is directing as if it's a live-breaking news report. He's got Dr. Burns huddled by a football goalpost. "For those of you just joining us, shots were heard moments ago. They appeared to be coming from somewhere in the immediate vicinity. However, we've neither heard of nor seen any injuries." Burns touches his earpiece, taking instruction from Rittenhouse. "I've just received word we are going to switch over to Sister Rosemarie, who has been collecting guns on the south end of the park here. Sister Rosemarie, can you hear me? Are you all right?"

"Split 3 and 6!" yells Rittenhouse to our camera editor.

"Yes, I can hear you, Dr. Burns, and I'm fine, but very nervous. Very concerned. I am praying that everyone here is safe, and that those shots didn't hit anyone."

"So you've seen no shooting victims in your area?"

"That is correct. Everyone in this area appears to be safe. As soon as we heard the shots our security team and police officers had everyone get on the ground. But it is terrifying."

Sampson is talking to his NOPD contact. "Please have your men holster their weapons until a target is identified. Every single weapon. With safeties on."

Little Ricky sits next to me. He hands me his smart phone. "Sampson, come look at this."

It's a Twitter post. A fucking tweet from guy named @Beretta1313.

"Dealer blasts gun shots at #Nunswithguns thru P. A. #hilarious #riot."

"Motherfucker!" says Sampson.

"Ditto," I say.

"Per Twitter," Sampson broadcasts on his walkie-talkie, "we have reports that gunshots were an amplified recording. Repeat: Gunshots may have been an amplified recording through a P. A. system. Please investigate the dealers set up outside the stadium. Look for anyone with a large speaker or stereo system."

"I hope it's true," says Little Ricky.

"Of course it's true!" I say. "Gun-crazy fucks."

I move next to Rittenhouse at the console, put on a headset and relay the possibility of a sick prank to Burns so he can report it in his broadcast. Then my phone rings. A local number. It's the mayor.

"I want to evacuate. I have a call into the governor to bring in more state troopers."

"I understand your concern, Mr. Mayor, but it appears to be a hoax. No shots were actually fired."

"I'm here, Salter. I heard them."

"I heard them, too. But someone on Twitter says the shots were coming out of a gun dealer's sound system. And so far we've seen no victims and no gunmen. Zero. It appears to be a prank."

"You're kidding."

"I'm as serious as mass fucking murder."

Five more minutes tick by. Rittenhouse does a superb job weaving reports together from the nuns, and from Burns and Maggie Driscoll. And then a sound rises up as Burns is interviewing a woman with a small child. "Oh, my, listen to this! Viewers, can you hear this? The voices, the singing? Here, I'll shut up."

And yes, we can hear it in the control room. It is coming through the microphones of the other crews.

This land is your land, this land is my land
From California to the New York Island
From the redwood forest to the Gulf Stream waters
This land was made for you and me.

"Holy shit!" I say, "Film them singing. Get 'em all singing! Every fucking camera. Incredible!"

People are scared and crying, but you can hear them singing through their tears. And the nuns are standing up—they've been told of the Twitter post—and belting it out:

As I was walking that ribbon of highway
I saw above me that endless skyway
I saw below me, that golden valley
This land was made for you and me.

"This is amazing," I say to everyone and no one.

Sampson pulls off his headset. "Suspect apprehended with a hand truck wheeling speakers and amp to his car!"

"Rittenhouse," I say, "Tell them all. The situation is over!"

And soon, on screen, we can see the nuns are lifting their hands, palms up, motioning the crowd to rise up, while returning to the first verse, because, let's face it, nobody knows the rest of the song.

This land is your land, this land is my land
From California to the New York Island
From the redwood forest to the Gulf Stream waters
This land was made for you and me.

What a fucking hymn to America! On my show! I can't remember being so proud, so close to a heroic moment, to unity. There are tears in my eyes. Of joy. Of relief. I leap out of the remote truck and run into the crowd. "It's okay!

It's okay! Nobody's hurt. It wasn't a real gunshot. It was a recording! They caught the jerk with his P. A. system."

I head toward Sister Rosemarie. I'm running, jogging. I never do that. But this is a special event. Like a wedding or a christening. It's celebrating life! The cops are smiling. Everyone is smiling. At about the 50-yard line, there are a bunch of food trucks. I stop at the hot dog stand. "Excuse me," I say, "I'd like to run a tab. Everything is now free. Okay?"

"That's like $7,000 for everything."

"Fine. I'm the producer of the show. Feed everyone. Here's my card. I'm serious."

I repeat this spiel to the taco stand, the ice cream truck, the beignet stand, the po'boy purveyor and the cotton candy flosser. Sister Constance Grace is closer to the food than Sister Rosemarie. I stop by and tell everyone that the food trucks are now free. "So donate your guns, and then go get some ice cream or something."

When I get to Sister Constance Grace, I fling my arms around her. "Am I allowed to do this?" I ask. "Hug a nun?"

"No law against it," says Sister Constance Grace. And she hugs me back.

• • •

Sampson Smith, Little Ricky and I are eating in my suite after the New Orleans show.

"This is a fucking travesty!" I say, as room service rolls our food in. "Some of my favorite restaurants in the world are in this town and we're eating room service."

"I never been to New Orleans before," says Sampson.

"Me neither," says Little Ricky.

"There are some great old joints. Like Galatoire's. I'd love to take you guys there. They have waiters who look like they started working there during Prohibition. And the Rock 'n' Bowl, one of the greatest bars in the world. Bowling and zydeco bands. It's heaven. We should go."

"We should go to bed," laughs Sampson.

"Fucking nut jobs," I say. "But at least we got that jerk-off."

"Do you think everyone that loves guns is a jerk-off?" It's Sampson.

"No. I didn't say that. Don't put words in my mouth."

"Sorry."

"You love guns, don't you, Sampson?"

"Love? No, I don't love them. But I enjoy them. I *like* them."

"I can see that. Is this show hard for you? This job?"

"It's a challenge. I believe in safety, in security. I believe in doing what I'm hired to do. I'm here to keep everyone safe."

"You and your team were fantastic."

"Thank you."

"Listen, Sampson, I get it. I get it more than you know. America has been taught to love guns. Shit. Everybody mentions John Wayne and Charlton Heston. But it goes way, way back. Five generations have grown up watching gunslingers at the movies and on TV. Tom Mix, Bronco Billy Anderson, Hoot Gibson, Roy Rogers and Gene Autry. And those guys used peashooters compared to the thugs and gangstas played by James Cagney, George Raft and Edward G. Robinson. When I hit the business there was Richard Roundtree as Shaft, Clint Eastwood as Harry Callahan and Charles Bronson as whoever the fuck Charles

Bronson played. And James Bond! Christ, James Bond was like weapons porn for me. I practically wanted to fuck that guy, and I'm straight."

"Which Bond?" says Little Ricky.

"I don't know. All of 'em, but that's not the point, Ricky! The point is you watch those movies and you are hooked. All those actors, you know what they do? They make bad guys disappear. Like a myth, like in a bible story. Good blows the shit out of evil. Who wouldn't love that?"

"I never saw those Westerns until I was older," says Sampson.

"But you saw Eastwood, right? Dirty Harry?"

"Eventually. Yeah."

"You really think these movies, these images are to blame for gun worship?" asks Little Ricky. "The blame-the-media thing again?"

"Oh, the 'it's just images' argument. I fucking love that one! You know what the world spends on TV ads? The ads that drive what they call 'brand awareness.' The ads that fucking sell cars and Coke and iPads? *The ads that basically keep the world's economy going?* They spend billions and billions. And why? Because those images work. They fucking get into your head and stay there. So images in the media aren't the only reason. But they are a major reason."

"I didn't have a TV growing up," says Sampson.

"You didn't have a TV?" Little Ricky says. "Seriously?"

"Sampson, were you sent here by Boyle to prove me wrong on everything? Here, try the seafood gumbo. Pretty fucking good."

"My mother was a Jehovah's Witness. No TV. No movies. No nothing. When I joined the army, I got an M-16 and I loved it. It was powerful. I felt powerful. You know how great it is to just hold a baseball bat? Why is that so fun, so addictive? It's just a piece of wood, right? But a gun is even better, man. Metal, lethal, a machine. I was in awe. It's pretty light—it weighs about 8 pounds holding 30 rounds. And that motherfucker can put out a lot of lead. The bullets move *800 yards in a second* when they leave the muzzle, man. See? And if you're feeding it, you can shoot 800 rounds *in a minute.* When you get good at it, you feel like, I don't know, a pitcher, a surgeon, a fucking expert. You can hit anything. It's like the next best thing to…"

"Sex?" asks Little Ricky.

"Flying. Everyone can have sex. This is super-hero, super-power stuff. I don't know. I never thought that much about it until I started working on your show. But that's the thing for me. I'm sure everybody's got their thing. Family tradition. Heirlooms. Safety and fear. Libertarian bullshit. For me it's power. Super-powers, that's why I like guns."

I nod.

"It does sound cool, when you talk about it like that," says Little Ricky.

"I know."

"I used to feel the same way about cameras, if you can believe that," I say. "Film cameras. Beautiful machines. Projectors, too, knocking out 16 and 24 frames per second. That's 86,400 fucking frames in 90 minutes. Incredible, too, right?"

"Are you mocking me?"

"No, Sampson. I'm serious. I get that people worship objects. That they love them, savor the details, the design, the form, and the technology behind them. I totally get it. And you know what I think about those people, those collectors?"

"Jerk-offs?"

"Nah! 99.99 percent of them are fine. Look, you're a fine, upstanding gentleman who loves—sorry, likes—guns, Sampson. But that 0.01 of a percent, those are the crazies. The nuts. The misfits. The real number is probably even lower, but even .001 percent is too high a number when you are talking about machines that fire 800 rounds in a minute. Or even 60 rounds. Or even 10 rounds. One person can do a lot of fucking damage."

"Yes, that's a problem."

"You know what else is a problem? That prick today, he's going to jail. He basically yelled fire in a movie theater that wasn't burning. How the hell does someone that stupid and irresponsible get a license to sell guns?"

"He's going to say it was a form of protest," says Little Ricky. "Free speech."

"Fuck him," I say.

Sampson has a more eloquent take: "Then he doth protest too much."

• • •

For the next 24 hours, the news focuses on the show, the scare, the heroism and the singing. The Vatican even weighs in, praising the sisters for their bravery and commitment to making the world safer. In terms of positive PR, I don't see how we could have done any better had we tried to engineer a publicity stunt ourselves. This was not just a prank, this was terrorism. And we had it all on film.

But a second-day story in the *New York Times* changes everything. While I was busy hugging the nuns and celebrating all our New Orleans contestants, a reporter asked me what compelled me to feed everyone. And in the joy of the moment, this so-called—according to the article—"legendary crusty producer" said: "These people here today have suffered enough, waiting on line to do a good deed and make America safer, then getting terrified by those fake gun shots. They are heroes. They deserve a lot more than a hot dog, but this is what we have, and life is generally better when it's catered, right?"

Am I a fucking moron or what? Instantly that quote confirms me as a card-carrying champagne socialist, a let-them-eat-cake exploiter. So the pro-gun lobby and right-wing blogosphere now has a new story, a new angle. Not about the guy who terrorized thousands with a gun shot, but about my supposedly insensitive, out-of-touch rich man's words. Now the calls for interviews come pouring in. And guess who leaves a message for me at the office with Jasmine. My old pal Kitty Andropov from CNN.

I call her back because, hey, Walter Fields lifted my gag order for the press conference. I feel good dialing her number. I really haven't done a damn thing for *Nuns with Guns* press-wise. Between the network promos and the fact that the show stomps directly on the nation's hot-button issue—I mean, really, what other issues can inflame like gun control? Women's rights? Freedom of religion? The right to fuck? The right to drive?—we really haven't had to do PR besides sending out video clips and press releases.

"Rrrick, good to hearrrr from you," she says when I call her back.

"Yes, I just can't resist you, Kitty. But I need to be totally off the record for this conversation. Agreed?"

"Surrre." She laughs her flirty TV journo-babe laugh. "I'm just trying to book you for the show. You can't stop making news."

"Your colleagues can't stop manufacturing it. I'm not a story. That little quote about feeding people? I say far more offensive things than that in my sleep."

"Save it forrr the show. Would you honorrr us with your presence?"

"Kitty, what's with the strong Russian accent all of a sudden?"

"I went back for a visit. I tried to get to Snowden. Four weeks there, and the accent comes back. Will you come back, too?"

"I can't right now, too busy. How about in a few weeks? Right before the New York show. We'll be red-hot then."

"I want you now, Rrrick."

"Me, too, Kitty, me, too." God, she is such a tease. "But you have to wait for me. I swear, I won't talk to anyone else. How's that?"

"Call me soon, Rrrick."

Chapter 17

Sister Rosemarie shuttles to Las Vegas whenever possible leading up to the Miami show. She and Andray train and jump for 10 out of 14 days. But nothing beats that first day, and the awkward moments before her first jump, which we capture on film.

"What to you mean, we jump together as one?" Sister Rosemarie asks.

"Well, Sister, I mean that we are going to be joined at the hip."

"Really? Side-by-side."

"More like back to front."

"Show me."

"Um, without the harnesses on and the parachutes someone might get the wrong idea."

"What do you mean, Andray? Come on. I need to know."

"Maybe you guys should turn the camera off. I don't want people getting the wrong impression."

"Just show me."

So Andray walks up behind Sister Rosemarie and pulls her against him, so his pelvis is pushed against her backside.

"That's a problem!" says Sister Rosemarie. "I can't do that."

"Everyone does it. Paratroopers do it that way the first time."

"But I'm...I can't do that."

Eventually Sister Rosemarie agrees to do it as long as no cameras film them together. "I don't want people to get the wrong impression."

• • •

On a beautiful sunny Thursday afternoon, three rival nuns drive up to South Beach in an open-air double-decker bus, trying to keep cool in their Kevlar as they wave to the crowds and urge them to attend the gun exchange on Saturday. And then they make it to the beach, where they watch, oohing and ahhing as two tiny figures jump off a plane.

My heart is in my throat as I watch Sister Rosemarie descend, her habit and the oversized wimple we outfitted over her crash helmet flapping in the wind. She and Andray King free fall for a few seconds and then, positioned over the water's edge, release the pilot chute which in turn quickly leads to the release of the main canopy. When the rectangular chutes—which are a far cry from the giant, balloon-shaped ones that I picture from World War II photographs and movies—open, their descents slow dramatically. And they begin pulling on what Andray later explains are toggles, seatbelt-like swatches that you use to steer.

There's a Coast Guard cutter out monitoring the situation in case our stars get blown into the sea. But the rookie skydive goes perfectly, and Sister Rosemarie and Andray King touch down before a sun-bronzed crowd waiting on a strip of beach next to the Delano Hotel.

At her seaside landing, Sister Rosemarie is a glowing, breathless wonder.

She stands, her wimple blowing in the sea breeze and with her Made in the Shade "No Gun" sunglasses on, talking to the cameras with Maggie Driscoll and Dr. Burns. Maggie sets her up with the homerun question: "Was this hard for you? Were you nervous?"

"Nervous? That's an understatement," Sister Rosemarie laughs. "I was terrified. I hate flying and I have a fear of heights."

"How did you beat it?"

"When the idea for a flying nun came up, I thought, fear is a terrible, crippling thing. I must conquer it. And then I started to think about why so many people have guns or think they should have a gun. Because of fear. Fear of the unknown. Fear of violence. Fear of danger. And that's ironic because most gun deaths aren't good guys killing bad guys, like in the movies. Sixty-two percent of all gun deaths in America are suicides and at least three percent of all gun deaths are accidental. So thought: I have to conquer my fear if I expect others to give up the guns they bought out of fear. So I opted to be brave and put my trust in my instructor and common sense. And you know what, Maggie? I feel so wonderful and alive!"

• • •

The skydive leads newscasts all over the nation. Sister Rosemarie is on the cover of *Time*, *60 Minutes* orders an instant profile. Random House offers $2 million for "any book Sister Rosemarie wants to write."

The stunt helps move her into third place ahead of Sister Iron Iris and just 200 guns behind Sister Constance Grace. She beats Sister Teri on her own turf by 500 weapons. That night I meet Sister Rosemarie and Wilson Cliff for celebratory drinks in the show's hotel suite, and I tell them they need a huge enticement for Baltimore, something that will really motivate gun owners.

Wilson says, "Rick, I'm a publicist, not a market researcher. How the hell should I know what people want?"

In a way, I'm totally sympathetic. He's a middle-aged, cat-loving man who has never touched a gun in his life. Why should he know how to entice gun owners to give up their weapons? But seeing as how I just saved his career by thinking up the parachuting stunt and he hasn't even thanked me, I'm about to rip into him, cameras rolling, when Sister Rosemarie says, "I have an idea."

"Thank God!" says Wilson Cliff.

"Every Christmas we get wish lists at the mission. Not just from little kids, but everyone. And this year the number one request after clothes, food and a job were these special headphones. BASSick. Like Bass and Sick. 'Basic,' get it?"

"That sounds great," says Wilson. "How much do they cost?"

"I think they are pretty expensive."

"Get on the phone, Wilson," I say. "See how much it's worth to them to be featured on America's #1 show. They will beg to give us 10,000 units. And if they don't, their next biggest competitor will."

The next day I have Dr. Burns and Maggie Driscoll visit the other sisters to shoot footage about their marketing plans. "Get as much nun footage as you can," I tell them, "because I'm shipping the nuns out to an undisclosed location until Friday night."

Burns visits Sister Iron Iris. Her flack Felice Donatti has been working the phones. "McDonald's refuses, but Burger World will do two free kids meals. What do you think?"

"Not good enough. After that stunt by Rosemarie, I'm not even sure coupons to heaven would work."

"I know, Sister Iris. I know. I'm sorry."

"We've just seen Sister Rosemarie," says Burns, "and I agree with you, Sister Iris. I'm not sure kids meals are going to do it. I think you need to come up with a higher-value gift."

"Burns," I call in to his earpiece, "Suggest they think big. Sneakers or something."

"I'm wondering, " Burns says, "If you've approached the bigger athletic wear companies. Perhaps they'd like primetime exposure if we could give away sneakers."

"That's perfect. Sister Iris was a marathoner, too!"

"My thoughts exactly," says Burns.

Maggie Driscoll moves down the corridor to the next suite where Sister Constance Grace and Oona Strike are asking themselves hard questions. "You're giving up a gun," says Sister Constance Grace. "What do you want in return for that? Safety, right? That is part of the exchange. You give us a gun, and we'll give you the means to protect yourself. What makes people feel safe?"

"Bigger guns?" asks Oona.

"Locks?"

"Alarms?"

They look at each other, searching for the answer.

"Phones! Cell phones! Right? You call for help. You

can track your child. You can photograph an assailant."

"Sister Constance Grace, that is brilliant! I can't believe we were so pleased with streetwear before. What were we thinking?"

A huge smile spreads across Sister Constance Grace's face. "We were new at this way of thinking. Or at least I was."

The show cuts to the co-hosts in the studio.

"This is amazing" says Dr. Burns. "The sisters are turning into expert marketers."

"It's not that surprising when you really think about it, James," says Maggie Driscoll. "These women are constantly asking themselves what their communities need. And they spend a lot of time trying to deliver on those needs."

"Well, they are certainly doing it now. They've got seven days until the next episode of *Nuns with Guns* in Camden Yards, Baltimore. And when that show is over, only two of these wonderful women will be left in the competition."

"The thing I'm wondering about," says G-Mac, "is how much more can they do to boost their causes? They tweet and post, and shoot videos and stop at schools and churches. What's left for them to do?"

"Well, I'm not sure," says Burns. "The show's producers just sent all four of the nuns to a secret location to work on a special project. Of course, they haven't told us where they are going or what they are going to do. Only that they are working together."

"So the nuns are missing?"

"Yes, America. The nuns have vanished."

"Until next week."

• • •

That night Marta calls. The June wedding—our rewedding, I guess—is on. Her mother just got a passport, which is wonderful news. Just as wonderful, she knows where we can do it.

"Where?"

"Hector and Mikey's new Guaco-Taco in Santa Monica!"

"Is it going to be big enough?"

"It fits a hundred and fifty people."

"Marta, don't you want to invite more than 150 people?" I mean, really, she is such a nice person she wants to invite practically everyone she's ever met, including the guy who mows our lawn and the guy who brings our wine deliveries. Not that I care... but the point is capacity.

"Maybe..."

"Marta, it's okay if you do."

"I want a big party, papi. Dancing, your friends, my friends, our family. That's all. Oh, and the sisters from the show."

"Okay. That's great. I only have my staff, my pals, Rittenhouse, Jay, and couple others. Maybe 40 people on my side."

"And Rick? I don't want no gifts. Just everybody donate to Omar's mama and his son, they got nothing."

"Marta, you are too good for me. I would have never thought of that."

"That's not true, you doing a good thing. How many guns you collected?"

"About 25,000 so far."

"That's so good, Rick. How is the next show?"

"The Network has promos for 'The Big Gundown' that they are airing like crazy. You'll love this spot, Marta. The sisters are on a set of a fake western as if they are going to duel, but as the tension builds, they toss their guns into a basket and start dancing. But I'm a little worried about Sister Rosemarie getting to the second round. She doesn't deserve to play second fiddle."

"They all good, the sisters. Be careful, papi."

"Thanks, hon. I got this. We are all going to be fine."

• • •

But it turns out many things are out of my control.

Little Ricky calls me. The Gun Shop, Baltimore's #1 weapons emporium, has started running a major ad campaign. They'll be buying guns during the week of our show for "Double our normal buy-back price—up to $500!"

"How can they afford that?" I ask.

"Good question. I imagine they are being sponsored or underwritten."

"Please get some quotes from the sisters about this that we can post on the web and send to the morning shows. And work up a release. These kinds of stunts are being pulled to deliberately hurt our show and run counter to our mission, which is to create a safer America."

"Got it."

• • •

Later in the afternoon Jasmine calls from L.A.

"We just had a bomb threat."

"Now?"

"About an hour ago."

"Holy shit. Everyone okay?"

"Yes, we are fine. But police evacuated the whole building."

"How do these assholes get our phone number?"

"Nothing is secret, boss. We sent out over a thousand emails to people with our new number. And I'm sure you can just hire some online service and they'll just hack or bribe their way into it."

"Listen, Jasmine, effective immediately, I am now promoting you to office manager. Talk to the security guys on the site and tell them we want to relocate offices at least temporarily, to a secret location. Everything is backed up online, right? Payroll, coverage, contacts?"

"Of course."

"And when we find a place, we can just get call forwarding. So call Lexi Jacobs, and tell her what we need. Go up to $15 grand a month and aim for somewhere that's no more than 15 minutes from our office."

"Do I get a raise?"

"Let's go to $1,500 a week. That's a pretty big bounce, right?"

"Oh my God. Thanks, Rick."

"Send me pictures of the contenders. And make the lease short-term with a renewal option!"

I'm about to put on my pajamas and watch mindless TV when my phone rings again. It's Walter Fields.

"That was genius, Rick," he says. "Sister Rosemarie's skydive."

"Wait until you see the insurance and security bills."

"It was worth it. Congratulations."

"Thank you, Walter. I told you this would work."

"Yes, you did. But give me some credit."

"Oh, I will. Which reminds me. You are still okay with

me talking to the press?"

"Yeah, you are on your own. You handled that press conference very well. We were all surprised."

I let that go. "Good. Because I have a standing offer from Kitty Andropov."

"Go ahead."

And so, Wednesday morning we—that is, my two security guards and me—end up flying back to L.A. for 36 hours so I can see Marta and do the CNN interview. Marta is very excited about me being on TV. She insists I model my clothes, which feels silly, but, to be honest, I love doing it. She wants me to look good. She's also invited the entire office staff to the house for a viewing party tomorrow night.

"We all be here when you get back."

"Okay. Good."

"Just don't insult nobody!"

"Thanks, coach."

"Who else is on the show?"

"I didn't ask. But I'm sure they'll have some gun rights advocate to try and trip me up."

"You are very smart, Rick. You just think with your heart, sometimes."

"Really? Is that what I do?"

"You used to think with your *verga*. But now more with your heart, *sí*."

We are in the kitchen. It's late, so for once there's nobody around. I go and nuzzle her nape. How is it this woman who has existed on a completely different social stratum from me—no movies, different language, no money, no leisure time, no connections—appreciates me, reads me better than anyone else? Is it primal? Or is it that I'm just an old guy, thankful and flummoxed that this woman 15 years younger than me not only tolerates me but seems to want to celebrate me?

"Leave the dishes," I say.

She turns and reaches behind my head with her wet, soapy hands and pulls me closer to her small, full-lipped, red-glossed mouth. Her tongue darts into my mouth, exploring and imploring. Or maybe that's my tongue darting into hers. And while I revel in the glory of the wet, soft warmth, I think, why is this a French kiss? Why not a Mexican kiss? What the fuck did the French do to get the trademark? Kisses like this, in terms of getting your head and your heart racing, are from a country deserving of its own name. As I get older I think kisses are right up there—and I really mean this—with fucking, which of course is what French kissing so often leads to. But right now my head and heart are wrapped on this perfect mouth, this coquettish tongue that dances, declares and disappears, the flirty white teeth that bite my lip, leaving behind a vanishing pinch. Christ, I'm hornier than a marching band. But then Marta pushes me away. "Go upstairs. I got to finish this. Five minutes. And don't fall asleep!"

I follow orders.

• • •

The next morning I'm in a buoyant post-coital mood. I grab Jared and take him out for breakfast at our favorite diner. Or rather Norbert North and Joe Russell, my bodyguards du jour, drive me, and Jared follows in his used Mini.

"Our page views on New Orleans were through the roof, Dad," he tells me when we've sat down.

"How did you guys hear about it?"

"I was off. But they called me when it broke. I think either Twitter or a wire reporter who was on the scene. They follow Twitter a lot."

"Interesting. So nobody leaves the office to actually report, right?"

"Most of the time we use the phones or the web. But there are crews going out to shoot interviews. People go meet sources, too. But I got overtime, 'cause I had a source on the scene."

"Really? Who?"

"Ricky."

"You called Little Ricky during New Orleans?"

"I just texted, Dad. He didn't have to answer."

"I'm not so sure. You're the boss' son. He might have felt between a rock and a hard place."

Jared chews his lip, thinking it over. I am, too. He says, "I guess so."

"Jared, I'm not mad at you. I just don't want Little Ricky to feel obligated."

Jared nods, but he's looking out the window at the diner parking lot.

"Jared?"

"What?"

"I'm proud of you. I'm glad you called Little Ricky."

"You didn't sound glad."

"You're right. I didn't. But that's your job. And if Little Ricky doesn't tell you shit, you should try me. And then you should try Jasmine, and everyone you know."

"Really? This is a big change."

"Life's too short. You did me a huge favor with that videotape girl. If you want to report, go for it. Be the best."

He's still not looking at me. He's playing with his

hash browns.

"And Jared, I mean it, mean it, mean it. It's great having you here. I'm fucking thrilled. And Nadia, God, she's a knockout. I hope you finish school, but I am overjoyed that you are here. Hey, are you okay?"

His eyes are a little watery. "Dad, you know what I asked Little Ricky first?"

"No idea."

"Is my dad all right?"

I am such an asshole.

"Then I asked some other questions for the story, but when I first heard, I was scared shitless for you. You are a target."

He's wiping his eyes with a napkin. I have to wipe my own.

"Dad, do you have your flack jacket on? The Kevlar?"

"Come on, Jared, it's 85 degrees out."

"You have to wear it, Dad. *All the time.* I'm on the Internet. There are people out there that hate you. Just read the comments of any article about you on CNN or Fox News. So many people with crazy conspiracy theories would be happy if someone took you out. They call you a Jew Hitler who wants to take away guns, so you can own America."

"*A Jew Hitler?* That sounds like a bunch of paranoid mental fucking midgets. They're probably seventh graders or something."

"You never know, Dad."

"I'll wear the Kevlar. But it makes me feel like an out-of-shape action hero."

"Thanks, Dad. Marta is terrified, too."

"You think so?"

"I know so."

"Look, I'm not the face of the show. The sisters are the ones putting their necks on the guillotine. And that's why we have the best team of security guys money can buy. But I hear you. I'll wear the Kevlar."

• • •

I get to the CNN building on Sunset Boulevard and a fast-talking segment producer walks me to the green room, telling me about all the promos they've been running "on air, online and on the radio. I hear we even bought time on Glenn Beck and Rush Limbaugh. We never do that."

"I'll try to live up to the hype."

"I'm sure you'll be great."

"Any other guests?"

"I'm not sure it's been locked down."

"You're the segment producer. If you don't know, who does?"

"I'm just helping out. Audrey is your segment producer."

"Where is she?"

"Good question."

"She's with whoever you're ambushing me with, right? I wonder who it is. Some gun lobby groveler? Charlton Heston calling in from Hell?"

"Now that would be something. I'm sure you'll do very well."

Fucking Kitty Andropov. She's trying to screw me again. Or no, that's not completely accurate. She's trying to get me to screw me, get me to crack up and spew some Salterian stupidity in the hopes it goes viral. That's her whole act: Confront one featured guest with a surprise hostile guest, and hope sparks fly, tempers fray and someone does something sensational.

"Oh, I will do very well," I say, "But very well for who? Me or you or whatever dirtbag opposition you've dredged up?"

She gives me a weak smile. It's one of those smiles that makes you want to throw it under a microscope and break it down: one part smug, one part sympathetic, one part laughing at me, and there, at its root, in the nucleus, five parts not giving a shit about anything.

So I turn to the small bar in the green room and pour myself what one of my ex-wives used to call a pure martini, a.k.a. straight gin.

I hit the studio and get mic'd. I see an empty chair on the other side of Kitty Andropov, who smiles at me.

"Rick," she says, no longer rolling her Rs. "So glad to see you. You look different."

"Living with a clean conscience. That's my secret."

"It suits you."

Of course I have no idea what that means. It's the verbal equivalent of the segment producer's smile. But I say, "Thanks. Everything suits you, Kitty."

"Oh, Rick, you are such a charmer." She's taken it as a compliment, but I wasn't just talking about her looks. The thing about Kitty is that she doesn't care what your point of view or belief system is. She's made a career of instigating arguments. She's a fire stoker, a gas pourer, a provocateur. A ratings magnet.

"I heard some stories about you, Rick."

"What kind of stories?"

"Old stories, new stories."

"Urban myths, most of them," I say, wondering what

is she getting at. "Except *Goldengrove*. All those stories are probably true. Unfortunately."

"That is admirable. To own up to the past."

"One minute!" announces the assistant director.

A woman comes over and sprays something on Kitty's sensational auburn hair, and Kitty checks herself out on the monitor in front of us.

"You know the drill, Rick? Right? Same as last time?"

"How could I ever forget? Who is here to take me down? Those NRA guys–Wayne Dubois? Nelson Perry?"

"They couldn't make it."

"30 seconds!"

"So who is he? What skel did you dig up?"

"Them."

"What?"

"We have two guests."

"God, you've become a high-brow hit woman, Kitty."

"10 seconds…5, 4, 3, 2, and …"

Kitty does her spiel, talking about the controversial ratings juggernaut that is *Nuns with Guns*, the recent near-riot in New Orleans, the floundering boycott of The Network. "Of course, based on Mr. Salter's past, none of these controversies are unexpected. Trouble and outrage seem to follow him." So she goes through my horrific past— skipping over my Best Picture Oscar for *Evergreen* and my brilliant, world-unifying, big money-earning kids comedy, *Diplo Dynamite Six;* but mentioning my studio-destroying bomb *Goldengrove*, mocking it for trying to tell the story of Genesis in reverse; recounting the alleged anti-Semitism in my comedy *Desperately Seeking Goldfarb*; and finally settling on *The King of Pain*, that "outrageous and bizarrely exploitative show featuring contestants willfully undergoing torture."

And then she shows last year's clip of me on this very set insulting the U.S. Surgeon General, Premshaw Choudry by calling him Apu.

"Excuse me, Kitty," I say, while the clip airs, "if you are going to show that, you might also show my profuse apology and mention that I won a multimillion-dollar settlement for wrongful termination."

"Good point, Rick. And I believe you made a sizable charitable donation to an Indian organization."

"Damn straight. $50,000 to the Indo-American Friendship Foundation."

"Okay. I get it."

"Thanks. I suppose it's too much to ask you to explain I was blindsided by Choudry's appearance."

"I'm not even going to answer that."

We're back on the air and Kitty provides some backstory to the clip so I don't look like a total jerk. Then she asks about the *King of Pain* lawsuit and the settlement.

"Legal issues prevent me from talking about the settlement. I'm sure you understand. But we brought the suit in the first place because I was wrongfully dismissed from the most-watched show in America—a show that didn't force or exploit contestants to do anything, I might add—which I created and would never, ever harm."

"I believe The Network claimed that you displayed frequent behavior detrimental to the show."

"I certainly offended people while defending *The King of Pain*, no question. I did it right here on this show in the clip you just aired. But I was protecting my baby. I think anyone can understand that."

"Well, we have a never-before-aired clip of you, and it appears you are behaving badly. A clip that the owner says you paid to suppress. Here it is."

Holy fuck. There it is, beaming out to the world, the shitty phone video that Jared and I worked so hard to conceal; me defending Amanda and insulting an auditorium of people who accused the "the hunger episode" on *The King of Pain* of advocating starvation.

I actually sort of like the clip. It shows me asking the crowd if, instead of a hunger competition, they would like an eating competition in which contestants are forced to stuff themselves for three consecutive days. Unfortunately I ended my proposal saying, "Clearly that would be torture, but not for some of you."

That was me making a fat joke. A misstep.

"I'd like to bring Tom Danko, who obtained a copy of this tape, which was recorded at Valley High School auditorium in Orange County," says Kitty.

"Thanks for coming, Tom. Tell us about the video clip."

All I'm thinking is "Protect Jared, protect Jared, protect Jared," so when this kid, who can't be more than 20 years old sits down, I leap in:

"I was approached about the tape, which, by the way, is entirely misleading in that it fails to show that same audience booing Amanda Taylor, an associate producer on my show at the time, who was trying to explain that we don't, in fact, support starvation. I negotiated to buy this tape because it does not reflect the whole truth of the incident."

"Yeah, I heard that," says Tom.

"Really?" It's Kitty. "What did you hear, Tom?"

"That girl who filmed it and gave me a copy, she kind of leased it to Rick. You know, an, um, imbroglio."

"Embargo," I say.

"Why did you negotiate that, Rick?" says Kitty.

"I have been embarrassed enough in my life. My reputation—I have a reputation for being a hothead. But people do change. I still have a mouth on me, but I'm a much calmer person."

"You weren't trying to keep it from surfacing and hurting your lawsuit?"

"It was all about my reputation. Look, I kept paying Tom's girlfriend or whatever she is *after* I won my settlement. Isn't that true, Tom?"

"Yes, that's true, but not recently."

"Because she signed a deal for the last payment agreeing not to show this tape to anyone for the next five years."

"How do you think The Network will feel about this tape?" asks Kitty.

"Water under the bridge, Kitty. Nice try, but The Network was in last place until *Nuns with Guns*. Now they are in second and poised to finish first because *Nuns* is the #1 show in America. Translation: The Network may be a little pissed, but ultimately, they won't give a damn. That tape is completely out of context, anyway. The crowd I was berating, they had booed my colleague off the stage. And if you contact Amanda right now, she will back me up 150 percent."

"If this video goes viral, aren't you worried about a backlash from overweight and plus-sized people?"

"Not really. Nothing I said was untrue. It wasn't polite. But it wasn't wrong. I was making a point. They were upset with our starvation episode. So I suggested we make a contest out of the opposite idea: overeating. If they didn't like my suggestion, so be it."

"Let's look at it one more time, shall we? And when we come back we will focus on our guest Rick Salter's controversial and top-rated new show, *Nuns with Guns.*"

While the clip runs, I say, "Nice one, Kitty."

She shrugs. "We could do a week-long series on you Rick. Everyone has something to say about you."

Back on the air, Kitty recounts the clip again and lets me explain my side. Then she says, "Let's shift gears a bit. Your new show is now beating last year's show. Why is that?"

"Many reasons. The liberals love it, Catholics—and viewers of all faiths, really—love it because the nuns are so wonderful. Really, how can you not admire these women? Gun lovers may hate the show, but they watch it to see the guns that get turned in. Reality TV fans love it because it's an interesting show; it has drama and competition, heartbreaking sorrow, it's about media, messaging, getting the word out and making America a safer place."

"How did you come up with the idea?"

One of the reasons I didn't fight Walter Fields on his original media blackout for me is that I've wanted to avoid that exact question. And here, for some reason, I sense a trap. She's been digging. She's heard stories.

"Actually, Sister Rosemarie mentioned that she'd been approached to do a show called *Nuns and Guns,*" I say. "Apparently the producers were pro-gun and wanted Sister Rosemarie and other nuns to laugh it up, fire weapons and enjoy themselves."

"So that inspired you?"

"It *offended* me. But I saw possibilities in the name and asked my lawyer to trademark *Nuns with Guns,* because I thought it was catchier. And then I sort of forgot about it."

"Are you sure the title you heard was Nuns *and* Guns?"

"Oh, yes, 100 percent. We can call Sister Rosemarie right now if you want."

"What happened to reignite your interest?"

"My sons-in-law own a fabulous Mexican restaurant, Guaco-Taco, in L.A. Some thugs tried to shake them down for protection money. In the end, one of their employees, a hardworking young man named Omar Naxos, was shot dead during an attack on the restaurant. The final credit of the first episode says 'In memory of Omar Naxos,' in fact. And I thought, you know, there are a lot of reasons Omar is dead. Economic inequality, a shortage of police, greed, lousy education, stressed out social services, not enough jobs and too many guns. And I thought, I can't fix inequality, I don't have a plan or the smarts for that, and ditto for education and social services, but there must be a way to reduce the number of guns out there. To tell stories about the senseless tragic deaths that occur. And I remembered *Nuns with Guns*."

"That is all very interesting," says Kitty Andropov. "I'd like to bring out Nelson DeMire, Vice President of Business Development for G.U.N., Guns for a United Nation."

Out walks a tall, thin man with short-cropped blond hair and wearing a slick blue suit, looking like the poster boy of the Beltway faithful. He has lobbyist/politician written all over him, from the smarmy smile he flashes when Kitty greets him, to his overly friendly wave in my direction.

"Nelson, I believe you have a different side to this story."

"That's correct, Kitty. I am the one who called Rosemarie."

"Really? So you are the man who first thought up the title *Nuns and Guns*."

"Yes. Yes I did. But it was definitely *Nuns with Guns*. Not *Nuns and Guns*."

"How did it feel to see your idea up on the screen?"

"To be honest, Kitty, I was shocked and hurt. It felt like

I had been robbed."

I'm trying to stay calm, because this guy is spewing 100 percent Grade A bullshit. I vow to say nothing until Kitty calls on me.

"I mean," this kid Nelson goes on, "I wanted to do a show that highlights the importance of guns, the history of guns, the sense of responsibility and the joy they bring to everyone, not just hunters and collectors and security personnel, but everyone, even nuns."

"But instead the name of your show has been taken to the exact opposite."

"Right. So I feel awful, and frankly, a little angry. To have my creation co-opted like that, it feels like I've been violated."

"Rick, do you have anything to say?"

"First of all, I stick by my story. I heard a different title and adapted it. If Sister Rosemarie misheard the title, there's nothing I can say. But I did not mishear Sister Rosemarie. And you can ask her. I am a lot of things, but I am not a thief. And Sister Rosemarie, to me, is beyond reproach. All I can say is that even lesser minds think alike. Second, titles cannot, of themselves, be copyrighted. If I wanted to write a song called "Stairway to Heaven" or a book called *Fifty Shades of Grey*, or make a movie called *Citizen Kane* I could probably do that, unless they were trademarked. That's why people trademark things."

"So you weren't trying to snatch a show away from Guns for a United Nation?" asks Kitty.

"Hey, if I knew there was an organization with a ridiculous name like that—I prefer a nation united by compassion to one united by guns—I'm sure I would have wanted to cause some havoc. But the fact is, Sister

Rosemarie wasn't even told the name of the organization, or at least she didn't tell me."

"Why did Sister Rosemarie call you?" asks the boy wonder.

"Why do you think? Because I ran the most popular TV show in decades, which she starred in. And I helped her raise millions of dollars for her mission."

"So she kind of owes you, doesn't she?"

"Owe me? Are you kidding? I owe Sister Rosemarie Aria. We all do. She's one of the most giving human beings I have ever met. She represents what is good in the world. And now, even though she gets death threats from insane gun-rights activists who may well be members of G.U.N. for all I know, she works on our show every week, trying to reduce the number of guns out there, trying to build gun safety awareness and trying to save children from accidental death and injury. She's a hero. So please watch what you say."

"All I'm saying is it is interesting that she came to you after I called her."

"Whom else is she going to ask? It's not like her mother superior or Jesus gives out advice on syndication rights."

"Rick, please don't offend our viewers like that," says Kitty.

"Sorry. I was only trying to make a point. I'm the logical person for her to talk to. There was no concerted effort to go against your show, 'Nuns *and* Guns.'"

"Nuns *with* Guns."

"Honestly, I admire your moxie for even approaching her. Sister Rosemarie is all about welfare. And I don't mean welfare like government programs. I mean like general well-being. Is everyone okay? And let's face it, guns are not like food or clothing or education for most people in America.

We are no longer a nation of hunters who kill for food and wear the skins. You don't *need* a gun for your well-being. So the appeal of your proposed program must have been a little insulting."

"We offered her a large sum of money that she could use for her mission."

"Why? Who would pay for it?"

"Our organization."

"And what is the point of your organization?"

"To promote unity through gun ownership—"

"To protect gun and ammo sales, you mean."

"—and to protect the Second Amendment."

"That's the one that says that gun and ammo makers have the right to make a huge profit, right?"

"Rick! Please," says Kitty. "Your sarcasm is insulting."

"What this guy is saying is insulting, and *Nuns with Guns* is about making the world safer. There is no attacking the Second Amendment. I didn't bring it up."

"You asked me what my organization did."

"You could have said 'we're a lobby group for the gun industry.' You didn't have to mention the Second Amendment. But you guys always do, don't you?"

"Okay, gentlemen, let's calm down. We'll go to a commercial and then be right back."

The rest of the show is more of the same. Did I steal this guy's idea? How does he feel about it? Don't we really need Sister Rosemarie here to back me up? But I keep my cool. And I don't think I look half bad, even against a pretty boy who looks like he spends hours working out when he isn't busy oiling his Bushmaster AR-15 Semiautomatic Rifle or cashing in his paychecks from Colt and Remington.

When the witch-hunt ends, Kitty smiles at me. "Well

done, Rick, you made it through a show."

"Yeah. Sorry about that, Kitty. No fireworks this time. But you really brought it hard."

"Well, thanks for coming on. I'm sure the ratings were huge." She looks down at her cell phone. "Look, Rick Salter is trending on Twitter… and Facebook. That's about as good as it gets."

When I get home there are about 50 people in the house. A big "Rick, Rick, Rick!" cheers goes up, followed by "Speech! Speech!"

I've got a huge smile to fight off. "I'm sorry," I say. "I don't understand this reaction. I'm used to jeering."

Marta comes up with some champagne and a kiss for me. "You were great, Rick. Everybody was cheering."

"Thank you all. My anger management classes are really starting to pay off, right? Listen, I've talked enough tonight." I raise my glass. "Here's to the success of our show and to my lovely wife for putting up with me and bringing you here. Cheers!"

Chapter 18

There are two questions getting play in the press going into the Baltimore exchange. One is, what are the nuns up to? There are reports they've been spotted in Las Vegas. The other involves the hefty gun buy-back deal offered by Baltimore's biggest dealership. Will the big money trump our show? I don't think so. Here's why:

First of all, as *American Idol* has proven, people will do anything to get on TV for their 15 seconds of fame. Second of all, our nuns are now beloved figures. Fans want to meet them and pose for pictures. Third, there's no testifying at a gun dealership; nobody is going to listen to you talk about the misery firearms can cause at a gun shop. Remember Bradley Boardman in Texas? Well, with every show we get more and more people who want to testify about how guns ruined their lives or the life of someone they know. Everyone has a story. Okay, not everyone. But more people than I ever imagined. And you can't tell that story to a gun dealer, can you? You'll get no sympathy or empathy there. During registration at each exchange—when potential donors sign a waiver assigning us ownership of any footage shot during the event and are given an ID number to get their free photo—we ask donors if they plan to testify. If they say yes, the signup teams will ask for details so we can verify their stories. We get dozens of these from every show and we film as many as we can.

Turns out I'm right about not getting trumped.

Baltimore is astonishingly well attended, with over 20,000 people streaming through the gates at Camden Yards.

The most dramatic moment of the day comes when a gorgeous young mom wearing a "Debbie" name tag breaks down in tears without any warning and flashes a picture of "little Jessica, my cherub, my angel, my reason for living." She escalates from there, sobbing, kneeling at the feet of Sister Constance Grace, who bends over in concern. The woman leaps up and starts striking herself with the pistol she wants to donate, yelling, "She was an innocent! An angel! Why did you take her from me! Why, why! I can never go back home. They hate me there." At that point one of the security team steps up and subdues her.

The footage is incredible. It blows away Bradley Boardman for pure, heartbreaking spectacle. Her blood-streaked self-flagellation encapsulates the grief, the guilt, the pain that must come with the senseless death of a child. Rittenhouse, directing things from the remote truck, is beside himself. "This could be the most viral footage in the history of reality TV, Rick," he says.

Little Ricky agrees. "This is amazing. I wonder what happened."

"That's a good question," I say. "Did we get her story?"

"I don't think so. We try to move up the testifiers earlier in the day, so the sisters have the energy to deal with them.

This is pretty late."

"We need to find out who she is."

"Who cares? She's gorgeous!" says Rittenhouse. "She's a knockout. She'll be huge. Camera Two! Go tight on the picture of Little Jessica. We'll need that."

I turn to Sampson. "Have one of your guys down there get her I.D."

He gets on his walkie-talkie. I turn to Ricky. "Check to see if she signed up to testify."

• • •

Turns out there is no "Little Jessica." And there is no mom named Debbie, either. There was, however, a fledgling New York actress named Monica Moore, and a mysterious man who saw her photo on Backstage.com and contacted her. He sent her a round-trip New York to Baltimore train ticket, a $10,000 money order and a promise for another $100,000 if her stunt made it onto our show.

"I guess this won't make it into the episode?" says a very pale Monica Moore.

"Oh, it might," I tell Ms. Moore. "This guy who hired you…any idea why he would do that?"

"No."

"Come on! You didn't ask, 'What's my motivation?' You're an actress. We've caught you lying once. Let's try the truth."

"No comment."

"Ms. Moore," says Little Ricky, "Let's review some facts. We know you signed a waiver that warranted all your statements were true. We have you on camera saying tons of things that aren't true. You are looking at possible criminal charges and certainly civil charges. And, if you don't know your employer, you are looking at facing all those charges alone. We are not vindictive people. But the more you can help us, the less likely you are to become the fall guy. Or gal."

"I have nothing further to say until I speak to a lawyer."

"Sampson," I say. "Can you get some cops here? I'd like to press charges."

"Sure."

"What charges?" says Monica Moore.

"Fraud, fraud and fraud."

Needless to say, Monica Moore sings like a proverbial nightingale. A man named Thomas Vickers contacted her and said he was associated with an organization seeking to discredit *Nuns with Guns*. "The plan was for me to get on the show, fool you into airing my story, and then they would discredit my account, and accuse you of faking the stories," Monica tells us in an on-camera interview with Driscoll and Dr. Burns.

"And you agreed to this?" asks Maggie.

"I feel really bad. But I have a lot of financial troubles. And now I'm going to have credibility troubles. But I'm not lying! I'm happy to show you my finances. Do you know how much rent is in Manhattan?"

"But you were expecting to be discredited?"

"Yes, eventually. After the episode aired. But if that happened, I was going to get a lot more money. Like a hundred thou."

"Did you sign a contract?" asks Dr. Burns.

"No. They couldn't do that. Vickers said his group couldn't be implicated."

"Any idea what the name of the group he represented was?"

"No. I just got a sense it was a group that supports guns. And really hates your show."

"The NRA? Or maybe Guns for a United Nation?"

"I really can't say."

"How do you get in contact with this Thomas Vickers?" asks Maggie Driscoll.

"I have a cell number. And his email. He said he lived in Virginia."

"Can you give us them? We'd certainly like to talk to him."

"I'm not sure."

"Well, perhaps you want to discuss it with him? He is certainly implicated now."

"Yeah. I guess I should do that."

"We are going to ask the police to talk to you, too."

"Really? Oh my god. I better not say anything. I've probably said too much already."

Thomas Vickers is a real person. He lives in Alexandria, Virginia, and lists himself as a "political consultant and strategist." He refuses to answer any questions. The Baltimore police list him as a person of interest in pending conspiracy to commit fraud charges. This pretty much leaves us at an impasse. But we put Vickers' photo on the show, and report that the former clients listed on his web site include The Freedom Group, which owns Remington Arms and Bushmaster; Smith & Wesson; RJ Reynolds Tobacco Company; Halliburton; and some Frackers 'R' Us company I can't remember.

I ask Sampson to see what he can dig up on this asshole. "I know there are services out there that can magically produce data. Grey-area stuff, like who you've been calling, stuff like that. It would be great to see who hired this dirtbag recently."

"I'll see what I can do."

"Thanks, Sampson," I say, "Please just bill this as a run-the-business expense, petty cash, if you will. It's not a line item, if you know what I'm saying. More like a general consulting fee."

"Got it. Loud and clear."

Chapter 19

New York is really the perfect place for *Nuns with Guns*.

It's a city with mass transit, so anyone can get to the exchange. It's got millions of people. It has a large Catholic population, which never hurts when you are dealing with nuns. It is a much safer city than it was in the '80s and '90s, so there are probably tons of guns that people have just had sitting around. Perfect for donating.

Little Ricky and Sampson Smith have blocked out every aspect of the event with amazing precision, but the fact is that the New York episode is simpler to shoot, because there are now only two teams to film. Almost lost in the drama of Monica Moore's Baltimore unmasking was the fact Sister Rosemarie was the huge winner of that event, pulling in an astounding 4,500 weapons exchanged (how is that even possible, you ask? About half the donors handed over two weapons at a time, plus donors who didn't want to wait in line could hand in their guns when checking in and receive their swag). That number vaults her into second place over Sister Constance Grace and Sister Iron Iris, who are now out of the running for first prize. Not that the runners-up are off the show; Sister Constance Grace joins Sister Rosemarie, and Sister Iron Iris joins Sister Teri. Filming our giant Citi Field jamboree is now a lot easier. Not only are the nuns paired up and staying in close proximity, but we don't have to worry about giving all four equal time.

Although we've announced the gun exchange date—the third Saturday in March, before the Mets start playing every day—the whereabouts of the sisters have been largely unknown. I mean, we have footage of them plotting and planning, booking music acts as a special entertainment enticement to come to the stadium and turn in your gun. And their Facebook and Twitter pages are updated with words of inspiration, prayers and news of tragic gun deaths, of which there is at least one per day. But their Big Apple arrival has been shrouded in mystery.

That ends three days before the event. We send out a press alert to meet at the merry-go-round in Central Park at noon.

There's a media mob in the park when Little Ricky informs the crowd of a slight change of plan. He directs them to nearby Sheep Meadow, the grassy 15-acre haven in the southern half of the park. Journalists being journalists—or rather, TV journalists being TV journalists—there's some grumbling and grousing.

"Couldn't you have given us a little more notice?" whines a talking head.

"Get there in 10 minutes!" Ricky calls. "Or you'll miss the big event."

Not long after, we hear the unfamiliar buzz of a plane—a rare sound over mid-Manhattan in these post-9/11 times. The small plane circles over the city. This probably the most nervous I've been since we started the show. But the weather is supposed to be perfect. It should all work.

By now all the press have walked or driven to the west side entrance for Sheep Meadow. The plane approaches.

"Ladies and gentlemen of the media," says Dr. James Burns into a P.A. system we've set up, "please welcome the cast of *Nuns with Guns*, floating through the air with the greatest of ease."

Our four nuns in full habits jump from the plane, wimples outfitted over their crash helmets, fluttering, soaring. A fifth jumper, a much more aerodynamic figure with no wimple, leaps out, too, and zooms toward the nuns. It's Andray, of course, pointing them into position overhead.

You can hear the journalists and photographers, the TV talking heads and their camera crews all oohing and aahing as the sisters zoom in the sky for a few seconds—it feels like an eternity to me—and one by one pull their cords. As the chutes open, I breathe a sigh of relief. In order to make it to the meadow, which is only a couple of acres, and not get blown off course, they had to make the jump from a low altitude, so getting the chutes open quickly was key.

It is a great PR stunt. The footage of the jump, the joy and hugs after the successful landing, the joyous invitation to come to our New York exchange and donate guns, meet the nuns and listen to a great concert—it's all perfect. It instantly leaps to the front of the worldwide news cycle. The photos are tweeted like mad and #NunswithGuns is the top trending term in the webverse or whatever it's called. Ninety minutes later, I am on top of the world. I walk with Little Ricky, David and Tabitha out of the park toward the Pierre, where we are all staying. We've got two guards with us, one in back and one slightly in front. We walk down

Fifth Avenue, and I'm breaking it down for Little Ricky, David and Tabitha. "In the annals of marketing stunts, that's got to be at the top of the heap. How much did it cost us? The lessons, the plane, Andray, the insurance? Maybe $350,000. And we end up with millions of dollars of PR? This is going to be the story of the week and one of the images of the year!"

Yes, I'm soaring, bursting with pride. My flying nuns.

"High fucking five!" I say, turning to David.

And then, out of nowhere, there's a strange metallic swooshing sound. And suddenly David, instead of slapping my hand in celebration, is teetering off balance, like he's having a stroke or a seizure or something.

And part of his face is missing.

I don't even realize I'm splattered with blood until much later.

"Holy shit!" yells Ricky.

"David!" screams Tabitha.

"Jesus Christ!" yells some guy heading uptown, toward us. He crouches down and breaks into a run.

David's fallen to the pavement by the time I've lowered my un-high-fived hand. Tom, the security guy in front of us, is all business. "Down! Down! Mr. Salter, get the fuck down." He clicks a button on the wireless monitor on his belt, and talks into his mouthpiece. "Security alert! Team member shot. Secure all possible targets immediately."

"911! Call 911," says Nelson, our security guy who was watching our backs. I'm on the ground now, but I peek to see him pulling his sweatshirt off and jamming it against David's face

Little Ricky is on his phone. "I need an ambulance now at Fifth Avenue and 64th Street. Yes, a man just had his face blown off! Only one shot…I don't know who. We didn't see a shooter. It was a sniper, I guess. A hit. An assassination attempt…Yes, just one shot. My name is Ricky Garcia. Yes, I'm not going anywhere. HE IS A FRIEND OF MINE!"

Tom is in a crouch behind a parked car, looking across the street, trying to figure out where the shot came from.

"Oh my God! David! No, no!" Tabitha sobs.

And me? I'm in shock. I'm lying there listening to Ricky trying to explain the inexplicable, to Tabitha sobbing, to Nelson the security guy saying, "Hang on, buddy! Stay with us! Stay with us. Here, hold my hand. Please, man, stay with us. WHERE'S THE FUCKING AMBULANCE?"

I hear sirens. I have to fucking stand up. That bullet was meant for me. I high-fived myself into surviving and got another man shot in the process. Those should be my brains on the ground, not some 28-year-old kid who wants to make the world safer. I force my head up.

"Mr. Salter, please stay down," says Tom.

"They only fired one shot. They must be gone."

"We don't know that."

"Well, the ambulance is coming. Aren't we safe?"

"Who the hell knows? In Iraq, there are scumbags who detonate one bomb to hurt people and then a second bomb to take out the medical help."

"Fuck it. I'm getting up."

I stand up, look at David, his face obscured by Nelson's blood-soaked sweatshirt and hand. His body utterly motionless. I run to the curb and start to puke.

Tom is up now, too. He's got his phone out and is snapping photos of David.

"What the fuck are you doing?"

"The medics are going to come and haul him away.

This is for the investigators, to help them figure out where the shot came from. The splatter and shit. Here." He points the phone at me. "You got splattered. That's evidence."

Cops arrive and two ambulances pull up. EMTs are out and moving in their careful and quick manner. I get it. They are professionals. They have studied crisis. They have a method. But of course, I want speed.

"Come on, guys," I say. "We're from *Nuns with Guns*. Save him and you'll get the bonus of your life."

There's nothing else I can do but try and give Tabitha a hug. Then I look down at my shirt and realize I can't do it without getting David's blood on her.

"It hit me, too," she says, when she sees my hesitation. And she buries her head in my chest and sobs.

• • •

While I'm waiting at New York Presbyterian hospital, I call Marta and Jared and leave messages that I am safe and sound. Then I turn to Tabitha. "Do you know anything about his family?"

"His parents are teachers. Science and English. I met them once when they came to visit."

"Did he have a girlfriend?"

"Cathy. Somebody has to call Cathy. Jesus."

"Do you have her number?"

"Me? No. But it must be on his phone."

"What's her name? Cathy what?"

"Simmons. She works at a non-profit. Teach for America."

"Ah, fuck." I turn to Ricky. "Can you get me Cathy Simmons at Teach for America in L.A.?"

"Santa Monica, I think," says Tabitha.

"What about his parents?"

"They are high school teachers in Carmichael, a Sacramento suburb. Really nice people."

"Ricky?"

"On it."

"Thanks," I say, still focused on Tabitha. "I'm no expert. But this doesn't look good."

"No kidding."

"Tabitha, for what it's worth, I want you to know that I think you and David are both inspirational figures. And I just want to say, whatever David needs, whatever you need—time, money, therapy—you will get it from us. From me."

The eyes narrow at me. Does she blame me? Does she hate me? She doesn't say anything.

"Tabitha, that bullet was meant for me."

"I know."

• • •

Years ago, filming *Goldengrove* in Hawaii, we were doing aerial shots and the helicopter went down. We lost a cameraman and the pilot. I was already borderline insane from having my starlet on bed rest due to pregnancy complications, a tropical storm that obliterated our set, copious amounts of drugs and booze in my system and running $80 million over budget. These days, that amount can cover the marketing campaign of a blockbuster, but back in the early '80s, that was a number that led to the collapse of the studio that backed it. So I went completely insane after the crash, suspended production and smoked about a half-pound of Maui Wowie in two weeks while counting waves on the beach. I left it to my associate producer to call the families of the deceased.

I remember this as I dial to get Cathy Simmons on the phone. No wonder I ducked out back then. Who wants to be the messenger for the misnamed angel of death? How the fuck is the angel of death an angel? Rittenhouse films the call on his fucking iPhone, the bastard. We use the footage later. It is nightmarish TV to watch. I have zero awareness of being on camera, and you can see me, a collection of awful, nervous, weepy tics. Rubbing my forehead, scratching my head, shifting my weight from side to side nervously, as I tell her, or try to tell her, that her boyfriend is dying.

But as soon as I tell her my name, she already knows.

"What happened? How is David?"

"I'm calling from the hospital and—"

"Ohmygod, ohmygod, ohmygod."

"The doctors are operating now. They are doing everything they can to save him."

"Save him from what? What the hell happened?"

"Cathy, this is very hard stuff. Do you have friends or family nearby?"

"WHAT THE FUCK HAPPENED TO DAVID?"

"He was shot, Cathy. I'm so, so sorry. In the head. He has lost a lot of blood. There's an army of doctors trying to save him."

I hear the phone clattering to the ground or the desk and a shriek, the wail of a mourner's anguish. She knows. We all do.

• • •

While I'm pacing around the hospital, a cop sees my anxiety and informs me that, in general, New York City is a very good place to get shot in. That's because they have a bunch of Level One Trauma Centers in New York. Level Ones, I am told, are hospital emergency rooms equipped and staffed to handle major trauma events on a 24/7 basis. So, this loquacious police officer tells me, "If you plan on getting shot and surviving, New York is a pretty good place to be."

The heroes at New York Presbyterian fought hard, they kept David on life support, they transfused him, they removed fragments. But the .223 Remington bullet that was meant for me, and that crashed into his frontal lobe, had done the damage it was built by ordnance and ballistics geniuses to do.

Kill.

• • •

I meet with NYC detectives. I say I saw nothing, have no clue who the shooter was or where the shooter was. I say our route was totally spontaneous. I say everyone associated with the show has signed scary, ironclad non-disclosure agreements and has gone through rigorous background checks and that we have received numerous death threats. And I say that the bullet was meant for me, not that it really matters, just that David was probably not the intended target. The detectives assure me they have a huge team working on the shooting, searching the park, confiscating security tapes in the neighborhood, issuing appeals, canvassing the Fifth Avenue apartments that face the park.

After the interviews, we gather at a large suite at the Pierre. Everyone from the show is there: the sisters, Burns and Maggie Driscoll, Rittenhouse and all his crew members, our 15-man security team, Little Ricky and his army of segment producers and go-fers. And of course there's a crew filming. There has to be. We have to show this. The horror. Not all of it. But some.

I sit, shocked and numbed, stunned that the threats to the show have crossed beyond the crackpot, hotheaded right-wing rhetoric and into action. I knew it was possible, but I'm an expert at denial.

People want to know if this is going to impact the future of the show. Walter Fields calls me to ask if we should cancel or postpone the New York episode. He's just dealing in the reality: trying to get ahead of the PR curve lest The Network be accused of profiteering.

I have already talked to Tabitha and Little Ricky and am ready for this question. It was not an easy conversation. Tabitha, of course, is a wreck, although Xanax has helped her a bit. She's normally pale, but now she seems ghostly. This makes her dark eyes seem even darker.

"No," she says when I tell her The Network is going to ask whether we should suspend the show.

"No what?"

"The show has to go on. That is what David would want. That is what has to happen. He's a martyr, Rick. A young man murdered in a country where we let crazy people have guns. Where we let *blind* people have guns. Where a fucking crazy blind person can have a gun! Where, in some states, you can bring guns to church or school. Where it's okay to shoot someone if you feel threatened. We must stand *our* ground. The show goes on."

"I agree. One-hundred percent, Tabitha. One-hundred percent. Here."

I hand her a napkin for the tears dripping off her face.

So when Walter Fields calls, I say, "I appreciate the sensitivity here. But David Ryan believed passionately in the ultimate purpose of *Nuns with Guns*. I'm sure he would want us to push ahead at all costs and continue the fight to get as many guns—like the gun that killed him—off the streets. Gun control and gun safety had been his mission for the last seven years, since he got out of college. And I'm sure—as are the people who worked with this heroic young man—that he would want the show to continue and get more potentially lethal weapons out of circulation."

The Network takes it, tweaks it and releases it as a statement.

• • •

"What's this, Sampson?" I say, as he hands me an envelope.

"I think it's pretty obvious, Rick."

"I told him he's being ridiculous," says Little Ricky.

It takes me a minute. "You want to resign? Are you fucking kidding me?"

"I don't *want* to resign, Rick. I am offering my resignation. Something happened today under my watch that should never have happened. You offered maximum exposure with minimal coverage. Four high value targets walking down Fifth Avenue with two guards? That is not acceptable."

"I was being me, Sampson. I was celebrating the moment. I was loving life. I was careless. But I'm the boss. You couldn't know that I decided to walk. You were watching the sisters, as you should have been. I saw the plan. A team of 25 assembled around the perimeter, the four men covering at each nun as they landed. The cops spread around the edges of the meadow, looking outward, not upward. It was beautifully done."

"You must have been followed. We didn't spot it."

"Sampson, this is not your fault. You are not the fall guy. Did you discuss this with Lance?"

"Not yet. Not about resigning. Just about asset allocation."

"Excuse me," says Little Ricky. "But you are our number one asset. I couldn't do this without you. I'm moving people and crews and handling legal and you are in lockstep every second of the day. Actually, you are thinking far ahead of me. You should be getting a production credit, not trying to resign."

"I don't want to resign. I'm *offering* my resignation."

"Well, I'm not accepting it, " I say, tearing the unopened envelope in two, and then into four. "Let's get the fuckers who did this. And move on. We have a show to do."

• • •

"Mr. Salter, you should get some sleep." It's Tom from the security team at about 2 that night.

"Nah. I'm too wired."

"I don't blame you. I'm really sorry about this. About not doing my job."

"Jesus, not you, too. I talked to Sampson about this. You and Nelson did everything you could."

"I'm supposed to prevent the shot, sir."

"There's 150 million crazies out there, Tom."

"With all due respect, they're not all crazy, Mr. Salter."

"Oh, come on, Tom. Like we really all *need* guns. Like we're all going to join a militia to keep America safe from who? The British aren't fucking coming! Al Qaeda isn't even fucking coming. They're stuck in Waziristan and Yemen and ISIS is busy going nuts in Syria and Iraq."

"Mr. Salter, this country was raised on guns. We love guns. I guess it's not the time to talk about this, but maybe after the show…"

"Shit, Tom, if we don't talk about it now, when are we gonna talk about it? Go ahead. Enlighten me."

"All I'm saying is that we get taught to love guns. I loved 'em as a kindergartener. I had toy six shooters. Didn't you have those?"

"No, I didn't, actually."

"Nobody watches westerns anymore. But my dad and his dad, man, they'd sit through anything with a gun in it. It didn't even need to be a John Wayne movie. And now, instead of John Wayne, we've got video games where you can just kill entire armies like you are Rambo. And we've got action movies and bullshit rappers talking tough, spinning fantasies about mass murder. And you know what makes the games and movies and raps thrilling?"

"It's crazy. Make-believe. A sickness."

"The guns. My dad taught me to shoot. My dad loved his guns, especially the Remington his own dad left him. What do you have of your father's that he loved?"

I think for a minute. "Nothing. The man collected nothing. He loved listening to the radio. What I have from him is a sense of, I don't know, broadcasting. No, not broadcasting, but an appreciation of stories. But, Christ, I don't even have one of his ties."

"Mr. Salter, where I come from, people send out Christmas cards that have the family posed around the tree, all loaded to the gills with guns and ammo. You know what the caption usually is?"

"'If Santa Claus comes down the chimney we're gonna put a cap in his ass?'"

"'Merry Christmas and have a *safe* new year.'"

"'To celebrate the birth of Jesus?'"

"'Yup.'"

"'Kill me now.'"

"'They're trying.'"

• • •

I'm collapsed on a sofa in the Pierre suite when Marta walks in on Friday morning and crouches down beside me.

"You look terrible," she whispers in my ear.

"Oh, Christ. I feel terrible. I started drinking at midnight. What time is it?"

"9:30."

"Jeez. I am so glad you are here."

"We couldn't just stay in L.A., papi. We wanted to see you."

"We?"

"Hi, Dad."

Jared is in the suite, too. Watching from the food table. I struggle to get up, kiss Marta, and then go give him a hug, my taller, handsomer son.

"This is a surprise."

"A good one, I hope."

"D'yes. We had to come, because, you know, you didn't tell me," Marta says. "And Jared asked, and so did Mikey and Hector."

"Asked what?"

"You know. The shooter. Who was he aiming for?"

"I need coffee."

"Dad?"

"Jared, is there any coffee in there?"

"Dad, answer the question."

"What the hell am I supposed to say? I don't know if they were aiming at me. But, probably. Maybe. I mean, yes. Yes, the bullet had my fucking name on it, okay? But I'm here and David Ryan is dead. All because I turned to high five him the exact moment some fucking nut job pulled the trigger."

"Oh, Rick!"

"I'm gonna be okay. I got my body armor on. I just need to add a helmet now, is all."

The sisters come into the suite escorted by their bodyguards. Last night they sat here in a circle and prayed. This morning, they are looking for Little Ricky. They are scheduled to tour NYC for photo opportunities, including a visit to a school in The Bronx, a stop at St. Patrick's Cathedral on Fifth Ave., and a trip to the Metropolitan Museum of Art, which the Mayor requested as a little tourism boost.

"We don't think we should be doing anything," says Sister Teri, "except honoring David's life and work. And mourning his loss."

"I'll go visit St. Patrick's and see the children, but I'm not going to a museum," says Sister Iris.

Little Ricky shows up and they start in on him immediately. "I hear you. I hear you. We are going to have a press conference on the steps of City Hall with the mayor and the governor at 2 p.m. They will speak. And the nuns are invited to speak as well."

Sister Rosemarie stops to say hello to Marta. "I feel like I'm living in a dream state," she says. "One minute we are flying over New York City, one of the most amazing events in my life. Two hours later my heart is torn apart."

"I never got to tell you yesterday," I say. "But that was brilliant. The skydive was perfect. Did you see the newscasts?"

"Yes," says Sister Rosemarie, lowering her voice to parrot the modulation of your typical newscaster. "'What began as a wonderful, dramatic entrance into the city—the stunning sight of four nuns soaring through the sky—now serves as frivolous footnote to the deadly attack that was to follow.'"

"I know how hard you worked," I say. "It was magnificent. I was a fuc—I was a wreck worrying about you guys. I guess I should have been worrying about other stuff."

• • •

Naturally, David's death, not the nuns' skydive, is the story of the week. The sisters' tearful appearance at City Hall talking about this shameful, cowardly, murderous act—an assassination—is all over the web. Politicians weigh in. The governor of New York reminds everyone that this still happened even though New York State has some of the toughest gun control laws in the nation.

And you know who makes the same exact point? The NRA, GUN, A2AA (American Second Amendment Association), the FGS (Freedom for Guns Society) and every other gun-crazy group that is secretly funded by the Gun Manufacturers of America Association and assorted neo-con organizations. But the governor and the gun lobbyists take the same point to entirely different conclusions. The governor, God bless him, says the shooting means that we need to pass even more stringent laws in New York and elsewhere. The gun lobby says this proves that gun control doesn't work and we need deregulation so we can all protect ourselves.

I'm hanging out in the suite that evening when we hear this last bit of deranged logic. "Listen to this gutless, disingenuous NRA shill," I yell at the TV, outraged that the reporter isn't challenging him.

"Gutless and spineless," says Sister Constance Grace.

"And totally unsurprising," says Sister Iron Iris.

"Amen," I say.

• • •

David died on Wednesday. Saturday we run the greatest gun exchange in the history of the world at Citi Field, in Queens. DJs spin throughout the day and three great bands—Trending, The Public Option and Deny, Deny, Deny—play in the evening. Plus, we feed everyone free pizza, care of Dingle's Pies, which is amazing, because their owner is an archconservative. But it turns out that Dingle's is a giant target for robberies all across America, since they have one of the most visible delivery services around. Apparently most people pay cash on pizza deliveries—taking credit cards slows down the whole process—and these drivers zip around with a couple hundred bucks in their pocket and get mugged all the time. So the Dingle's head of marketing calls us up and says, "You guys are speaking our language. Pizza is on us, just mention us on air." Between the bands and DJs who wanted to play for free and the free food, Sister Rosemarie and Sister Teri don't offer any new trade-ins, but they do have the surplus booty from previous episodes to hand out. So, really, *Nuns with Guns* is about the best entertainment deal around: dinner for two, a concert and a T-shirt or sunglasses. All for the price of a gun you should never want to use.

The turnout is insane. The event goes from 10 a.m. to 10 p.m. About 14,000 donors show up, most with a friend. At donor registration the weapons get checked to make sure the chambers are empty, and everyone is searched and then given a ticket with a seat number—we can't have 30,000 people crammed on the field for the concert. Amazingly it all works. No doubt thanks to the thousand-plus cops, ushers and security team members circulating inside and outside the stadium. Also at registration, we tell donors that we are selecting at random which nun they will meet. If you want to donate to Sister Rosemarie there is a one-in-two chance you will see her "assistant" Sister Constance Grace instead. We also stress that, given the huge crowd, they'll be lucky to get 30 seconds with their nun. Finally, we say that we'd be happy to take their guns right now, attribute the donation to the nun of their choice and give them a ticket to the festivities. Most people are cool about it and opt to wait in line. But about 20 percent hand in their weapons and take the tickets.

By 10 p.m., when the crowd is throbbing to The Public Option, we stop collecting guns. And Dobson McMaster-Jones, the lead singer, announces the tally. "You people are amazing! You've set a record for the show with your donations. You turned in more than 16,000 guns today! 8,219 for Sister Rosemarie and 7,792 for Sister Teri. That is fantastic. That is something to dance about. That's something, in fact, to sing about."

The steady 4/4 thud of a house beat shakes the air and

McMaster-Jones leads the crowd through a series of chants: *Less guns, more life; The NRA is not OK; If you wanna shoot play basketball!*, and, as the video screens show a handsome, familiar face: *David Ryan, ray of light, David Ryan, always fight!*

Rittenhouse edits the show—the flying nuns, the murder, the shock and the concert into two hour-long segments, which The Network runs on Tuesday and Wednesday. Half the TVs in America tune in. But it's hard to get excited by the ratings. When Little Ricky emails me our #1 ratings data, I email him back:

"This puts the numb in numbers."

Chapter 20

Back in L.A. I don't go into the office immediately. Fortunately, we have a compilation show planned after New York—*Behind the Scenes with Nuns with Guns*—which is nothing more than a narrated recap spiced up with interviews with the stars and hosts about their favorite moments and surprises. That leaves two weeks before our next show in Newtown, Connecticut. I sleep late. I lie in, listening to the babble of sports radio discussing the upcoming football draft, the NBA playoff hopes, and the problems with the Dodgers and Angels. I even watch Scooby-Doo en Español with the kids. A day passes. Two days.

But it's no use. I think about David Ryan even when I'm trying not to think about him. David is buried in a private ceremony. Only his immediate family and his girlfriend's family. But of course some paparazzo nabs a photo of his tear-streaked girlfriend and his collapsing mother. And of course, I study them and think about how it could have been Marta and Jared crying instead, if not for my infantile burst of enthusiasm. A high-fucking-five.

A bonding celebration. The slap of skin. The wrong man murdered. My life saved. I surf the Internet to monitor the progress of the investigation. There is very little. Detective Roger Dixon, the officer heading the investigation, reports they are combing through videotapes from hundreds of buildings and businesses, as well as the video files of tourists who were in the area around the time of the shooting. They have a person of interest—a tall man with a guitar case who was seen talking urgently on a cell phone by a doorman on 65th Street just before the shooting.

While I'm lying low, Marta clucks sympathetically, cooks for me and even gives me a massage, which is a first. Turns out she's pretty awesome; she even brings me a hot towel at the end.

"How do you know about this? You're like a professional masseuse."

"Oh, no, Rick. I just called Yumi and Yoko and asked how they did it."

"Oh," I say, a little stunned. Yoko and Yumi used to come to the house and give me four-handed massages. And some, shall I say, additional personal care. I'm wondering just what exactly they told Marta.

Fortunately Marta changes the subject.

"You need to start a what you call it, a foundation, papi. For David. So his parents and everybody can keep him, you know, in their mind."

"What about his girlfriend?"

"Her, too. But you know, she's young. She has more life still to come. It's different if it's your children that dies. Your children is special."

I remember Marta smacking the shakedown thug at Guaco-Taco. "You are right. I'll get on that tomorrow," I say, and then I moan in appreciation. The hard rubbing and pummeling has stopped. Her fingers are now caressing me. I moan some more.

• • •

That afternoon Jay calls. "How you doing?"

"Shitty, angry, depressed."

"I figured. I'm really sorry, Rick. I don't know what to say, so I haven't said anything."

"I appreciate that."

• • •

The mail arrives. There's a hand written note from Amanda.

> *Hi Rick,*
>
> *I am so sorry about what happened in New York. My heart goes out to David Ryan's family, but also to you and Marta. I know you must be furious and you should be. But please, please, please be cautious and careful. I lie awake worrying about Ricky and about you. And I know Marta does, too. I know you, so I know you will never stop pushing this show. But I pray it is over soon.*
>
> *With love and admiration,*
> *Amanda*

• • •

The next day I see the City of New York is offering a $10,000 reward for information leading to the arrest and conviction of David's murderer. I'm in my pajamas when I read this, and I blow a gasket.

I hop into the shower and put Little Ricky on speakerphone. "Ricky!" I yell through the streaming, steaming water.

"Is that you, boss? You okay?"

"No I'm not okay. I'm fucking furious! Did you see this reward New York is offering for David's killer?"

"Yes. I saw it. Where are you calling from? I can barely hear you."

"I'm in the shower. I'm coming in. You call up that fucking sheriff, I mean, that detective and tell him to make it $100,000. I'll pay for it."

"Rick, maybe we should announce it ourselves. You know, on the show?"

"Right, right. Good idea. Listen, let's tag it on the end of the show that airs this week. Can we do that?"

"Why don't you call Walter? And have Rittenhouse cut it in."

"Genius. Of course. I'm sorry, Ricky. I've been out of it. I was lying here feeling sorry for myself, but that is over. I'm coming in."

"Great."

"And sorry for the speakerphone, Ricky."

"Just proof you're back."

"I am. Nowhere to hide."

• • •

When I get to work, Sampson hands me a sheet of phone numbers with two dozen calls highlighted in yellow or green ink.

"Great, Sampson, what the hell am I looking at?"

"Thomas Vickers' phone calls to the NRA main office. And repeated calls to a number in New York. All right before and after our show in Baltimore."

"Holy shit. Smoking gun, huh?"

"More circumstantial, I think. We don't know who he talked to there or what they talked about."

"But we can use our imaginations."

"Imagination doesn't stand up in court."

"Can you look up the New York numbers?"

"Yes. I'll get on that."

"Who do we tell?"

"Let me think about it."

"Good. Are you surprised there might be a link here?"

"Maybe a little. I'm surprised anyone could think they could fake something like this to make the show look bad."

"Still, we were pretty ready to fall for it. We all hoped Monica Moore was real."

"Yes. You were more suspicious than all of us."

"Well, this is great work, Sampson. A great start. We need to find something solid and pass it on."

• • •

Initially, the visit to Newtown is not planned as a gun-collecting episode; it is going to be a healing tour. We booked Friday so we could visit schools, and Saturday so we could visit hospitals, attend religious services and meet with the families of the victims. The general message was going to be one of safety and recovery. But as our show gains steam, the selectman—which apparently is what they call the mayor in New England towns—calls Little Ricky and asks that the gun exchange continue. He is furious at

Congress' failure to legislate more gun safety measures across the country. And furious that, in the immediate wake of the senseless massacre that has scarred his town, gun sales across America actually increased.

"You guys have the most proactive, visible gun exchange program in America," the mayor says. "We want you to continue."

The selectman then goes one step further, announcing that gun vendors will not be welcome during our event. "This is an event for a community that is still and forever in mourning. On Saturday, we will join *Nuns with Guns* and channel our grief into the reduction of weapons. Gun dealers will not be welcome."

He might as well have said, "Hey NRA, come on down!"

Why? Because, as Little Ricky later explains to me, a mere 3.3 miles from Sandy Hook Elementary school, the scene of the deadliest mass shooting at an elementary or high school in U.S. history, sits the National Shooting Sports Foundation, which bills itself as the trade association for America's firearms industry. Its supposed mission: to "promote, protect and preserve hunting and the shooting sports."

"Are you fucking kidding me?" I bark into my cell phone while Tom and Nelson are trying to drive me to the high school field where we are hosting the exchanges.

It's 9 a.m. and traffic in this sparsely populated town is crawling at about one mile per hour. Little Ricky, who is already at the exchange site, brings me up to speed:

"Last night, apparently, the NSSF sent out an email protesting the selectman's statement and invited all gun-rights supporters to stage a rally at their office today at 11 a.m. The thing is, if they get 300 cars, that's a lot for this place. Just a few slow-moving cars can tie up traffic."

"Did you know this? That the NSSF was here?"

"No, Rick. I've never seen it in any coverage. And none of the people we talked to during planning mentioned that this goddamn town is one of the epicenters of gun rights. I checked the NSSF website. They represent 10,000 gun manufacturers, distributors, retailers and shooting ranges. That's a big fucking mailing list, I'd imagine."

"Jesus. Well, they've got the message out. We've moved about 40 feet in 10 minutes, Ricky. Where are the sisters?"

"We picked them up early. So they are here ready to work."

"Thank god."

"And so is most of the crew."

"Any donors?"

"Sure. But not like we planned."

It takes us an hour to go the two miles. I want to walk, but Tom says it's too dangerous. "You are safer in here, sir, behind tinted windows."

It's hard to argue. When we get to the grounds, we march—Tom in front of me, Nelson close behind—to the remote truck. There, we learn that the chief of police has shut down the rally at the NSSF, because the gun-lovers have failed to get the correct permits from the town, and state troopers have been stopping traffic on Routes 6, 25 and 34, informing drivers their rally has been canceled. But traffic is still a total shit-show. It actually doesn't take that many cars to create a tie up, if you think about it. Just flood a bunch of cars into a five-block area and have them circle around, and you've created a nightmare of crawling traffic.

But donors keep coming, hundreds of them parking their cars on the side of the road and walking miles to the grounds. They are taunted as they walk by gun-rights fanatics who call from their cars. Cops are sent along the road to keep the peace as the gun lovers deliver drive-by insults:

Pussies! Faggots!

You are giving up your rights! I'll buy your gun!

You deserve what you get if you give up your weapon.

You wanna give up your rights, fine, but don't take mine.

When the communists take over, don't blame me, fucking faggots.

We capture a lot of this civilized discourse on camera.

Most of our donors turn the other cheek. But we capture some of them giving as good as they get.

I'm giving our gun in because my husband is okay with his penis size, unlike you, tough guy!

The right to bear arms means the right not to bear arms, nimrod!

Your guns really helped those kids in Sandy Hook!

That last one doesn't make it into the show.

As we learn from on-camera interviews, people have been driving down from all over New England to hand in weapons. We have testifiers from Portland, Maine; Newton, Massachusetts and Rutland, Vermont, who wait for Sister Rosemarie in one end zone, Sister Teri in the other. The lines are long, snaking back and forth across the field, guided by yellow police barriers.

And many of them are wearing the My Favorite Nun T-shirts we've been selling on the website for $30—ten of which go to Tabitha and David's organization, eight of which goes to the nuns, five of which goes to me, and seven of which goes to the company making the shirts. Our nun-wear has pictures of the smiling nuns on the front, and the *Nuns with Guns* logo on the back. We have sold tens of thousands of them, which is pretty damn amazing. And pretty damn gratifying.

Going into today's competition, Sister Rosemarie has closed the gap considerably. She's less than a hundred guns behind Sister Teri with two shows left. She now tweets like a bird, hammering out good tidings, scripture quotes, Pope quotes, show updates and gun death facts.

> *Montana has a higher per capita suicide rate than New York City. Why? They have much higher per capita gun ownership. #dothemath #NWG*

> *The number of gun owners in U.S. has gone down. But the number of guns sold continues to rise. #lethalarsenals #NWG*

> *How do I define tragic? 20,000 gun-related suicides annually in the U.S. #getthemoutofyourhouse #NWG*

> *Shame: One year after Newtown, 70 percent of new gun bills eased gun restrictions. #insane. #NWG*

Of course, Sister Teri is no slouch. Her tweets are half in Spanish and half in English. Sometimes in the same tweet: "Yo peeps, te amo, and Jesus does too!" #letloverule #NWG." She quotes rap lyrics, pop songs and gives shout outs to fans. She also has a new YouTube hit, "Muzzle Yo Muzzle," which she made with DJ 5-2-10, an ex-con who served—you guessed it—5 to 10 years on gun charges. Here are a few lines from the new track:

> *Want a medal? Don' be mental*
> *Drop that metal before it gets fatal*
> *Havin' it around, you know that's bent*
> *Meant for some tragic accident*
> *Muzzle yo muzzle*
> *Do it now, hustle*

Muzzle yo muzzle

Although you might expect a rap hit to bring out the youth market, the Newtown event feels slightly older than it has in other towns. Probably because you have to drive to get anywhere in Connecticut, but also, I think, because the Newtown tragedy is so resonant. No, that's not the right word. The right word is fucking tragic. It is every parent's worst nightmare. Who wants to deal with that? So Teri's massive outreach, as good as it is, doesn't quite translate into donations. She does well. But Sister Rosemarie closes the gap some more, gaining 60 guns.

The score so far:

Sister Teri: 15,596.
Sister Rosemarie: 15,556.

• • •

I'm in New York after Newtown. I'm about to head out of the Pierre to fly back to L.A. when Kitty Andropov calls my cell. "Rick, can you do our show tonight? We'll send a crew to you. Anywhere."

"Hi Kitty, nice to hear from you."

"Can you do it, please?"

"What's the rush? Someone cancel?"

"You didn't hear?"

"What?"

"Thomas Vickers was shot dead last night."

It takes me a moment. "Vickers? The NRA consultant?"

"Yes, the guy who hired that actress, Monica Moore."

"Where?"

"Parking lot. In Virginia."

"Why? Robbery?"

"It's not clear. Could be a carjacking. Or maybe it's related to his work, but that's just conjecture."

"Wow."

"Can you do it?"

"I'm getting on a plane, Kitty. Sorry."

"Shit!"

"But if you need a quote, our hearts go out to Mr. Vickers' family over this horrible act of gun violence. Gotta run."

· · ·

What Kitty says turns out to be right on the money. What's more, it looks like the perfect crime. No witnesses, no nearby surveillance cameras, no strange prints found in Vickers' car. The murky circumstances and the victim's connection to the *Nuns with Guns* scandal lead to an explosion of conspiracy theories. The most popular is that one of his clients had him silenced to prevent him from naming names about hiring Monica Moore and trying to dupe our show. "Whoever paid him to hire Monica Moore would definitely be a person of interest," one anonymous investigator tells the *Washington Post*. This tells me it's only a matter of time before they look at Vickers' phone records and discover what Sampson did: that he was talking to the NRA around the time of the Monica Moore debacle. And then I read reports of geniuses that hold the opposite opinion: that some liberal took him out because "he was such an amazing Second Amendment defender." I know: ridiculous. Other suspects include a recently divorced wife, a former business partner and, of course, Monica Moore herself. The thing is, nobody can find Monica. She's gone missing, which just feeds this theory. "It's not like her," her mother in Minnesota tells the Associated Press. "She called me every Sunday for the last five years."

There's another theory, too, which is that Monica killed David Ryan, which is why nobody has seen her. She's gone totally underground. The investigation into the Ryan murder has stalled. Investigators are still arguing about where the shot came from: a moving vehicle, a public telephone across the street, an apartment window? The whole sniper idea seems strange to me. Who knew we'd be where we were? Nobody. I didn't even know. Unless someone was following us, and called an accomplice.

As Sampson points out, they might have been tracking my cell phone.

This is all very scary shit. So many unknowns. But I put on a brave face because we have the final episode to shoot.

In Columbine.

Chapter 21

"After three months of being on the air, we finally have some numbers," Tabitha says, sitting down at our production meeting and dropping a sheaf of papers on the table. There's a faint hint of a smile on her pale face. "So I've got good news and bad news."

"Let's accentuate the positive," I say.

"For the first quarter of the year, new gun registrations—that's for new gun owners—are down 15 percent year over year. And handgun sales have dropped 10 percent over the same period."

"I don't see how there can be bad news."

"Semi-automatic rifle sales rose by about 10 percent."

"Oh."

"But that always happens when there's any perceived attack on gun rights, which is what, unfortunately, *Nuns with Guns* is viewed as by a certain audience segment. So the people who are preparing for Armageddon or just love hardware and want to add more firepower drive the sales up, especially because they assume that those weapons will be the first to get shut down."

"Have you ever seen a decrease like this?"

"No. Never. Sales, registrations and background checks all *increased* after Newtown."

"You're sure about this?"

"The NRA lobby lumps the Second Amendment with the right to privacy to get the libertarians all riled up, so data can be hard to come by sometimes. But the background checks and a few new state registration laws have helped us monitor things. Also, a few gun manufacturers have issued guidance to investors saying they expect sales to slow this year."

"This is huge! We can have the sisters announce it. You can tell them yourself. We'll film it. They are doing the impossible! They are changing the attitudes of Americans."

"That's what it seems like," says Tabitha.

"Wow," says Little Ricky.

"Amazing," says Sampson.

"Tabitha," I say, "this is *astounding* news. Are you okay? We should be breaking out the champagne over this!"

"I know," she says, her eyes growing watery. "I was just wishing that David could hear it. He would have been so happy."

• • •

Sampson comes into my office with more phone records.

"You look tired," I tell him.

"I am tired. But I'm also excited. Here." He tosses the papers on my desk. "These are records of Vickers' calls to New York, with addresses attached. Some of them are to Monica Moore. But look at the address highlighted in red."

"Grant Matthews, 834 Fifth Avenue?"

"The apartment building opposite where David was shot."

"You're fucking kidding me."

"No, Rick. To quote a friend of mine, I'm as serious as mass murder."

"Who is Grant Matthews?"

"He appears to be a corporate lobbyist. But I think at this point, it's time to turn over what we know to the NYPD, and let them find out who Matthews is."

"Why? They should have nailed this themselves, but they didn't."

"We don't know that. And remember, they have legal hurdles that we sidestepped. I obtained these records in a totally illegal manner. But now, if a source tips them off, they can gather the evidence legally, and run this down."

I think for a minute. "Okay. So donate this information anonymously. I don't want us getting in more trouble. We're already in these fucking nut jobs' scopes."

Sampson leaves, and I get up out of my chair and start throwing punches in the air. I'm shadow boxing, even though I've never boxed in my life. Finally! Good news. Tabitha's statistics and Sampson's investigation. I feel like we've done something to get David Ryan's killer, besides offer reward money. I feel exhilarated. Like we are fighting and maybe even winning.

• • •

Is it possible I'm more proud of my TV shows than my movies? I hate TV. Small screen, annoying aspect ratio, commercials, sneaky fucking cable bills, addictive and easy.

So much of it sucks—and yes, I'm aware of the recent super-hyped series on cable that people are calling TV's new golden age. I like some of it. But honestly, are any of these acclaimed drama series better or more important than *12 Angry Men*? Maybe. I'm not sure. Can anyone match the physical comedy of Sid Caesar on *Your Show of Shows*? Again, it's not that clear to me. Yeah, there's some good stuff out there. Jared and I love *The Simpsons*. But part of me wonders if the hype is so thick because there's so much cheapo supposedly unscripted Real World/Kardashianized TV shit that gets poured out, that good drama just seems better than it is. But whatever. TV just pulls in everyone. And despite my contempt for the medium, it seems that my greatest work, my greatest achievement isn't the Oscar-winning *Evergreen* or my other movies. It is these reality TV shows. Or at least *Nuns with Guns*—a show that affects the way people think.

Damn. I wonder how Frank Capra felt. Sure, he made *It Happened One Night* and *It's a Wonderful Life* and other tremendous films, but nothing was more important than his *Why We Fight* war documentaries, which changed and charged America, stoking and unifying our armed forces during World War II. Okay, I'm *not* Frank Capra. That's ridiculous. The man was a god. But still. I'm making something that is changing the world for the better. I'm fighting my own private war. How do I celebrate this? What do I do? I want to tell someone about Sampson's discovery, about this guy Grant Matthews. But I can't; telling someone is the equivalent of confessing to a crime. Since we leave for Columbine tomorrow, I go home.

The kids—my step-grandchildren—are in the pool. I change into a swimsuit and join them. I launch the little ones in the air. They scream with laughter, they protest, they mock fight me, they taunt me, they trash talk—"you can't get me! You poopee head!" I catch them, tickle them and gently dunk them.

"Papi," laughs Marta from the side of the pool, "Don' give yourself a heart attack. You got a big week and then the re-wedding soon after that."

"Just tell me where to go, when to go and what to wear, and I'll be there," I say, getting out of the pool.

Marta hands me a towel, but instead I grab her and give her a giant, bend-back-over-my-knee-so-I-can-ravage-you kiss.

"Ooh! Abuela! *Beso grande.*"

"Ooh la la!"

Then they all say it and giggle. "Ooh la la!"

"'Ooh la la?' Who taught you that?"

"I don't know."

"Yeah, we don't know. Poopee head!"

"I'm not finished with you!" I thunder at them.

"Why you home so early?" Marta asks.

I tell her about Tabitha's research. "I know people say I'm a cynic. I'm exploitive. That I pander to the lowest common denominator with shows about terror and fear and violence. But it's all B. S. This show is doing some good."

"Sí, of course, Rick. Like everything you do. All the charity. Me. My boys, they look up to you. Ever since they were little. An' look at the sisters. They make a lot of money for the missions, all because of you. I marry a crazy prince."

"Thank you, honey. You were the one I wanted to tell first. You and Jared."

"So call him."

Jared is elated. "That is fucking awesome, Dad," he

says. "It's amazing. I am so proud of you. But you know what? Don't get lazy. Watch your back. The show is almost over, and when it is, I can't tell you how relieved I'll be."

"Well, the season will be over, but not the show."

"You're going to do it *again?*"

"A new version, yeah. I can't just let two #1 shows die. That's bad for my reputation. What little I still have."

"You are getting maximum respect around town. And you've done something huge. You've put a cap in the ass of the NRA."

A cap in the ass of the NRA. I can't help smiling. Who does he sound like? Who would say something like that?

Me, that's who.

"Jared," I say, "You just made a good day even better."

I hang up in time to see Marta gingerly lowering herself into the pool. "Niños!" I yell to the kids, before leaping into the water. "Let's get Abuela!"

Chapter 22

Turns out that Colorado, for all its tragedies and mass killings, is not exactly the hot zone for gun lovers that you might expect. When it comes to national statistics, they are in the middle on gun ownership and gun deaths. Still, Tabitha tells the cast that the state presents significant challenges.

"Coloradans have a reputation for being more independent-minded. It's a little bit of the Wild West and the state has attracted its fair share of hippies, ski bums, hunters. Pot is legal, which I think speaks to the state's libertarian streak. There is a lot of hunting, and hunting, as I see it, is one of the gateway drugs to gun addiction and having firearms in the house. Not that I think we should ever attack hunters. That is a total non-starter in policy discussions."

"It's really amazing they are even letting us do this in Columbine," says Maggie. "Aren't you surprised?

"We got lucky."

She's not kidding; we hit a trifecta with a mayor in his last year in office, a sympathetic D.A., and a sheriff whose cousin was one of the Columbine victims. So the people in charge love the idea. In fact, the departing mayor says he hopes it will become an annual event. Little Ricky works with the town government, and we make a hefty donation to the Columbine Memorial, which is located in Clement Park beside Columbine High School and is the perfect spot for the event. And in the wake of the Newtown traffiic tie-up, the mayor and chief of police have arranged to have state troopers conduct traffic stops on all major approaches to the area. Donors need to pre-register on our web site and will have to show their weapon and their printed pass to gain admission to the actual exchange. The chief of police also announces that any unlawful assemblies will be broken up and participants will be arrested.

The four sisters all want to arrive by parachute. But Little Ricky nixes this immediately. "We can't have you floating up there like giant skeet targets," he says. "Frankly, I can't believe we let Rick talk us into the other jumps. It's a miracle you survived."

But we throw the flying nuns a bone and helicopter them into Columbine from the Denver airport on the day before the giveaway to attend a pre-show rally.

A breathless, radiant Sister Rosemarie tells the crowd that has gathered just outside the Columbine Memorial that they are blessed. "Flying in was such a treat. This is a beautiful part of America."

Iron Iris is even more amped. "It's been said for many years that I put the fun in funeral—especially when I taught math. But my goodness, being here is a blessing. The grandeur and the glory of God exists in these Colorado Mountains that surround us, in this beautiful park, and in the wonderful crowd that is here to greet us."

That wonderful crowd, however, is a wonder, all right—a wonder of polarization. It's amazing. Somehow all the gun-rights and Second Amendment literalists mass together facing stage right. Facing stage left are gun control advocates. I am pleased to see the gun safety advocates, as some of them have started to call themselves, clearly outnumber the gun fanatics.

"Thank you for coming today to meet us," says Sister Teri, who pauses to wait for a big cheer and a chorus of boos to pass. "I'm glad so many people are excited about making our communities safer. I see that there are some signs in the crowd of gun dealers offering money for your guns. That is not what the spirit of *Nuns with Guns* is about. Selling your gun—which is your absolute right to do—won't make the world safer. That gun can go on to be part of the thousands of suicides or accidental deaths that occur each year in our great nation. Or even become part of something larger, more harmful, heaven forbid, like the kind of tragic event that has scarred this lovely town."

"Why do you people keep reminding us?" cries a voice in the crowd.

"Did you hear that?" says Sister Rosemarie. "Someone in the crowd just said, 'Why do you keep reminding us.' And that's very painful isn't it? Being reminded of tragedy. Or senseless death. I can't imagine the pain and the loss. So why do you think we keep reminding people? Not just of Columbine but of San Ysidro, of your suffering neighbors in Aurora; of Blacksburg, Virginia, or Newtown, Connecticut?

"My sisters—not just the ones on the show, but all sisters everywhere around the planet—we remember the brutal senseless death of our Savior. We remember His sacrifice for all of us. His passion for life, for humanity. And that's part of what drives us. That love. That sacrifice. And so yes, we want to remember the lost, stolen children and all the victims of all these horrible gun deaths, the thousands of accidental deaths and injuries every year and the senseless rampages. All these victims of powerful, unnecessary weapons, they tell us something. They say, 'Hey, you don't need guns in your house. You don't need them in your life.' Selling yours will not accomplish anything. The gun still lives as a threat to someone. Melt it down. Make these killing machines go away! So please, wait on line, meet us, take your picture, be part of not just a TV show, but a serious movement. A movement to support and sustain life."

"Fuck you!" screams a voice.

And it becomes an instant refrain. "FUCK YOU! FUCK YOU! FUCK YOU! FUCK YOU!"

"SHAME! SHAME! SHAME!" starts the other half of the crowd.

Sister Iris comes back to the microphone. "Excuse me," she says, "Settle down, people. Settle DOWN!" the chanting stops, and she looks toward the pro-gun section of the crowd. "We don't come to the annual gun show in Las Vegas, or the NRA convention and harass speakers there. So I'll ask you not to insult my good friend Sister Rosemarie or the rest of us in attendance with such bullying words."

But someone yells, "Teri's uncle was a communist!"

Sister Teri hears this and rushes back to the microphone. "Excuse me, I just heard someone say that my uncle, Father Inglasio Hector Alves, was a communist. No. He was a Catholic who believed in helping the poor. If that is communism, then I guess you could tar the Holy See with the same brush."

Dr. Burns steps out. "Sister Rosemarie, Sister Teri,

tomorrow is our last event of the season. One of you is going to win a $2 million donation to your mission. You are locked in a tight battle to collect the most weapons. Do you have anything to say? Why should someone donate to you, Sister Rosemarie, instead of Sister Teri? Have you cooked up any special rewards for the donors?"

"I can't believe you're asking me that question!" beams Sister Rosemarie. "You should donate to whomever you feel more comfortable with, right, Teri? Or whoever's line is shorter! As for rewards, Teri and I have delegated the swag to the wonderful Sister Constance Grace and Sister Iron Iris."

"And what would that be?"

"They've arranged to repeat two of our most popular giveaways: BASSick headphones, or Samsung cell phones."

"Wow!" G-Mac has joined them. "I have to ask this, Sister Rosemarie and Sister Teri, are you two feeling that competitive?"

"What do you expect, G-Mac?" says Sister Teri. "Of course we are both competitive. But this show, this cause, is bigger than the both of us."

"We are, you know, 'sisters,'" says Sister Rosemarie.

"Touché," smiles Dr. Burns, who turns to the crowd. "Really, ladies and gentlemen, how can you not want to give your Kel-Tecs, Colts and Cobras, your Brownings, Berettas and Bushmasters, your Walthers and Wilsons, your Mausers and Magnums, your Remingtons and Rugers, or your Sig Sauers and Smith & Wessons to these wonderful women? Be sure to come out tomorrow to see which of these pistol-packing prioresses will win $2 million on *Nuns with Guns*!"

• • •

It rains all morning before the Columbine exchange. I'm pissed. You work and work, and bust your ass to make magic happen. You get death threats, bomb threats. You get cursed at, spat at and shot at. And your friend gets murdered. And then, because you haven't suffered enough, you get shitty weather for the finale.

Marta calls as I peek—very quickly, because I stay away from windows—through the curtains of my hotel window. Sheets of rain are coming down.

"Hi, Rick, honey," she says. "It's me."

"I know, Marta. Your face comes up on my phone when you call."

"I want to say some things."

"I'm listening, darling."

"Good luck, I love you. And don't do anything estupid. And wear the vest."

"Just 12 hours, honey. And then I'm all done with this."

"Thank God. Everybody is scared for you. Especially me. How it is there?"

"Raining fucking cats and dogs. Really pissing down. But maybe it will clear up."

"The people will come. A lot of Catholics and Mexicans in Colorado. They love the sisters."

"I know. But this is pretty big gun country, too, Marta."

"You got your vest on?"

"Not yet. But I will."

"Good. If you don't wear it, I'll keel you."

• • •

The rain stops. The pro-gunners come out, but not in droves. Compared to yesterday's rally, the crowd is relaxed.

Security in the form of police, state troopers and our team is everywhere, and everyone is patient. "This Land Is Your Land" breaks out spontaneously on the lines for both nuns. Dr. Burns, G-Mac and Maggie rhapsodize about the perfect finale: the warm sun, a unified crowd, the important mission. It's moving television.

A tearful donor tells Sister Iris her cousin was killed in 1999 by the kids whose incomprehensible actions still haunt the national memory—or at least my memory—Dylan Klebold and Eric Harris.

"Would you say time heals the wounds?" Sister Iris asks.

"Heals? No. It buries the wounds, but they are there, ready to open up, like, like….like what just happened when I started bawling a few minutes ago. The nature of tragedy, the nature of memory is that pain grows duller. That's how we go on. But if I go back and think about the loss, oh my god, I'm going to break down again. Not on TV, please."

The last hour, the sisters are moving like robots, *smile-greet-shake-take-pose*, *smile-greet-shake-take-pose*. They race to move the line. Sixty guns separated them at the start, and we've been monitoring the donations like exit pollsters on the first Tuesday in November. Sister Rosemarie appears to be catching up. Her line is longer. The donors are coming with more guns. But then a woman shows up with 10 handguns from her late husband's collection—Snubnoses, a Glock 22G, a Kimber Stainless Raptor II, and a Smith & Wesson .357—and gives the heavy bag to Sister Teri. So it remains neck-and-neck. Dr. Burns issues a final warning over the event P.A. "You must be on the exchange line in the next five minutes to submit."

I'm in the remote truck with Rittenhouse and Little Ricky.

"Camera Two," says Rittenhouse. "Give me a tracking shot of Sister Rosemarie's line."

"The competition has come down to this," says Dr. Burns. "Twelve cities in eight states, over 55,000 guns collected from over 30,000 donors over a period of four months, and now, only 10 guns separate Sister Rosemarie from Sister Teri. Maggie, how many people do you have on your line?"

"Switch to Maggie on camera 3!" says Rittenhouse.

"It's hard to tell, James, because some people are here with friends or family members. But I'd say about 20."

"We've got three more minutes for donors to line up. Can you believe how close this is? Excuse me, sir? Let me see your nametag. David Lerner! Hello, David. Did you just donate a gun?"

"Yes. Yes I did."

"Can you tell us, what made you choose Sister Rosemarie over Sister Teri?"

"That's easy. My wife is a huge fan of Sister Rosemarie. She is going to be totally shocked when she sees this. And when I give her my picture with her favorite nun!"

"So it was your wife that shaped your decision?"

"Oh, yes. She's been after me to do this ever since your show went on the air."

"How do you feel?"

"Pretty good, actually. I paid good money for that gun. $225. But what the hell? I never even used it."

"G-Mac!" Rittenhouse barks. "Please grab a donor and find out what is motivating Sister Teri's fans."

"Hi, there," says G-Mac, approaching a young woman. "Can you tell us why you wanted to donate to Sister Teri? Is she a favorite of yours?"

"Of course. I love Sister Teri. She's so cool and tough. I like Sister Rosemarie, too. But, you know, she already sort of won on *The King of Pain.* Sister Teri got attacked a lot more, it seemed to me, on this show."

"You mean those negative ads?"

"Exactly."

"What kind of gun did you donate?"

"I don't know. It was my mom's."

"Really? Does she know?"

"No. She's been depressed though. And so I didn't want it around. Especially after hearing what Sister Teri said about suicide. Not that my mom is *that* depressed."

"What a great daughter. Are you going to tell her what you did?"

"No. Hopefully she'll never notice. Of course—is this live?—maybe you could edit all this out."

"Burns," says Rittenhouse, "Give us the countdown."

"Ladies and gentlemen, the donor lines are now closed. The guns donated by the people in these two lines will now determine who will get the prize money of two million dollars."

The camera pulls back and wide.

"Whoa, whoa, whoa!" yells Rittenhouse.

"What the fuck?" says Little Ricky.

"What is he doing there?"

At the back of the line of donors for Sister Rosemarie is a familiar face.

Sampson Smith.

"Ricky, call him and give me your fucking phone," I say.

Ever the good soldier, Sampson picks up on the first ring.

"Hi Sampson," I say. I'm trying to be polite, but I just

can't do it. "Exactly what the fuck are you doing?"

"I'm going to make a donation."

"Seriously? I thought you loved guns."

"I do. But I have a lot. I can do without one or two."

"But Sampson, this is the last show. You work for us. You can't do this."

"No, Rick. I work for Lance Boyle. He hires me and tells me what to do. Not *Nuns with Guns*."

"Yeah, but that's all sort of inside baseball. You have been our head of security. That's a fact. And we are paying your salary, either directly or indirectly. We have language excluding people affiliated with the show from participating in the exchanges."

"Usually that kind of language is about excluding friends and family from winning. There ain't nothing for me to win. I just want to give up some guns and refuse the swag."

He's right about that. But I don't tell him. I'm busy trying to figure out his angle. Have we been infiltrated? Is he an NRA wingnut who's been acting like a double agent? Is he just a wacko who wants to be on TV? Or is he genuine? "Why, Sampson?"

Sampson is silent. I hear Rittenhouse tell Maggie: "Interview Sister Teri, she's done. Let her know that Sister Rosemarie has seven more people on line. So it's too close to call."

"Sampson?"

"I'm doing this because—"

"Oh my word!" It's Burns, doing his on-air-report. "This is a surprise. Ladies and gentlemen, it appears that Sampson Smith, a leading security expert, is the very last gun donor on the show. Are you even allowed to be here?"

Sampson pulls the phone away from his ear and addresses Dr. Burns. "I was just discussing that with your producer."

"And?"

"I am not an employee of the show."

"Really."

"I work for a security consulting firm, not *Nuns with Guns*."

"Did you fill out a waiver?"

"Who cares about a waiver? I'm a military man. I'm a member of the NRA. I'm the donor you guys dream about. And I'm here to donate a gun to Sister Rosemarie."

"Nobody put you up to this?"

"I can't fucking believe this guy," I tell Rittenhouse and Little Ricky. "We can't have him do this. People will scream fix."

"Nobody put me up to this," says Sampson. "I was just watching it unfold, like a viewer with a ringside seat. And I saw that Sister Rosemarie, well, she's running behind, right? And I thought, I have some guns. In fact, I have too many guns. For real: I walk around with two, three, even four guns all the time, man."

"Well you *are* a security guard."

"I'm a security *expert*. I have more degrees than you do, *Doctor* Burns."

"I see, Sampson. My apologies. Are you worried about what will viewers think? That this smacks of collusion. Or something."

"Hey, you're the judge with G-Mac and Maggie. I'm just a citizen who works for the show indirectly."

"Indirectly? You are responsible for all our safety. The entire day-to-day security operation."

"Maybe, but right now I'm a fan of both the sisters. And I thought I'd give up some guns."

"You're a fan of both, but you're only donating to Sister Rosemarie. Why is that?"

"I can't be on two lines at once. And hey, wouldn't it be great if they finished in a tie?"

"A tie?" bleats Dr. Burns with a laugh. "Are you trying to complicate things?"

I smack my head. "Fucking guy!"

"I suppose that is a possibility," says Dr. Burns.

"Hello Sampson!" calls Sister Rosemarie. "What brings you here?"

"I have two guns for you, Sister Rosemarie. If they let me donate them. I have a gun right here—" he bends over, hikes up his pant leg and pulls out a small handgun, cracks open the chamber and dumps out the rounds. "A beautiful peashooter and—" he puts his hand inside his jacket "— one of my first 9 millimeters." He pulls out the clip and hands both guns to Sister Rosemarie.

"Thank you, Sampson. How kind." She looks at Dr. Burns. And then over at Maggie and Sister Teri. "Am I allowed to accept these?"

"NO, NO, NO!" I yell to Rittenhouse. "Tell Burns no fucking way!"

"Let's let it play, Rick," Rittenhouse urges me. "This is great stuff."

"It's fine with me," says Sister Teri. "Every gun is a welcome gun in our mission."

"Kill me now," I moan.

"It'll be okay," says Little Ricky. "Either way we play it, we win."

"But Sister Teri," says Dr. Burns. "You were in the lead

today. These two guns could lose the show for you."

"The competition is secondary for us."

"What do you mean?" asks Maggie.

"The competition is a major part of the show!" I cry. "And now the world will be crying fix!"

"Whether Sister Rosemarie wins or I do, the bigger win is gun safety awareness," Sister Teri says. "We are working toward reducing loss of life and the pain and suffering that comes with it. We win no matter what, because America wins, because we have less guns. Would I love to earn $2 milllon for my mission? Of course. But if I lose, I'll ask viewers to open their hearts and their wallets and share with the less fortunate."

"The media will love this," says Little Ricky. "The producers have lost control of their show. The contestants take it over—that's the storyline. Unscripted good. It's a reality TV revolution."

"Someone is going to sue us. That's what I'm worried about," I say. "The NRA is going to demand an investigation. It'll be like *Quiz Show* or whatever that TV game show scandal was about."

"No they won't. We reserve the right to change all rules and regulations at any time. It's in the boilerplate."

Back on the monitor G-Mac is asking, "Sister Rosemarie, do you feel the same way?"

"Oh, certainly. The greater good is what is important. And there's always next season, right?"

"Take the fucking guns and count already!" I yell.

"Well, this is certainly quite a bizarre situation," says Dr. Burns. "Sister Rosemarie, since there is no objection from Sister Teri, please take the weapons and we will add it to your tally."

"And don't worry, sisters," says Sampson, patting his right hand over his heart, "I'm not giving up the complete arsenal."

"Oh, dear," says Sister Rosemarie. "Thank you, Sampson. Something tells me we haven't made a big dent in your collection."

"It's a start. And I never thought I'd see the day, truth be told."

"Do you hear that, viewers?" says Sister Teri, "A security expert, a marine veteran, an officer and gentleman has answered our call!"

"Thank you, sisters," Burns says. "The moment of truth has arrived. Have these two guns closed the gap? Can Sister Rosemarie overtake her friend Sister Teri? We'll be right back."

"What's the score?" I ask. "I'm not sure which is better now: to have Sister Rosemarie win or to have her lose."

"Well, it's neither nor," says Little Ricky.

"What does that mean?"

"It means they are tied."

"Goddamn it. Why can't I ever finish a show the normal way?"

I step up to the console and hit the talk button. "Burns, Maggie, G-Mac, if it's a tie, they both win $2 million."

And so it is. A. Fucking. Tie. The sisters all embrace and they hug the judges and the soundmen and the camera crew and anybody within hugging distance. And then, as if the magnitude of the situation suddenly hits them, they huddle together, heads bent.

"O Lord, thank you for giving us the strength and inspiration to help and heal. And thank you for watching over us on this dangerous mission. We are truly blessed to live and love in your service. Amen."

• • •

Amen is right. The finale draws the highest ratings in reality TV history. Sixty-three million Americans tune in. An insane share in the Internet era, which has seen TV ratings plummet.

"How many watched with the hope or expectation that someone was going to get shot, or a gun would really go off?" Little Ricky asks me when the numbers come in.

"Impossible to know. Ask your data pal at The Network. But I'm betting it was a tiny fraction. We have fans, Ricky. They buy T-shirts. They download their pictures. I'm sure the danger attracted some viewers, but screw them. Our early 'life-or-death' ads were the only times we flaunted that."

Some TV pundits criticize the show for poorly defined rules and allowing the interference of a tangential show member. But more of them embrace the meaning of Sampson's donation, not as a game changer, but as an example of "socially transformative TV." They love it and take it as proof that reality TV isn't all bad and mindless— some of it, after all, is artful and mindless. And now it can be socially impactful as well, in a positive manner. "As shocking as the idea may be," opined one op-ed scrivener, "*Nuns with Guns* now stands among the most important TV series to ever grace prime time."

Those words for me, Rick "The Prick" Salter, the man who "seemingly aspires to find the lowest common denominator in TV history," who "has launched two of the most exploitative shows in the annals of television," are truly gratifying.

I cut the article out. I have Jasmine get it blown up,

framed and hung in our office.

Then I take the original clipping, fold it up and put it in my wallet.

Chapter 23

The summer is amazing.

The Network approves a second season. The show will be called *Nuns with Guns: Battle of the Cities*. Each of the sisters will work with a new nun to collect the most guns in the city of their choice. Cleveland for Sister Constance Grace, Detroit for Sister Teri, L.A. for Sister Rosemarie, and Chicago for Sister Iron Iris. I won't have much to do with *Nuns with Guns: Battle of the Cities*. It's going to be a 12-episode season. Little Ricky will executive produce this himself with Rittenhouse on board. Sampson will handle security.

The casting for *The Gizless Days of Thomas Binder* is in place. Funding comes in from Wanderlust Pictures where CEO Noli Gianelli is a firm believer in teen entertainment. "Every year like clockwork," he tells Amanda, echoing my own philosophy, "A new crop of kids ages up, ready to be spoon-fed teen stories. It never fails." So we are looking at an October production date. I am thrilled.

On the domestic front, Marta and I have our second wedding. Her mother flies in. I had expected her to be this elderly woman, because Marta was so reverential about her. But she's only 16 years older than Marta, which means, she's a year older than me. She has Marta's sweet, full-toothed smile, but seems a great deal more reserved than her daughter. We can't really communicate, but Marta is thrilled to have her with us. When "Granmami" is around there are actually four generations of Marta's family in the house: Marta, her mom, Mikey and Hector, and the little ones.

"So what?" says Marta when I point this out.

"What do you mean, 'So what?' Don't you think it's incredible?"

"Nah, Rick. I think it happens a lot in the world."

"Really? I'm thinking this is the first time I've seen it."

"You aren't normal, Rick. You got three wives, and only one kid. In most places, three wives is gonna be ten kids and you be a great-grandfather by now."

"Four, Marta. You are wife number four."

"See? You just making my point."

Marta's mom and I mostly just smile at each other. In my other marriages I always resented the fact that I felt like I was supposed to kowtow and genuflect before my beloved's parents, as if I should apologize for invading their family and *schtupping* their daughter. As if that was a big no-no. But maybe I was just projecting. Not that there's anything wrong with paying some parental fealty, some dues, some dowry, to the people who raised the woman who gets your mojo rising. With Granmami, I don't feel any guilt or pressure. Maybe I'm growing up. Or maybe it's a class thing, as horrible as that sounds. I was always slightly intimidated and guilt-ridden meeting my exes' hoity-toity families. Conversely, rich men banging the help has been the way of the world since…forever. Although it wasn't like that with me and Marta. We delayed gratification for years and years.

The wedding is just what Marta ordered: a giant white dress, her adorable grandchildren tossing flowers, her mother walking her down the makeshift aisle in the new Guaco-Taco, me looking sharp in a silver tux, with Jared as my best man. We have 300 people crammed into the restaurant, which isn't open yet, so Hector and Mikey can do whatever the hell they want; it's a private party. We've got a huge tent up in the backyard, with fountains of chocolate to dip strawberries and a small stage upon which a versatile Chicano band bounces out one song after another. And Marta, in her wedding gown, looks radiant. It is quite a gown: white, backless, with a slit in the front to show some leg, a poufy train that is almost as long as she is. It's her party. I follow her lead. I hold her hand and she pulls me around, laughing, chattering, hugging, kissing, introducing me in English then zipping into Spanish. It's my party, too, of course. I'm a lucky man. Lucky to be alive, lucky to have Marta, lucky to have money, lucky to do what I want with whomever I want.

Fucking lucky.

And the luck continues on our honeymoon in Europe and Mexico. A booze and shoes tour of the old world's finest museums, restaurants and hotels. I spoil her. And she spoils me, too, but I'll spare you the details.

Not long after we get back, I get a call from Nathaniel Blatt, the FBI agent who came to visit after the first death threats went up. He's working on the murder of David Ryan.

"I thought it was an NYPD investigation."

"It was, but given the threats against your show, it also came under FBI jurisdiction. Domestic terrorism, conspiracy across state lines—these are things we take very seriously."

"Me too."

"Mr. Salter," Blatt tells me, "I just got off the phone with David Ryan's parents and they asked that I call you. We have made great progress in our investigations. Today we arrested two men on conspiracy and murder charges relating to the killing of their son."

"That is fucking great! Who?"

"As you know, forensic and ballistics investigators suspected the bullet hit Mr. Ryan from a high trajectory. But proving that, what with the body being moved and all the principal witnesses moving, was difficult. But we found a connection between a gun lobbyist who was involved in your show."

"You mean Thomas Vickers?" I say, playing stupid.

"Exactly. We received an anonymous tip that Vickers was connected to Grant Matthews, a lobbyist in New York who lived in an apartment on 64th and Fifth, overlooking the park."

"So Matthews took the shot?"

"No. He claims he wasn't even in the city. But we have videotape of a man named Max Ulrich entering and leaving the building on that day. Are you familiar with that name?"

"It sounds familiar, but I can't place it."

"I believe you might know him as Mr. Bowl Cut."

"That moron shot David? What a fucking psycho!"

"Well, he was trying to shoot you."

"Why didn't he shoot again?"

"According to evidence we've obtained, he was worried about being seen. He thought someone would look up after that first shot."

"See? He is a moron. Any word on Monica Moore?"

"No, sir. She remains a person of interest."

"So did this guy Ulrich know Vickers, or just Matthews?"

"It appears both."

"The plot thickens. Hey, I have a question."

"Yes, sir?"

"How did they know we would be there on Fifth Avenue?"

"They didn't. But they knew you were in the Pierre, which was only three blocks away from Matthews' apartment. Apparently, it's been reported that you always stay there. It seems that Ulrich was on stakeout duty. We think there's a good chance they had you under surveillance and alerted Ulrich."

"Christ. Why didn't they take out the nuns in the air when they were over Central Park?"

"I believe they thought shooting the nuns would not help their cause. Murdering a nun would be a PR nightmare."

"How do you know that? Tape recordings? Emails?"

"No comment, Mr. Salter."

"Very interesting. Thank you. Will this be announced soon?"

"Yes. In a matter of minutes."

"Thank you very much. This comes as a huge relief for everyone involved in our show."

"Not at all."

"Do I pay you guys the reward?"

"I don't think so. The tip-off was really what broke that case."

"Wow. I wonder who that was?"

"A good citizen, no doubt."

"A prince," I say.

• • •

Toward the end of the summer, the Emmys arrive. Awards shows always start early on the West Coast. I mean, ridiculously early. And the Emmys are no different. The red carpet parade starts at 3:30, so they can get everyone seated and stoked by 5 p.m., which of course is 8 p.m. on the East Coast. But it's pathetic, trying to match the money and energy behind the Oscars. It can't be done, even though Marta is wearing a dynamite dress by Halstar Rieger that puts the lunge in plunge.

Our plan is to meet up with the four sisters, who have spent the day under orders to be pampered at the Beverly Hills Four Seasons, where two stylists are on hand to help with makeup and maybe add a little glow to their sensible shoes and boxy outfits.

When the limo pulls up at the Nokia Theater, my security guards get out and when they give me the okay, I step out wearing a black tux and a pair of the No Guns shades that we gave away on the show.

Right away the chorus of "Rick! Rick! Mr. Salter! Rick!" comes from beyond the police barrier where a battalion of paparazzi and fans are taking photos. I turn and give them a wave, and then Marta and I are ushered together for our slow walk down the red carpet.

It really isn't that bad. We amble. A reporter for *Entertainment News* asks me who the favorite is.

"I like Bang a Gong in the fourth race," I joke.

She looks at me blankly.

"He likes *Nuns with Guns,* of course," says Marta, "The sisters are the bravest women in television, right, Rick?"

"Yes," I say. "If we are here to honor important, thought-provoking television, then I don't think there's any question about it. *Nuns with Guns* must be the favorite."

"Well, you were the number one show in the country by a mile," says the TV lady.

"I was trying to take the high road, but since you mentioned it, you are correct, we were the most popular show of the year, but more important, not many reality shows actually *change* reality. I think *Nuns with Guns* did some of that."

Inside the auditorium we are seated in the seventh row and Marta adores every minute of it, from the giant TV screens, to the celebrities surrounding her, the live cameras, the cues. She is so wide-eyed that I get a little sad. "Marta," I whisper to her. "I'm sorry. All these years, I should have brought you here."

"Oh, Rick. Don't worry. This is a happy ending."

And it is. I look around. I see the gorgeously full-lipped and insanely funny Steffi Morgan, from that Las Vegas sitcom *Loaded Deck*. Two rows ahead of us is *Undisclosed Location* star Daphne Spindler with her heart-stopping red hair and green eyes and killer legs. And across the way is Natalia DeChristo, the Latina bombshell on *Foreign Exchange*, who has this killer accent that reminds me of Marta. And you know what? I don't care about any of them. I don't care who they are boffing or if I would even have a hundred-to-one chance to boff them. I. Do. Not. Care. I've got Marta and grandchildren, one of whom is named Zorro. I'm doing important work. I'm getting rid of guns. Can anyone in this room say that? No way.

"Yes, Marta. More happy than I deserve."

"Shut up, you. You a hero."

• • •

The competition is pretty tough for the Outstanding Competitive Reality Show, which is our division. I'm not worried about *Baker's Dozen* or *1% Wannabes,* but *America's Best Athletes* certainly is a fine showcase for some of the most famous sneaker salesmen in the world, and *Dr. Jekyll and Mr. Snide's Horror Costume Freak Show* is about as loud as it gets and has strong ratings in the 15-30 year old demo.

But when the clips are shown, you know that the thunderous applause that greets Sister Teri as she faces down NRA criticism and Sister Constance Grace as she hugs Bradley Boardman can only mean one thing.

And, still, when the envelope is opened and the words *Nuns with Guns* boom through the PA, it's hard to believe. Marta plants a big national TV kiss on me, and then I stand up and usher Little Ricky and the sisters into the aisle. I have no idea what the protocol is with kissing nuns, but I don't care, and grab each one of these wonderful, brave women for a peck on the cheek.

Up on the dais I don't waste any time: "I accept this award in the name and memory of two men. Omar Naxos, a victim of gun violence whose senseless death inspired the creation of this show, and David Ryan, who was murdered purely because of his association with our show. Omar was a hard-working young man of 20 who will never get to see his 2-year-old son, Markus, grow up. David was a heroic young man who educated and inspired us every day as he worked to combat gun violence, implement background checks and make America safer. We mourn David and Omar every day, and curse the cowards who killed them. There were others who helped *Nuns with Guns* do such important work. Thank you, Walter Fields for being the bravest man in television. Thank you, Jay Thanda. Thank you, Ricky Garcia, and

Tabitha Harding and Sampson Smith and the entire Lance Boyle security team. Thank you, Marta and Jared and my new *familia*, I love you. Thank you to all the civilians and law enforcement agents working to make our nation saner and safer. Thanks to our fans and believers. And mostly, thank you to four of America's bravest women: Sister Rosemarie Aria, Sister Teresita Maria Alves-Rodriguez, Sister Constance Grace Odikobu and Sister Iris Shaughnessy, who prove that it is possible to stand up for safety and sanity despite opposition from the most powerful, wealthy and greedy lobby in America."

And I step away from the microphone and listen as Sister Iron Iris steps to the mic. "I speak for all four of us, who have made it our life mission to love God and to carry out His lessons. This show comes from a place of love. It strives to make men, women and children of this nation safer. It's really simple: Guns are dangerous, America. And we will be back next year to continue our mission to reduce the danger. Goodnight, and God bless."

The crowd erupts, and the sisters blush and wave, and start blowing kisses. The get-off-the-stage music starts, but there's a standing ovation that has started, so we stay up there a little longer. I can't remember when I felt so good. So fulfilled. America was watching this. Well, maybe 15 percent of America. And they were seeing the love. For us. For our show. For our mission.

• • •

We go backstage for the requisite victors' press schmooze. I let the sisters have the spotlight; they earned it. And they will need to earn it again next year. They are a parade of platitudes and gratitude, thanking voters and everyone who donated time and money and, of course, guns.

"This is just the first step in the march to a safer America," declares Sister Rosemarie. "I want to thank Emmy voters for their support. And also Rick Salter, who takes a lot of abuse, but has shown the world that reality TV doesn't just have to be about dance contests or catty women or cooking shows. It can also be about causes."

"Yes!" seconds Sister Iron Iris. "I agree completely with Sister Rosemarie. I think we all do."

"I will say one more thing," says Sister Constance Grace, "While I'm very excited by the opportunity to lead Cleveland to victory in next year's show, I will miss working side-by-side with these wonderful, dynamic women."

"Flying nuns!" says Sister Teri.

The reporters and the talent hanging in the room give them an ovation. That doesn't happen too much. It's almost as rare as someone calling me a "do-gooder."

"Thank you, Sister Rosemarie," I say as she walks toward the exit with Marta between us.

"What for?"

"The compliment in front of half of the world's entertainment reporters. I really appreciated that."

"Well, it was true."

"I wonder if you are the first Emmy award-winning nuns," I say, changing the subject. I'm being modest. Falsely modest, actually. Tonight is a fucking triumph and I could happily spend the whole night hearing about how true Sister Rosemarie's comment was, how the award is a total vindication of my original idea. How all the tension and the death threats and the fear and anxiety and sleeplessness have been worth it, because, yes, our show showed America itself, showed the stupidity, the needless fear and the driving greed and the deadly power we cling to. I could bathe in it. How the end justifies the means.

Or almost justifies it—I'm not sure David Ryan's girlfriend or parents would agree with me, though. But even if I steered things to win a $40 million plus residuals settlement from Walter Fields and The Network, even if I "borrowed" the name for my hit show, even if I've made some money by flirting with the edges of disaster, it's all been worth it. More than 55,000 guns collected. That is an insane amount of weapons, and yet it is a drop in the ocean, because the U.S.A. has *300 million guns* floating around. We have collected a tiny, infinitesimal percentage of the guns in the US. But it feels like an enormous first step.

"I'm sure someone in the press room is digging into that question right now," laughs Sister Rosemarie. "There must have been someone else before us. Where are we off to next?"

"The Network is having a victory party. We all need to stop by and then you are free to go to the Viper Room or wherever you ladies live it up."

We step out the side door of the Nokia where all the limos are lined up. There's a valet captain and I tell him who we are. On both sides of the door are police barriers holding back photographers and stargazers.

"Sister Rosemarie, Sister Rosemarie!" the shutterbugs call, hoping she'll look in their direction.

"Sister Constance Grace! Sister Constance Grace!"

I have no idea what the car was or who our driver was. I'm just waiting for the valet captain to steer me clear, and my eyes drift over the crowd when I see someone raise a hand in our direction.

A hand with a gun in it.

The shooter looks vaguely familiar but I can't place the face in that paralyzing nanosecond where everything happens at the same time: this person who I recognize but don't actually recognize is pointing a gun at me and I better fucking move fast, so I yell "Down! Down!" and hear the noise, the huge repeating clap of a gun at close range while I'm pushing Marta down and reaching across to Sister Rosemarie.

You've seen the pictures and footage, right? It might be one of the most photographed crimes in history. That is fear in my eyes and terror and pain on my face, as I dive to cover the falling Marta and Sister Rosemarie, who is turning away from me and going into a crouch. Something slams into my side, a tiny, diamond-hard rocket burning into me as I hit the ground. "Ah, fuck!" I yell. You can hear that on some of the tapes, in between one of the shots. I'm thinking that I have a flak jacket underneath, something called Narcowear, which is why I looked like such a gorilla on the red carpet and up on stage. The camera adds ten pounds? Well, Narcowear adds 20. It also adds a false sense of security because while the jacket helps, it doesn't turn you into Iron Man. No how, no way.

I'm fucking leaking. Onto Marta.

"Ay, papi, you are hurt!" she says, rolling from under me. "Someone call 411! *Ay mierda*, I mean 911. My husband has been hit!"

The shooting has stopped, I can hear men yelling and garbled voices on handset radios. I'm glad Marta is up, because it means she's okay. But I'm worried about the others.

"Sssister?"

"I'm okay, Rick. You just relax."

"I can't fucking believe this."

Jay is at my side. "Are you okay, Rick?" It's a stupid but key question. I have no idea. I think I'll be okay but I'm breathing heavy and it hurts. I close my eyes. I'm squeezing them tight. I hear cops saying, "Get away, back away! Move! Move!" But it's hard to know who they're concerned with because I can't see anything, being on the ground. Jay strips off his tuxedo jacket and presses it against where he sees blood.

"Jay, what are you doing? That fucking hurts!"

"Sorry."

"Are you a doctor, too?"

"No, man, but this is what they do in the movies. Plus, I got to do something. HEY, WHERE ARE THE EMTs?!"

"Pray," says Sister Teri, "that can work, too."

"I think… breathing…" I gasp. I want to say breathing is the thing that works for animals in general. But it hurts too much.

"Move back, everyone, move back," says a cop-like voice. "The EMTs will be here in one minute."

"That's my husband. I'm not leaving."

"Sorry lady, please move back. Help is on the way."

"Jay, you gotta tell them."

"Hey, officer," he says. "She has all his information for the medics."

"Okay lady. But you gotta go, Mister."

"I can't go, officer. I'm holding his fucking innards in place, and I'm his lawyer."

"Oh papi, stay with me! Please!"

"Uh, sister, if you don't mind…"

"Please officer, I want to be near him," says Sister Rosemarie. "He's very dear to me. I'll just pray. And, oh dear, someone may need to give him his rites."

"He's not dying, Sister Rosie!" cries Marta. "Don't say that."

I shut my eyes tight, to help with the pain. And then something strange happens. I notice this ultra bright shining clean light. I can't believe it. "Marta, Jay," I gasp. "I think I'm done here. There's this light. That's what they say, right?"

"Nah, you're not dying, Rick," says Jay.

"How do you know? Look at all this blood, Jay. Don' lie to my husband. *Mierda.*"

I'm thinking: Christ, I don't even believe in this shit. If you had asked me at any time over the last 25 years if I was going to get into heaven, my answer would always be the same. "There is no heaven, and if there is, I'm not getting in." But maybe I was wrong. Maybe these lights are heralding the big show in paradise. And maybe *Nuns with Guns* has saved me, has cleaned my slate of all the abuse and greed and squandering of wealth and steamrolling over anyone who gets in my way. Maybe I'm fucking redeemed.

"He's not done. They just hit his lower stomach."

"Ooooh!" I wince. Jay is pressing hard.

"Sorry, man."

I can hear sirens.

"If you see the light, it's supposed to be peaceful," says Jay. "Are you peaceful?"

"No, it hurts like a son of a bitch."

"Well, that is not heaven then. Sorry, man."

"What do you know about heaven, Jay?" I grimace. "You're Hindu. You just come around again as a cow if you're lucky."

"We got the Good Kingdom, bro. Where all the big wigs chill. You'll like it. And watch those Indian stereotypes, *bhaisahib*. Don't you ever learn?"

"If you die, you going to heaven, Rick," says Marta. "Don't worry, even if you Jewish, the sisters is praying hard right now."

"She's right," says Jay. "I saw sparks coming from those rosaries."

Finally, I can hear voices and the opening of doors and the crash of metal gurney hitting the pavement. The medics are here.

"You gotta save my husband! Hold on, papi! Please stay with us, please!"

"I'm trying!" I say, calling out, my eyes clenched. "I'm trying and trying and trying, even with these lights calling…"

"We're going to cut away your clothes, sir. So we can see. Is that the only wound?"

"I think so," says Jay.

My sleeve is sheared away. "Hey, I didn't get hit on my arm!" I say, and then I feel a prick on my shoulder.

"This is gonna help you relax, sir."

"Papi, they are fixing you! Stay strong! I love you."

"I'm trying, Marta!" I cry. "Fuck it, fuck those lights, fuck the pearly gates, the heaven. I want to stay here. I—"

Chapter 24

When I come to—I mean, really, truly wake up in an only mildly narcotized state, not the post-anesthetic, clueless haze that everyone first surfaces in and no one ever remembers—I can't fucking move and I'm terrified.

Instantly, I think: not again. Not the Accident. This can't be happening again.

"What the fuck?" I rasp. My throat feels like someone has been peeling my esophagus with an acid-coated knife. It burns. It sears.

I'm in a totally unfamiliar room. In a bed.

Tubes are everywhere, connecting into my body—my chest, my stomach, both my arms. And pain is everywhere, not just my throat. I try to turn to the left, and my entire torso is one collective mass of agonizing sensations: stabs, cramps, burns and aches. "Jesus," I gasp. My voice sounds like the equivalent of an acoustic scab.

I hear Spanish. The TV on the wall at the front of my bed is on at a low rumble. A soap opera, it looks like. One of those telenovelas Marta likes.

"What the fuck?" I rasp, a little louder.

"Ooh, Rick! You're awake!" It's Marta, her oh-so-pretty face leaning over me, to kiss my forehead. "Thank god! I was worrying like crazy."

Of course, she's beaming now, expressing the complete opposite of worry. She grabs my hand and immediately a machine starts beep-beep-beeping an urgent SOS.

"Oh, damn. I just knocked this thing off your finger. Sorry. It tells about your blood."

"Here." A nurse zooms into my field of vision. Asian. All business, no smiles.

"Oxidation monitor. It records how much oxygen is in your blood," says the nurse, placing it on my middle finger and silencing the beeps.

"Yeah," Marta nods. "I tole him."

The nurse looks at a stack of machines at the side of the bed and says, "Your heart rate just spiked. You just wake up and try to move?"

"Yes."

"How are you feeling, Mr. Salter? Are you in pain?"

"Yes. It hurts just to talk."

"That's because they intubated you during surgery. That's perfectly normal."

"This is nurse Jane, papi. She's from the Philippines."

"If you are in pain, you have a morphine drip right here. Look, you can even press this button and give yourself some more."

"And don't worry. It has a timer, papi, so you can't overdose."

I try to turn again, and it's just like the Accident from last year: Pain is everywhere: my throat, my arms, my chest, where, I discover later, the tape from electrodes monitoring my heart is pulling at my body hair, my stomach where—surprise!—there's another fucking tube, and, moving further southward, even my dick feels strange, like it has something attached to it.

"God damn it!"

"Aw, don't cry, papi," says Marta, grabbing a tissue from the standard-issue square tissue container on the standard-issue rolling hospital table that can traverse the width of my standard-issue mechanized bed. She wipes my watering eyes. "You are going to be fine! You are alive, honey. And the doctor tole me you are going to be better than before. He cleaned up some polyps while he was in there."

"Yes, Mr. Salter. Sleep and rest for now."

My hand gropes for the opium feeder. Marta gets it into my hand.

I click it five times in a row.

"He always like drugs," Marta tells Jane.

• • •

I wake up. It's much darker. The light from the corridor streams in. I hear voices, murmurs outside. A nurse comes in.

"Good morning, Mr. Salter."

"Hi."

"I'm Agnes. I'm going to check up on everything. Take your temperature, check your bags. The doctor will be by later. Probably around 7:30."

Check your bags? I'm still pretty hazy. But what does she mean? It's not like I packed anything.

Agnes takes some device and sticks it in my ear and it beeps in a second. She reads it and repeats the procedure again. Then she writes something on my chart at the foot of the bed

"How am I doing?"

"No fever."

She looks at my tubes, disconnects something and then I see her take a bag with yellow fluid and dump it in the bio-waste disposal bin. My urine. From my catheter.

But then I see the brown bag.

"What the hell is that?!!"

"What, this? It's a colostomy bag. It's for your solid waste. You just have to use this while you are healing. Did your, um, did anyone tell you? They had to take out a piece of your intestine, and so we need to keep it clean while you heal."

I know what a colostomy bag is.

It's the most humiliating fucking thing in the world.

You think I'm exaggerating? I have never been more embarrassed in my life. There, hanging for anyone to see, is my personal refuse, my excrement, my shit... gross, brown liquid. The same, I'm sure, as anyone else's, but tied to me. An albatross, a unholy umbilical cord connecting me to my own vile, toxic essence.

My shit for all to see. I can't even take care of myself.

"How long will I have that thing?"

"The colostomy bag?"

"Yeah."

"That depends on how you are healing. Dr. Morris will tell you."

I mumble to myself, going soft on the "f."

"You're welcome, Mr. Salter," Agnes says.

I wasn't saying thanks.

• • •

So much for those celestial lights I thought I was seeing. Turns out they were the blaring, blinding lights of CNN, *L.A. Hunt* and *E! News* shining down, as cameras rolled in the hopes of nabbing million-dollar snuff footage. I know this now because Jay and Jared have been in here, showing me the footage filmed from both sides of the Nokia Theater exit door. You can see the light beams of opposing camera crews zapping me on the ground.

So, no, I didn't get to heaven. To hear the doctors tell it, I wasn't even in shouting distance of paradise, which is to say that as far as lethal wounds go, mine weren't even close: just two, one above the right hip, slowed by the body armor, that pierced the skin and barely went an inch in and hit some large intestine, and a second even shallower wound about three inches over. Thank god I've still got that spare tire around my hips. The only way it could have brought me down? Infection. You can say the same damn thing about a blister on your foot.

As for the other victims on the scene, there were none. It turns out that Monica Moore was a great actress and a terrible shot. None of us recognized her in the heat of battle. But given her bald wig, mannish clothes and fierce scowl, who could blame us? She's in a psychiatric ward now, where she reportedly spends her days ranting about how our show ruined her life.

• • •

One night in the hospital I have this dream. Normally, I try never to bother anyone with my dreams. My experience with listening to dreams consists of my ex-wives struggling to recount rapidly dissipating memories. It's like watching someone try to grab steam. But I've pretty much got the details down on this one.

In my dream, I'm walking onto a stage to address the national meeting of the NRA. I'm decked out in a tux and Little Ricky is pushing a giant contraption behind me that bears an enormous, swinging colostomy bag.

I approach the dais.

"Good evening, you short-sighted motherfuckers," I say. "You see this? This thing I'm yoked to for life? I have to carry around my excrement!"—interesting, isn't it, that somehow "excrement" is a more vile word than "shit"—"because you want to carry around guns. Anyone want to switch?"

"Get off the stage!"

"Who let him in here?"

"I was granted two minutes to speak. I'm an NRA member, too!" I hold up my membership card.

"Bullshit!"

"Faggot!"

"Communist!"

The boos keep coming, but I push on. "I'm here with a new idea. I've rethought the whole issue. The so-called gun problem is part of a larger entitlement problem. It's not about the Second Amendment or the Constitution. It's about that earlier document—the Declaration of Independence. About those inalienable rights: 'the preservation of life, liberty and the pursuit of happiness.'

"I used to love that phrase: *The pursuit of happiness.* So sweet, so true, so noble. But one man's happiness—a Bushmaster AR 15 semiautomatic rifle, for example, or a Kel-Tec PF-9—can lead to a huge amount of misery. So the Second Amendment, that's just constitutional camouflage, an extension of the fact that we are a nation founded on a sense of entitlement."

The crack of gun blasts is deafening. I flinch. I think I'm going to shit myself on stage and then I remember that I can't, because everything is flowing into the gargantuan colostomy bag, Except the huge bag is getting smaller, because it has been shot instead of me. My shit is leaking onto the NRA's stage.

"Thank you for your excellent aim," I say. "My bag over there is leaking like I'm leaking, like thousands of other gunshot victims leak. They leak blood, bile, urine, excrement. But I'm not here to attack guns, my fellow Americans, because guns are not just the problem. Listen, guns are a problem just like pollution is a problem, just like global warming is a problem. And the problem for all these things is that entitlement—the pursuit of happiness—is being urged on by the pursuit of profit. The guns you love and cherish more than anything in the world? The cars we drive with their newer, more expensive designs? The sodas we drink and toss away? They exist so you can buy them to make stockholders rich. It's not about you or the gun. It's about making people who don't give a damn about you rich. That's what the NRA does. You think they are fighting for your rights to have weapons? That's bullshit. They are fighting for the right to sell you weapons and get rich. And so we are fighting for the right to help them get rich. There's a word for this. You know what the word for that is?"

"Communist!"

"Almost. The word is 'suckers'!"

There are more shots. The bag is obliterated. The stage reeks. Two guards come and haul me off stage.

I wake up and look to my right.

The colostomy bag is still there.

• • •

My surgeon Dr. Morris stops by.

"Mr. Salter, you look much better."

"Thanks. I bet you say that to all your post-op patients."

"Just when it's true."

He looks me over, examines his stitch work, and wields his stethoscope.

"Listen, Dr. Morris, if I had gotten an infection, say a staph infection, and it beat me, what would have happened?"

He frowns. "You mean if you died?"

"Exactly. What happens? What would be the cause of death?"

"Oh! It depends. Technically, your death would have been due to a highly aggressive strain of staph infection."

"Is that what you would tell the medical examiner?"

"In your case, yes."

"But what about the surgery?"

"You mean complications of the wound?"

"Exactly."

"I wouldn't say that's the cause of death because we took care of the wound. You are healing beautifully."

"But it would be the wound that led to the infection!"

"I suppose there's some logic there."

"You suppose? Are you fucking kidding me?"

"Rick! Don't curse at the doctor," says Marta. "What's wrong wit you!"

"You are right, Mr. Salter; it's up for debate. As a surgeon, professionally, I'm interested in saving you from the wound. Honestly, a staph infection could come from anywhere. Just inserting an IV could do it."

"Really?"

"Sure."

"Well listen, Doc, if I take a turn for the worse, do me a favor and make me a gun death statistic. I think that's more accurate in my case. The wound sets the whole thing in motion."

"I'd have to think about that."

Is it okay to yell at the man who saved your life? I'm about to launch into this guy when Marta looks up from her phone.

"Ooh, Rick, the *niños* want to come visit! That's okay, right?" She looks at Dr. Morris. "His granchildren, they can come here, right?"

"Sure," says Dr. Morris. "As long as they can get by Mr. Salter's security guard outside."

"The kids can't see me like this. It's too scary. Plus, I've still got the friggin' colostomy bag."

"Oh, Rick. They miss you. It will help them understand."

"No. I'm a mess."

"I'll leave you two to work this out."

"Hey, wait. When does the colostomy bag go away?"

"We'll send you for a scan tomorrow. If it looks good, we'll remove it and let your system flow."

• • •

The guesthouse is finished when I get home from the hospital, and Hector and Mikey are living there with their families. Two fences are going up around the property, one is short and wired to a security system, the second is tall and meant to guarantee privacy in the backyard. Marta has hired a tennis pro to teach the little ones. "There's no Chicano tennis players," Marta says, announcing her plan. "They are going to be stars." We love watching the four of them stand in front of the net and practice footwork, swinging at invisible balls, running laps around the court.

Jared spends most of his time at Natalia's, which is 2,000 percent understandable. He's now an associate editor for the website. But I think he's getting the Salter bug. He says he thinks Salter Entertainment should get into the documentary business. We're negotiating. My plan? He works for Little Ricky for a year or two, and then he does whatever he wants.

I'm back at work in mid-October. We still have Lance Boyle's security teams watching my house, my car, the office building, Marta, the kids, the nuns and Little Ricky.

I drive to the new office digs with my guard of the month, Davis Taylor. The gun-lobby nut jobs have found us and are out with their signs and songs, including the big behemoth, Mr. Gun Crazy, who is strumming a guitar. I notice the guitar case at his feet, and it hits me. Cops were looking for a guy with a guitar case! He must have been there, and tipped off his buddy, Mr. Bowl Cut. Motherfucker. I call Sampson Smith, who is now Salter Entertainment's full-time security and operations chief, and I point out the guitar case.

"I'll contact Blatt at FBI and let him know," Sampson says.

After Davis gives me the all clear, I get out the car and head to the office, doing what I always do, ignoring them as they call out "Fascist!" "Nazi!" "America-Hater!" "Liberal!" But then I think, "not today." I turn around.

I walk toward them, this goon squad. This mob. A thought occurs to me: Are some of them actors, too? Like Monica Moore? I mean, this is Hollywood, right? But the invective gets louder and more alliterative as I approach, and it doesn't feel like an act at all. "Scumbag son of a bitch!" "Traitor!" "Fucking Fascist!" "Democrat douche!"

I'm standing there, five feet from them, and the volume, the fury, the rage seems to increase. I can see their spittle flying, finally they hit a crescendo, a chant! *"U.S.A.! U.S.A.! U.S.A.! U.S.A.! U.S.A.! U.S.A.!"*

I watch this brain trust, these aces of activism, these stooges doing the work in support of billion-dollar corporations and thousands of inevitable early deaths, and they smile at me. They've got me. What can possibly be wrong with chanting U.S.A.? It's unassailable. Who can argue with such primal patriotism?

After a minute or two I turn around. Davis is about eight feet behind me. Jasmine has come out the building. Mo Nathan, our lobby security guy, is watching from the building entrance. People on the upper floors of the building are looking out their windows.

The volume of this quartet goes up a notch when they see me turn—*"U.S.A.! U.S.A.! U.S.A.!"*—as if these all-powerful three letters will push me away, vanquish me and all I stand for. But it doesn't. I'm beaming now. I raise my arm and wave my staff toward me. It's the come-on-down swoop. There's only one thing to do.

"U.S.A.!" I chant, turning back to the gun club. *"U.S.A.! U.S.A!"*

I move closer so that I'm right in front of them, wondering if they get it. If they understand that I'm cheering for the same thing, but a totally different thing. Jasmine is out there beside me now. And so is Davis and Mo and they are chanting, too. *U.S.A.! U.S.A!*

We hold hands. We form a small circle that gets bigger as the rest of the office comes out to join us, Little Ricky, Amanda, Tabitha and Sampson, our mail and filing clerk Dennis Shea, two more of the security staff, and people I don't know from other offices.

"*U.S.A.! U.S.A.! U.S.A.! U.S.A.!*" we chant, and then we start to move, to dance. It's a rag-tag, slow version of the hora. Each hip-turning counter stride punctuated by a "U.S.A!" And the gun club? They don't want to chant with us. They've fallen silent, watching us, some scowling, some blank. Me? I'm smiling. I'm dancing. I'm happy! Maybe I am kidding myself. Maybe hope won't overcome fear. Maybe the NRA and greed are more powerful than all three of our government branches, but for right now we have used three letters to take away a major weapon from the arsenal of these gun goons and pointed it right back at them. "This land is our land!" I yell. "This land is *our* land! *U.S.A.! U.S.A.! U.S.A.!*"

The disarming has begun.

Thanks

Numerous organizations advocating gun control and gun safety provided me with hours of maddening reading and gun violence statistics. Thanks to all the staffers and volunteers fighting to make a safer, saner America.

Gun policy veteran Arkadi Gerney discussed exchange program decorum and gun culture in America and was very helpful.

Nuns with Guns went through more drafts than I care to count. Thanks to early readers Jenny Taylor and Rebecca Kaufman. And extra thanks to Gary Marmorstein, Michael Lundy and Markus Hoffman for their insightful feedback.

I am also indebted to copy editors Mark Schwartz and Eliza Kirby, book designer Sarah Masterson Hally, and graphic designer Kevin McLaughlin, who created the fantastic cover.

Finally, eternal thanks and love to Susan, Theo and Hilary.

SETH KAUFMAN is a writer whose work has appeared in the *New York Times*, NewYorker.com, *NY Post*, *The National Enquirer* and many other publications. He has worked as an ice cream maker, musician, entertainment reporter, editor and ecommerce executive. He lives in Brooklyn with his wife and two kids.